Blind Bet

Tracey Richardson

Bella
BOOKS
2010

Bella Books, Inc.
P.O. Box 10543
Tallahassee, FL 32302

Printed in the United States of America on acid-free paper
First Edition

Editor: Medora MacDougall
Cover Designer: Linda Callaghan

ISBN 13: 978-1-59493-211-3

Also by Tracey Richardson

No Rules Of Engagement
Side Order Of Love
The Candidate

For anyone who's ever had to pick up the pieces…

Acknowledgments

My thanks, first, to all the readers who have supported and encouraged me and, secondly, to the Bella family—the wonderful women front and center as well as those behind the scenes. Also, to my fellow Bella authors for sharing the passion and working so hard doing what we all love. My love and gratitude to my friends and family. Specifically, thank you, Cris S., for sharing my very special book journeys with me and for helping me with them... Sandra, for your continued support and love; Maryann, for your encouragement and support as well; and as always Brenda and Stacey. I thank my editor, too, for helping me make this and all my books better.

About the Author

Tracey Richardson is also the author of *No Rules of Engagement* (a Lambda Literary Award finalist for Best Lesbian Romance, 2009, and a Golden Crown Literary Society finalist, 2009), *Side Order of Love* (a Golden Crown Literary Society finalist, 2009) and *The Candidate* (a Golden Crown Literary Society finalist, 2008). Tracey has worked for more than twenty years in the daily newspaper business in Ontario, Canada, as a reporter and editor. Visit www.traceyrichardson.net.

CHAPTER ONE

Proverb on gambling: Luck never gives, it only lends.

Courtney Langford hadn't run this fast since her softball days in college.

"Son of a bitch!"

Her breathless expletive echoed around the empty seating lounge—a lounge that minutes ago would have been congested with noisy, anxious travelers. She'd give just about anything to be in the midst of that bedlam right about now—spilled coffee, whiny kids, cranky people, luggage to trip over. All of that was preferable to the silence that greeted her now, because it meant only one thing.

Courtney summoned her trademark confidence and instinctive self-assertion and bounded up to the airline receptionists wearing regulation blue jackets and bored expressions. She was reasonably sure she could convince them to call back the damned plane, the one that was now reversing out toward the tarmac. There were no impossibilities to Courtney, only challenges.

"I need to be on that plane!" Sweat tickled her scalp and her voice was hoarse with adrenaline. The male and female duo, stony-faced and as bereft of personality as their starched uniforms, didn't raise so much as an eyebrow at her.

"Sorry, ma'am. There's nothing we can do." It was the girl who spoke, her tone as neutral as her brown eyes and brown bob. She wasn't a girl, actually. She was probably in her late twenties. But Courtney, at thirty-eight, considered any woman that much younger than herself to be a girl.

Courtney shook her head furiously. *Wrong answer.* "You don't understand. I *need* to be on that plane."

"What's your name?" asked the guy with a badge that identified him as Bill. *Bill as in bland. Bill as in not particularly brilliant. Bill, who's being way too fucking calm!*

Crap. They didn't need her goddamn name. They needed to get that plane back here. Frustration raised her voice even as she acquiesced to his demand. "Courtney Langford."

At his computer, Bill punched a few keys. "You were supposed to be on that flight."

No shit, Sherlock. With effort, Courtney held her tongue.

"We had to pull your bag when you didn't show. I can direct you to baggage claim."

"You don't understand, *Bill.* I don't need my bag. I need to be on that flight or I'll miss an important meeting. I have a colleague already on the plane waiting for me."

The plane was teasing her, rubbing her nose in her lateness, as it backed out further and further. Its silver fuselage gleamed with the shimmer of a coin under water, barely out of her reach.

Bill tapped the computer keys again, the *click click* reminding her of the seconds ticking away. "The best we can do is put you on the next flight, which leaves in ninety minutes, though you're welcome to try another airline."

Courtney's sigh came out as a groan. The two of them could

care less if she was going to be late for a wedding, a funeral, an assignation with a lover, a doctor's appointment, a job interview. Clearly they had heard it all before and then some. There was no point in explaining that she was to meet with one of the East Coast's top advertising agencies to work on the final ad campaign for Microsoft's newest Xbox game. The meeting would have to wait for her. Her boss would not be happy, though, because time was money. And right now she was wasting both.

"I'll check with a couple of airlines and get back to you," Courtney replied curtly. She was resigned to being late, but she would at least put up a fight.

It was far too early on the West Coast to call Nan, her administrative assistant, to help her sort out this fiasco. Danny was on the plane, but she wouldn't be able to reach him either. All the passengers by now would have been told to shut off their electronic devices. She would have to try and get to Boston as quickly as she could.

Oh, hell. She worried about Danny, but he wasn't a child. He would figure out for himself that she would catch up with him later. In her haste to try to make the plane, she'd forgotten to call him earlier—had even forgotten to turn her phone on. *Sorry, Danny boy, you're on your own for a while.*

At a bank of nearby courtesy phones, Courtney quickly tried three other airlines. Every flight to Boston out of Chicago for at least the next hour was filled, putting her back to square one. Contrite, but barely, she returned to the check-in desk and ordered Bill to put her and her luggage on the next flight to Boston. Rubbing weary eyes, she settled in for the wait.

Courtney slumped in a plastic chair that was about as comfortable as a church pew. She hadn't felt this tired in a long time, her limbs limp like noodles, her eyes as scratchy as sandpaper. She'd flown in late the night before—the routine she followed any time she had to go to the East Coast for a morning meeting. Spend the morning at Microsoft in Redmond, outside Seattle, catch an afternoon flight to Chicago or even Detroit, get a decent night's sleep, then take an early flight to her final destination. It worked seamlessly. Or had, until now.

Her big mistake last night had been going to the hotel bar for a couple of drinks. Well, *that* part hadn't been the mistake. Flirting over martinis late into the night with a very beautiful flight attendant on a layover had been the mistake.

When the proposition finally came, Courtney managed to resist, even though the voice in her head kept asking incredulously if she was crazy. For the first time in a long while, she had been truly tempted. The flight attendant was scorching hot, and the conversation, about all manner of things unrelated to computers and games, had been a welcome distraction.

But, stubbornly, Courtney wasn't the type to go for a one- or two-night stand. She never had been, really, and although she was totally single, she couldn't persuade herself to throw caution to the wind and go for it. It wasn't that she had some great moral aversion to it or anything, and she certainly liked sex as much as the next woman. It was the whole getting-to-know-a-stranger thing, fumbling around in the dark and then, she supposed, having to pretend to come, that put her off. It was much less complicated to read a book and drink a glass of wine or watch a late movie on TV.

And so, reluctantly, she'd said no thanks to the gorgeous blonde in the bar and dragged herself back to her room for a few hours of grumpy tossing and turning. She didn't fall into restful sleep until what seemed like mere minutes before her alarm clock sounded. She had a fuzzy recollection of shutting off the offending noise. She didn't wake again until thirty minutes before her flight was scheduled to take off.

Courtney glanced at her Movado watch—a tangible reminder of Celine's sudden and still-puzzling departure. She had given the watch to Courtney at Christmas. By New Year's, she was gone. Courtney blinked away the memory. She didn't need thoughts of her ex compounding her pissy mood.

She focused again on the dial. It was 6:12 a.m., still the middle of the night back in Redmond and too early to catch anyone at the ad agency in Boston. *Oh, shit.* She felt helpless, as though she'd stepped back thirty years in time. She was almost always attached to her BlackBerry or laptop, wired to the rest of the world, but now, there was nothing she could do but sit, wait and stew in her own regret for making such a stupid mistake. Hell, she hadn't slept in and missed something important like this since the math midterm she slept through when she was a college freshman. This was simply inexcusable. She was a professional, and professionals didn't make amateur mistakes like this.

Courtney rose and hurried to the nearest Starbucks kiosk, hoping a jolt of caffeine would get her back on track and smooth the nightmare this day was becoming. She took a long, satisfying sip of her large Sumatran coffee and closed her eyes for a moment. In her mind's eye she saw her mother, heard her telling her, as she always had in life, to stop being so hard on herself.

It was true, all her life Courtney had been harder on herself than anyone else. A bad mark in school, failing to make the softball team in her freshman year of high school, whatever. She hadn't cared in the least what anyone else thought of those things. She was the one who beat herself up for days over her failures, vowing to never let them happen again no matter how hard she had to work. She hated screwing up and would do whatever she had to do to make up for it. She knew she would be castigating herself over the missed flight for at least the next week. She pitied her colleagues and anyone else she'd be coming into contact with.

Courtney smiled to herself. "All work and no play" was what her mother would say to her if she were here now. *Does that mean I should have played a little with what's-her-name last night? Gone a few athletic rounds with her between the sheets?* Well, maybe she should have. But she'd still have been late, she'd still be pissed at herself and, what the hell, she probably still would have had to fake an orgasm.

She sighed to herself, not quite able to loosen the invisible chains she so often wrapped herself in. It was exhausting being so uptight all the time, so hard on herself and others too. Her mom had once told Courtney that she was more severe in nature than the Pope himself. Well, Courtney had proven that theory wrong at least once—at the women's Hot Flash dance in Portland three years ago. If her mom had been looking down on her that night, she'd have thought someone else had taken over Courtney's body. Somebody a hell of a lot wilder and crazier. Someone who most definitely did not resemble either her daughter or the Pope.

Courtney was still alternately amused and horrified by what she'd done at that dance. She'd had a few too many drinks after a day in the hot sun and, at the relentless encouragement of her boisterous friends, went absolutely nuts to Rick James' *Super Freak*. She'd been super freaky, all right. Stripping down to her sports bra and boxers and dancing on a table, air grinding like there was no tomorrow…she didn't even remember what all. *Oh, Jesus*. It'd been the most fun she'd ever had, but also the most embarrassing. For months afterward, women on the streets of Portland and even Seattle had smiled knowingly at her or winked in acknowledgment. A few had even handed her their phone numbers or tried to high-five her. She'd been so humiliated, she briefly considered asking for a transfer away from the Pacific Northwest.

There had been another reason to regret that night, unfortunately. For that was the night she met Celine, who, after witnessing that dance floor display, had decided that Courtney was the coolest, most adventurous dyke on earth. What a joke that turned out to be. By the time Celine realized what Courtney was really like—working sixty hours a week, then hiding out alone with a good book on her down time—they'd begun shacking up together like an old married couple. Dinner at eight, bed at ten, Courtney up by dawn so she could get a session in at the gym before her workday started. Weekends she spent on her BlackBerry or trying out game ideas from one of her developers. It was a routine that Celine couldn't accept, as it turned out.

Courtney glanced at the time again. Her flight to Logan Airport would start boarding any minute. *Thank God.*

At that same moment, in Boston, a loud thunderclap rolled in from the ocean and reverberated off skyscrapers tinged pink by the rising sun, breaking the calm of a glorious April morning.

Still at her Chicago gate, Courtney flinched, as though an invisible hand had given her a small shove. Shaking off an odd feeling of foreboding, she gathered up her carry-on bag and joined the others queuing up for the plane.

Courtney spent the entire two-hour flight on her netbook, working on budget projections. It occurred to her momentarily how right Celine had been about her being a workaholic. *Tough shit.* She could work as much as she wanted now. Celine was gone; there was no one to bitch about it. It was heavenly to work without the guilt.

Courtney felt her neck muscles relax. She enjoyed her work. It challenged her and made her feel like she had a purpose—a purpose much in demand by her company. She was the manager of the division that created Xbox games and was paid handsomely for it. She owned a healthy portfolio of company stocks and had been given an Audi S4 as a bonus a year ago. She was appreciated at work. Which was a hell of a lot more than she'd felt at home the last couple of years.

Courtney dismissed thoughts of her nonexistent home life. There was no point to the exercise. Instead she drafted a long e-mail to her department sub-head. She wouldn't be able to send it until after she landed, but it was one more item to strike off her mental to-do list.

No one on the plane suspected anything was wrong after they landed in Boston until the wait on the tarmac began to stretch out. The plane's door remained closed, keeping them trapped in that tin can like so much tuna fish. Fifteen minutes passed and still they weren't allowed to disembark. Courtney sighed loudly, unfastened a button at her collar to cool herself. This was going to make her even more late for her meeting, dammit. She flagged down a flight attendant.

"What's going on?"

She was answered with a shrug and a lame smile, as though

this sort of thing happened all the time. "Probably a ground crew issue, ma'am. I'm sure we'll be out of here any minute."

Yeah, right, Courtney thought. *It's just not my fucking day.*

No sooner had the thought begun burning in her mind than the plane's door opened and passengers began streaming out. *Finally*. Courtney breathed a sigh of relief, her thoughts catapulting ahead to her meeting and how she'd kept everyone waiting. Her long strides carried her through the enclosed ramp. She shot ahead of most of her fellow passengers, intent on getting her luggage and a cab as quickly as she could. She chose not to turn on her BlackBerry yet. She could do that in the cab.

She entered the terminal, searching for the sign that would point her to the baggage area, her mind going a mile a minute with all the things she had to do. It took several moments to register that something was terribly wrong. The sharp scream of a woman stopped her in her tracks. There were muffled cries and sobs too. Whispered conversation that was somber and urgent. The atmosphere was incredibly still, almost funereal, and there was a heaviness in the air, as though something had sucked all the oxygen out of the massive airport.

Courtney glanced around. There were small groups of people huddled together. Some were crying, others were comforting them. Priests and pastors sat or walked slowly with people, holding onto their arms tightly. Airline officials, looking grave and a little scared, clutched clipboards or cell phones like lifelines. They were trying to look helpful but clearly they were overwhelmed.

What the hell is going on?

Courtney had traveled many thousands of miles throughout her career, and she had never seen anything as bizarre as this. It was like being in the eye of a hurricane, because in spite of the stillness, it felt as though malevolent and chaotic forces were swirling around them. She felt her face drain of color. The metallic taste of fear filled her mouth. Something most definitely was horribly wrong.

"Excuse me." Courtney tugged the sleeve of the nearest

airline employee. "What's going on around here?"

The employee, a middle-aged African American woman, scrutinized Courtney for a long moment. She looked frayed, exhausted, like she was having a much worse day than Courtney. "Flight 351 from Chicago crashed into the ocean two hours ago. Families of the passengers are congregating here. If you have no further business here, ma'am, I respectfully suggest you move along."

Courtney blinked hard, taking in the tableau of sorrow around her. It was surreal...almost like a scene from a movie. Except it was all too real. These were real people, people whose loved ones had just been killed. They were devastated, horrified, lost. Some looked adrift, numbed by shock. For others, the reality of what had happened was painfully sharp.

It was too much for Courtney to comprehend. She resumed her trek to the baggage claim area, moving along at a much slower pace. She wanted to get the hell away from this place and yet she was inexplicably connected to it.

Halfway to the baggage area her legs suddenly gave out. She sagged against a wall, her heart pounding furiously in her throat. *Holy shit! I was supposed to be on that flight.*

She doubled over, fighting the urge to vomit. She forced deep, even breaths into her lungs, the way she'd been taught at a stress management workshop for managers a long time ago.

Except...I wasn't on that flight. I wasn't on it, and there's nothing I can do about it now.

A moment later another realization slammed into her. Danny *was* on that plane.

Oh, my God! She couldn't breathe. Couldn't think. Couldn't feel anything in all this emptiness. Her reality—the order of her world—had been neatly excised in the few seconds it took a plane to plummet into the sea. How could Danny, her young, hotshot game developer, that great kid with the killer dimples and teddy bear eyes, be dead? And how could *she* still be alive?

Finally, like a camera lens coming into focus, her thoughts began to coalesce. She had a meeting to get to, a job to do. Yes, the meeting she was two hours late for—that was what mattered now. She had to get her feet moving again, had to get there and get on with it. She did not want to be stranded here with the others who were trying and failing to make sense of it all.

Courtney forced herself to straighten up and take another deep breath, commanding herself to stay calm. She would not think about the alternative. *Couldn't* think about it. Could not fathom the fact that she could be dead instead of standing here. *Dead like Danny.*

She clenched her jaw, firming her resolve. She was *not* going to become part of the collateral damage of Flight 351's crash, dammit! She was not going to be a victim of this tragedy!

Courtney pushed herself forward, not even feeling the ground beneath her. She had places to be, things to do, people to see. Soon she was no longer walking, she was running.

The frantic e-mails from Nancy, her assistant, were heart-wrenching, but not as heart-wrenching as the e-mail that Danny must have sent when he got on the plane and saw that Courtney wasn't there. It had popped up the minute she finally remembered to turn on her BlackBerry in the cab. She couldn't get his words out of her mind. *Miss you boss, where the heck are you? Will carry on without you for now.*

His e-mail had been followed by a dozen more, increasingly frantic, from Nan, who was old enough to be Courtney's mother and who often watched over like a surrogate parent. Steeling herself, Courtney punched in Nan's phone number. She answered halfway through the first ring, sobbing uncontrollably when she heard Courtney's voice. She'd desperately been trying to reach Courtney and Danny ever since hearing about the crash and realizing their itinerary placed them on the fatal flight.

In the back of a taxi, her phone at her ear, Courtney tried to calm Nan down. The older woman couldn't seem to stop crying, however, especially when she learned that Danny *had* made the flight. Looking around her, Courtney realized she was only minutes away from her meeting. It was cold to cut Nan off and order her to liaise with the airline about Danny, but she had to concentrate on her meeting now. She had a multi-million-dollar ad campaign to organize. Unfortunately, business didn't grind to a halt because of personal tragedies.

Courtney knew that if ever there was a time to shelve her feelings, this was it. Luckily, compartmentalization was something she was an expert at. It was as easy for her as brushing her teeth or getting dressed. She could write a book on how to ignore a dying relationship or to put aside grief. She still hadn't really grieved for her mom because work was always a handy filler. It was her savior, her excuse, her raison d'être. The day Celine had left, Courtney had gone off to work as usual, only vaguely wondering throughout the day if Celine really was gone for good. She was.

Shocked faces and murmured sympathy greeted Courtney as she strode into the conference room of McKerroll and Stanley. It was obvious they already knew she was to have been on that flight and they were all eager to express their relief that she had missed it. They didn't know about Danny—she hadn't told them she was bringing anyone with her—and she didn't tell them now. It didn't feel right to have them express sympathy for someone they didn't know and care about. She let them fetch her ice water, pull out a chair for her. They treated her like someone's ancient aunt. The company's CEO, Roger McKerroll, offered, while patting her hand, to delay the meeting a week or two—whatever she needed.

Courtney stared at him, unblinking, and for a second felt a sob catch in her throat. It would be so easy to cry, to get angry, to be grateful, to be sorry, to be guilty—to give in to all of these emotions that now battled inside her. But she couldn't give in to them. She would not play the role of victim, someone to feel sorry for or to make special accommodations for, someone to be pitied.

No. She was the head of this project, the leader, the alpha dog. It would not do to crumble and cry like a baby. How pathetic would that be? Especially when there were probably dozens of others waiting, like vultures, to prove they could do her job and do it better. Well, the vultures would have to keep on circling, because she was tough. She knew how to get up after a fall. She'd been doing that all her life and she wasn't about to stop now. This was a piece of cake next to her dad abandoning her and her mom when Courtney was just a kid, Courtney having to help her mom pick up the pieces, emotionally and, later, financially. No, this meeting, she could easily do.

"I'm fine," she declared, her voice cracking from the adrenaline still coursing through her body. "I'm here now…" She smiled, though she didn't feel like it. *I will not think about Danny, I will not!* "This project is on a tight deadline, ladies and gentlemen, and we cannot afford to lose any time. We've shortlisted the ad campaigns down to, what, four I believe?"

McKerroll nodded.

Courtney opened the purple binder before her, no longer able to hold their questioning gazes. "Good, then let's take a close look at those. We'll narrow the campaign down to two today, then we'll test-market those. Understood?"

The heads around the table reluctantly nodded. They still looked like rubberneckers at a traffic accident, stunned and curious, constantly watching her to see if she'd crack or fold. Why the hell weren't they all getting on with their work? It was terrible that those poor people had died this morning, that loved ones were grieving. Courtney was absolutely sick about Danny. He wasn't married, she knew that. She didn't think he had a significant other, but she wasn't sure. He was young, eager, good at his job, a nice guy. He looked up to her, and his good work had made her life easier. It absolutely sucked that he had been on that plane. But hell, what was she supposed to do? Was she supposed to fling herself on the pyre? All the tears in the world couldn't change what happened, wouldn't bring Danny and the others back. Life went on. There was work to be done.

The direct flight back to Seattle wasn't quite as unnerving as Courtney expected it to be. The lorazepam she'd borrowed from someone at the meeting helped. It went down quite nicely with the vodka and orange she'd downed in the airport lounge, as a matter of fact. She was mostly able to banish thoughts of Danny and crashes and flying again. It was difficult to ignore the constant assault of the TV news, which was unrelenting, but somehow she'd managed it. She didn't want to hear another goddamned thing about that crash—not how it happened nor anything about the passengers. When she overheard her fellow passengers whispering about it in the row ahead, she got up and moved. She could keep it all together if only she didn't have to think or hear about what she'd narrowly missed—and about what Danny had not missed.

The rest of the week, back at work at Microsoft's sprawling headquarters, which was like a small city unto itself, Courtney stayed the course. She worked twelve-hour days, pounding her body at the gym for an extra hour each morning before work, taking a couple of stiff drinks at home before dropping into bed each night. She graciously accepted the acknowledgments of sympathy for her department over Danny's loss. She rallied her remaining troops, telling them that the best way to pay homage to Danny was by doing the kind of stellar work he had done. Showed them that strong people carried on and moved past their grief, that work was their salve. She was stoic at the memorial service for him, even as Nan and many of the others fell apart.

She was, in fact, the picture of dependability and strength—until eight days later when a phone call plucked her from the reality she'd created for herself. She answered the phone at her desk only because it wouldn't stop ringing, belatedly remembering it was past five and Nan had gone home.

"Is this Courtney Langford?"

"Yes."

"Bob Warren. I'm a reporter with the *Boston Globe*."

Courtney didn't deal with the media. Microsoft had a very

lovely and very large department full of people to deal with reporters. "I'm sorry, Mr. Warren. You'll have to talk to our PR department."

"No, it's you I want to talk to."

"Look, I don't talk directly to—"

"It's about the plane crash outside of Logan Airport last week."

Courtney's breath left her in a silent rush. Her ears began to ring.

"I'm sorry, but you must be looking for someone else." She knew she sounded weak and shaky. If he wanted to talk about Danny, he'd have to talk to public relations or human resources. She sure as hell wasn't going to talk about Danny to some stranger.

"No, I'm looking for the Courtney Langford who works for Microsoft. The Courtney Langford who was supposed to be on that flight that crashed."

Oh, God, what could this guy possibly want with that piece of information? And how the hell did he find out? Had someone at the company squealed? Someone at McKerroll and Stanley? The airline? It wasn't that she'd done anything wrong or unusual or heroic, or…anything at all, except miss a flight that her colleague had not been as fortunate to do. "Look, Mr. Warren. I don't know where you got your information, but—"

"My sources are reliable. Ms. Langford, there were one hundred and sixty-one people on that flight. You're the only one who was supposed to be on that plane but wasn't."

"Are you implying something?" Courtney was horrified. Did he think she had orchestrated some kind of plot to get Danny killed but not herself? Or that she was supposed to feel *bad* for missing that flight? Did he think she had received some sort of divine information that she should have shared with the other passengers or the airline to keep that plane from flying to Boston? *What?*

"Not at all. I just want to talk to you about how it feels. You know, to be a survivor and all."

14

Courtney couldn't speak. *Survivor.* The word hung over her like a guillotine.

So that's what I am now. That's what I'm supposed to be known ever after for...for missing a flight that crashed and killed everyone on board. Courtney Langford, airplane crash survivor. Or Courtney Langford, the luckiest woman alive. Not Courtney Langford, Masters in Business Administration. Or Courtney Langford, division head of Xbox games development for Microsoft Corp.

This Warren guy, and plenty of others, would not think of her as anything other than the woman who should have been on that doomed flight. Hell, she'd noticed that many of her colleagues were having a hard time looking her in the eye and that the ones who did looked like they didn't have a clue how to act around her. Or like they even wanted to be around her, because she might be some kind of ghost or bad luck charm.

Courtney tried to say something, but her voice had completely deserted her. With a shaky hand, she slammed down the phone instead. At some point in the conversation she had stood up, and now she rocked on her heels, dizzy, as the ringing in her ears intensified. She was shaking too. Scared that she would pass out, Courtney slumped back into her leather chair. She buried her face in her hands. Her chest hurt like a son of a bitch. Was this the way a nervous breakdown started? Or an anxiety attack? It was like a speeding train bearing down on her, and there was nothing she could do to get out of the way.

Courtney didn't know what was happening to her, but she knew she was in trouble. She had never felt so alone in her life. Or so damaged.

CHAPTER TWO

Gambling tip: You cannot force a winning outcome and should not expect to win every time.

Six Weeks Later

Ellen Turcotte was a most unusual air traveler. A freak of nature, her best friend Samantha called her, because Ellen actually enjoyed the airport experience. The crowds, the sterile, wide-open spaces, the adorable little shops with their gimmicky merchandise and souvenirs. She found it exciting... Well, maybe not exciting, but a pleasurable diversion at least.

Sam, on the other hand, was one of those people who always wanted to hurry up and get there, and damned be to hell anyone who tried to slow her down. The crowds, even the little kiosks plunked in the middle of the wide corridors, were unwanted obstacles to her, things designed to make her life hell. If ever there were polar opposites in the world, it was Ellen and Sam, at least when it came to traveling. Flight delays, missed connections, crying babies, harried passengers. Whatever. Ellen took it all in stride. In fact, she prided herself on always being able to handle life's obstacles while maintaining her easygoing nature.

Maybe that was why Ellen had never really come clean with Sam about how much her impending divorce had been straining her sanity, swallowing up that laidback nature and crushing it like a dropped flower on a busy Yonge Street sidewalk. Sam would be shocked to learn of the days Ellen had spent curled up in bed these last few months, of the constant wavering back and forth, the self-examining that left her wrung out like an old dishrag. Some days she barely knew who she was or where she was going. It was as much as she could do to put one foot in front of the other.

She had kept the worst of it to herself. There was no sense worrying or shocking the crap out of her best friend, especially since she lived two thousand miles away in Vancouver. No sense either in forcing a role on Sam that she was simply not hardwired for. Sam would freak if she had to play the enabling, comforting, reassuring best friend, someone who promised Ellen an eternal world of lollipops and sunshine. A kick in the ass Sam was more than happy to give, but a shoulder to cry on? Not so much. Nevertheless, Ellen loved and relied on Sam like a sister, differences and all.

Ellen took a seat in the gate area, which was quickly filling up. The Toronto-to-Vancouver route was a popular one. It was the perfect place for people watching and the growing swirl of people amused Ellen. There was a group of what looked like medical students knotted together, talking excitedly about their forthcoming adventure. They all wore bright red T-shirts that proudly proclaimed, "Medical Outreach, Philippines." There were a couple of air force officers in uniform, both gray-haired and older than Ellen would have expected. There was a cranky elderly couple, stiff and short with each other, worn down like old sticks from too many decades together. A young couple tried everything to quiet their crying baby. Seated several rows ahead of Ellen, a twenty-something-year-old guy was reading a magazine article called "Sexy Things To Do After Sex." Now *that*

17

was amusing. Tips on how to get a woman into bed would be more appropriate for a young guy than what to do afterward. A young woman sat next to him, their shoulders touching intimately. Ellen smiled. *Good for you, girl. Maybe you've got yourself a good catch there.*

Boarding interrupted her musings. Just as well. Ellen didn't want to think too hard or for too long about any of these people's lives and especially not about romantic things to do in or out of bed. Not when her own life was falling to shit.

As she fastened her seatbelt, Ellen caught sight of her bare left hand. The imprint from her wedding ring was still faintly there. Like the ring, Susan was gone, but her absence still lingered. The pain still branded Ellen.

The big bird taxied slowly out to the runway, stuffed to the gills with about three hundred passengers. Ellen loved taking off, getting airborne. It made her feel like she was leaving the world behind, which, in a sense, she was. It was the world she had known for the last thirteen years anyway, and good riddance to it. *Sayonara, baby!* She was more than overdue for a break, and visiting Sam for a month was exactly what she needed.

Ellen's heart beat faster as the jet sped down the runway like a torpedo, panic suddenly chasing her. Hell, who was she trying to kid, pretending to be so cavalier about the changes she'd recently made, like leaving her marriage. It was damn scary, like nothing she'd ever been through before. But try telling Sam that. Sam had little patience for Ellen's ex and even less for any signs of regret on Ellen's part. "Get on with it, Ellen." "Get back to living your damn life as it was meant to be lived." Those were Sam's overused refrains. It was all so simple in Sam's eyes. So black and white. Ellen watched the ground below grow smaller and smaller, felt herself grow smaller and smaller too. *If only I had your confidence, Sammy girl.*

The jet climbed quickly and Ellen closed her eyes. Where was that optimistic attitude of hers these days, when she needed it most? It had deserted her. Gone like a cold-hearted lover at dawn, claimed by that grim reaper called divorce. *Well, crap.* She'd get it back eventually. A verbal kick in the ass every day from Sam would certainly help.

Ellen opened the novel she'd brought with her, closed it just as quickly. Reading required more attention than she could summon right now. If it hadn't been for Sam's insistent pleas to come out for an extended visit, she'd probably be preparing to fulfill her obligation of teaching spring term at Seldon College. She'd been teaching English lit and creative writing for so long she could do it in her sleep. She'd plodded through winter term, taking some comfort in standing daily before a classroom of eager young adults and getting lost in literature. Work had provided a much needed escape, but she was smart enough to know that burying herself in her books and in her job weren't going to cut it much longer. It was time to do something different, to think positive again, to try to get some of that sanguine spirit of hers back. It wasn't impossible. She could go for long, restorative walks in Stanley Park, swim in the pool at Sam's condo, bike ride along the harbor, check out Granville Island, shop downtown, take a drive up to Whistler and admire the mountains. Let the outdoors clear her mind, replenish her strength.

Ellen closed her eyes tightly. She still blamed Susan for shattering her life, even though the rawest of the hurt had begun to wane. It was Susan who'd turned her life upside down. Susan who'd made her question everything about her existence and doubt everything about their thirteen-year relationship. It was Susan's fault she was now unsure about her entire future, save for getting up in the mornings. It was Susan's actions, Susan's decisions, that had led to all of this. *Maybe someday I'll stop blaming her, but it sure as hell isn't going to be now.*

At the airport baggage carousel, Sam enveloped her in a long, exuberant hug. "Oh, my God, girl, it's good to see you!" Sam disengaged and scrutinized Ellen, smiling so widely that Ellen thought her face might split in two. "Goddamn, though, you need to put on a couple of pounds."

"Please. My sweet tooth is firmly intact." She patted her tummy. By most people's standards it was tiny, but Ellen knew she could still pinch an inch on her smallish frame.

"How was your flight?"

"Good. But better that it was me flying and not you, especially so soon after that crash in Boston." Sam was a poor flyer, which explained why she only came to visit Ellen every two or three years.

"Tell me about it. God. That was terrible. Did they ever figure out what went wrong? I try not to read any news on it, or it'll be at least five years before I come see you again instead of the usual two or three."

Ellen shrugged. She hadn't paid much attention to the crash either. If she wanted to dwell on bad news, she had only to think about her own life. "I don't know. Something about the hydraulics, I think."

"So," Sam said, eyeing the bags dropping unceremoniously onto the carousel. "Hope you brought some sexy attire."

Ellen's mouth fell open. "What?"

"You know. Tight jeans, short shorts, lacy bras, maybe a halter top or at least a tank top or two." Sam laughed at Ellen, who was shaking her head. Sam's brashness could still surprise her sometimes. "Don't tell me after married life you've forgotten what sexy clothes are? Christ, you probably packed nothing but turtlenecks and baggy pants."

Ellen made a face at her friend before pulling her two bags off the carousel. She handed one to Sam. "And what would I need with sexy clothes if I did have them?"

Sam's chuckle was evil. "You're not going to sit around being a nun for the next month, I can promise you that."

"Oh, really." Ellen had no intention of hooking up with anybody right now. After thirteen years with the same woman and then the heartbreaking discovery that her monogamy hadn't been reciprocated, Ellen was nowhere near ready to think about being with someone else.

Sam, however, was a serial monogamist who was currently between relationships. Drifting from relationship to relationship seemed to come easy for her. Too easy, Ellen thought. Sam could take up with a new woman as easily as trying a new brand of wine. If only Sam had been drinking the same wine for thirteen years, as Ellen had, maybe she wouldn't find the transition so easy.

Sam slung her free arm around Ellen's shoulders as they headed for the parking garage. "Trust me, a little fun with someone new will make you feel so much better."

Ellen couldn't stop herself from smirking. She knew full well Sam's method of healing from a failed relationship was to jump right into another. It was her modus operandi, her coping mechanism. *Run fast enough and you can outrun the rain, eh, Sammy girl?*

"What?" Sam asked skeptically, taking in Ellen's know-it-all smile.

"Nothing." This was not the time or place to discuss their respective attitudes about relationships. Besides, Ellen's view was so jaded right now, it wouldn't be an objective conversation. She'd probably end up suggesting they become nuns for about, oh, the next eighteen years or so.

Sam halted at a silver Jeep Patriot and opened the back tailgate for Ellen's bags. "How do you like my new wheels?"

Ellen gave it a quick once-over. "Pretty nice. A little boxy, though, isn't it?"

Sam rolled her eyes before unlocking the passenger door for Ellen. "Still driving that boring little Mazda3?"

Ellen climbed in, rebuffing the insult with indignation. "It is *not* boring. It's reliable and cheap on gas."

"So is my bicycle, but that doesn't mean I want to ride it everywhere."

Ellen shook her head. A month with Sam was going to either kill her or cure her.

The marina restaurant was packed, but Ellen couldn't keep her eyes off the placid water outside and the way the sun's dying rays danced and rippled across it. She lived not far from the water

21

herself in Toronto, but it wasn't as peaceful and quiet as this. Toronto was much more of a rat race than Vancouver. Dirtier, smellier, louder and much busier. It also didn't have majestic mountains—nature's skyscrapers—hovering over it.

"See anything you like?" Sam gave her a suggestive leer.

"Samantha Calloway, you are incorrigible. I know you aren't talking about the scenery, so don't even *try* to play dumb with me."

Sam laughed from behind her martini. "I am talking about the scenery, but not outside." She leaned closer and lowered her voice. "There's a few sisters in here tonight."

Ellen took a quick look around. There was a table of five lesbians in the corner, young and carefree, getting louder with every sip of their drinks. At another table were two women who appeared to be a couple sharing an intimate dinner. At a third table was a woman flying solo. She was butch, handsome, and sending subtle glances Ellen's way. "So there are," Ellen answered with a small shrug.

"You could go for a little dessert with one of them afterward, eh? Maybe *her*?" She nodded toward the woman dining on her own.

"I think you're confusing me with yourself."

Sam leaned back, full of casual indifference. "Not my type."

"Well, even if she *was* my type, and I'm not saying she is, let's just say I don't have much of an appetite for dessert anymore."

"C'mon. You said yourself you have a sweet tooth."

"For sugar. You know, that white, refined, sweet-tasting, powdery stuff."

"Oh, Ellen. You're missing out, that's all. You're sittin' here being Mother Teresa, while you can bet your sweet ass that Susan is still getting plenty of sugar, and I don't mean the white, sweet, powdery stuff."

Ellen had known the conversation would get around to her ex eventually. She was surprised it had taken this long. She exaggeratedly looked at her watch. "Wow, that's a new record. It took you two hours and twenty-two minutes to mention her."

"Yeah, well, she's like gum on a shoe. No, wait." Sam screwed up her face. "She's like the smell of vomit in the backseat of a car that takes forever to go away."

Ellen laughed before disgust took over. "Sam, you're a horrible person."

"Yes, but you love me and you're lucky to have me in your life."

Ellen smiled. Sam was right. They loved each other like sisters and were lucky to have each other. The years and distance had done nothing to diminish their closeness. Her thoughts began to turn dark, as they always did when Susan entered them. Susan was the ghost always hovering in the room. "Maybe," she said quietly, "if we don't talk about Susan, she'll go away."

Sam was eyeing her suspiciously. She had to see that Ellen was close to tears. "I promise you, my friend, that by the end of this visit, you'll be asking 'Susan Who?'"

Ellen shook her head. She wished it were that easy. "Well, then, I hope you know a damned good hypnosis method. Or maybe you're planning to hire a hit man."

"Christ, I should." She pointed her glass at Ellen. "After what she did to—"

"Sam, stop. We've been over that many times, okay?"

"I know." Resignation was heavy in Sam's voice, but her eyes were fiery with an incinerating kind of hatred. "I hate the thought of anyone hurting you, El. It kills me."

"I know it does." Sam and Ellen had met at the University of Toronto when they were freshmen—Ellen an English major and Sam in the nursing program. They had been inseparable for years, until jobs, girlfriends and geography put distance between them. Their devotion and loyalty to one another, however, remained a constant in their lives.

Ellen softly placed her hand over Sam's. "I'm going to be all right, I promise. I just need time."

Sam had always been Ellen's protector—now more than ever. She looked at Ellen like she didn't quite believe her. "Well, I'm going to do my damnedest to make sure you're going to be okay. And you can take *that* to the bank!"

Ellen so wanted Sam to be right. She watched her friend pull out her cell phone and quickly glance at a text message. The simple act reminded her painfully of the first hint she'd gotten last year that something wasn't right between her and Susan. She'd taken Susan's cell phone by mistake—their phones were nearly identical—and accidentally discovered a suspicious text message from someone named Jessica. Signed with a bunch of x's and o's, it had said she couldn't wait to see Susan the next night. At first Ellen chalked it up to harmlessness. Probably an old friend from high school, she figured. Or maybe a colleague Susan was particularly close to and somehow hadn't mentioned in their thirteen years together. She'd come up with all kinds of possibilities and excuses until she was finally and explicitly hit over the head with the obvious.

"You look a little green," Sam interjected. "Are you okay? Was it the salmon?"

"I'm fine." Ellen wasn't really, but she didn't want to spend the whole evening talking about Susan. Trash talking her, more like. While heaping the world's troubles on her ex might be fun for a while, it wouldn't really help. Ellen knew that from experience.

"Ellen, look. I know you don't want to spend the whole month here talking about Susan. And we're not going to, but—"

"I know. It's that she's always here, even when she's not, and I'd just like a goddamned break from her, you know?"

"Yes, I do know. But I'm your friend. Your *best* friend. And I want to help. It's the first time we've gotten together since you two broke up."

Ellen reached across the table and took Sam's hand again. "I know, and you are helping, trust me."

"Good. But I'd feel so much better if I could beat the bitch up. Five minutes with her, that's all I need." Rage sparked in Sam's eyes again, making Ellen appreciate her friend's unyielding loyalty, even if it was rather juvenile and comical at the moment.

"I assure you, beating the shit out of Susan is not necessary, though I appreciate the offer."

"Might teach her not to mess with you. Or me."

24

If it'd been that simple, Ellen would have battered and bruised her ex months ago. Especially that afternoon when she'd entered their condo, her class having been canceled because of a bomb threat, and walked in on Susan, her *wife*, for Christ sake's, with another woman's bare legs wrapped around her shoulders. Even now, she could taste the paralyzing nausea and numbness, as raw as it had been that horrible day.

Tears sprang to her eyes as she recalled the sick smile on that Jessica person's face and then Susan's dumb-ass explanation. It was more than laughable. It was downright insulting. She'd been drunk, Susan said. *Yeah, right, in the middle of the afternoon.*

Jessica was some bartender who had practically stalked her, had thrown herself at her, Susan pleaded. She'd do anything if only Ellen would give her another chance. She'd begged. Cried. Practically done headstands. Then a week later, she was gone. Said she had to explore her inner self. Which was really just a bullshit way of saying she wanted to fuck around some more.

"Okay, look," Sam pleaded. "Let's leave Susan for another time. How about tomorrow night I take you out for a little night action on Davie Street. What do you say?"

Ellen narrowed her eyes. She knew from past visits that Davie Street was the city's gay area and that it could be quite lively at night. "As long as you're not going to throw me at some woman. God, how embarrassing." She pointed a menacing finger at Sam. "You'd better not treat me like some virgin on her first night out on the town looking to get laid, because it's not going to happen."

"What, me?" Sam feigned innocence, but she was grinning like a little troublemaker.

"All right." Ellen forced a smile and with it felt her tension over Susan subside a little. Maybe it wouldn't actually hurt to go along with Sam's antics for once. "I'm game for a night on the town. A *nice* night on the town. And you'd better be good!"

"Oh, I'm always good, honey!"

CHAPTER THREE

Gambling tip: Gamble only what you can afford to lose.

Courtney's spirits soared at the feeling of solid, bone-rattling metal between her thighs. Each vibration made her feel at one with the road, reminding her in a tangible way that she was connected to the earth below her. It was perfect, because she was never going to fly again. That was the only thing she was certain of right now. That and the open interstate stretching out ahead of her like a map unfurling.

She reached down and patted the metallic midnight blue tank of the Indian Chief Roadmaster. Only days old, it was her baby now. It was just her and the Indian and the I-5 leading to Vancouver, Canada. Everything else she had sold or was leaving in storage.

If someone had told her two months ago that she was going to quit her dream job and take to the open road, she would have told them to go to hell. Angelina Jolie in a negligee, flinging open her office door with a come-hither look, would have been much more likely. Nevertheless, one day Courtney was living her life the same way she'd been doing for years and the next it was suddenly like she was looking through a porthole, watching someone else going through the motions of her life. She no longer recognized herself, had no idea what she was doing or even where she was anymore in her life. It was as though she'd been transported to another land or another time, like being thrown into some crazy fairy tale.

It had happened shortly after that newspaper reporter's phone call. His questions had nudged open the door to thoughts about the crash she hadn't let herself consider before. Then the airline called her, asking if she needed support and suggesting that she should come to them first if she needed anything. Her colleagues gradually began asking her questions about the crash too and about how she was doing. They were timid at first, then grew bolder. The breaking point occurred in a meeting with other department heads. Someone made a joke—*a goddamned joke!*—that since she seemed to have a lucky horseshoe up her ass, she might nab the CEO's job next. Courtney slammed her laptop shut and wordlessly stalked out of the room, never to return to work again, as it turned out.

For two days she sat in the dark of her living room. She didn't answer phone calls, didn't log into her e-mail, didn't even turn on the television. And then she did the only thing she could think of, which was to run like hell. She quit her job over the phone, called a realtor. Suddenly, what she was doing was the easiest and most necessary thing in the world. No more rat race, no more working on computer games. Meaningless shit, those games were anyway. No more strings, nothing holding her down anymore.

Nan tried so hard to talk her out of it. Took her out for dinner, her tears dotting the tablecloth like inkspots as she pleaded with Courtney to stick with the status quo for a while longer.

"You can't quit, honey." Nan practically begged.

"Actually, I can." Courtney stifled a giggle. She was high on being alive and ecstatic with the knowledge that her life was hers to do with as she wished, no matter what anyone thought or expected of her. Nan couldn't take that new sense of freedom away from her. Nothing could.

"Why not take a leave until you can sort yourself out? Please, Courtney."

Courtney stubbornly shook her head. "There is nothing to sort out. Besides, it would be putting off the inevitable."

"And what is that, exactly? What plans do you have?"

Courtney shrugged her answer.

"There must be something…"

"Nope, not really. Other than buying the motorcycle I've always wanted and hitting the road."

"To where?"

Courtney was coy. She didn't want anyone hunting her down in Vancouver, trying to urge her back to Seattle and the life she could no longer live. "I don't know yet."

"What about money? Won't you have to work eventually?"

Courtney had made a nice six-figure salary for years. Made a tidy profit on her condo too. She wouldn't need to work for at least a couple of years, maybe even three or four if she was careful. Nan should know that, but she was grasping at straws, saying anything to make Courtney reconsider.

"Look, I can't do this crap anymore, okay? I can't come to work and pretend that these stupid video games mean a damn thing to me anymore. I can't pretend that work is all I care about, that it's my life. I feel like I'm trapped in a goddamned box. I have to get out."

"But honey, that's all you *did* care about for years. How can you not care anymore?"

Courtney couldn't explain it, even if she'd wanted to. She was different now, the way a day could begin sunny and then end stormy. The old things didn't mean as much to her anymore, and new things did, like listening to a good song or lingering over coffee instead of gulping it down like pumping gasoline into a car. Even the damned birds singing could captivate her now, and watching grass grow had never been more fascinating. As silly as it all sounded, it had become true for Courtney. Where she used to sprint, she now crawled in slow motion. Of course it didn't make sense. *But why does it have to?*

"You wouldn't understand. I'm not the same person I was a few weeks ago, Nan. Things are different now." She didn't want to get further into the subject of the plane crash with her.

"But maybe with time things will get back to normal," Nan suggested hopefully. "Maybe you're right to take some time off. Do some fun things for a change. There used to be a daredevil in you when you first started here." Nan laughed uncertainly. "I remember you belonged to the company's skydiving club, and every Saturday for a while, you'd be up in some plane, then hurtling toward earth. Remember that?"

Courtney did. Years ago she had tried all the things a young game developer was expected to do…skydiving, waterskiing, downhill skiing, squash every week. And then she got serious about her work and serious about climbing the corporate ladder. She grew up and stopped stretching herself so thin and living wildly and began concentrating more on her job.

"I haven't been that person for a long time. And I'm especially not that person now."

Nan nodded somberly. Maybe she did get it. "Courtney." She took Courtney's hand across the table, patted it in a motherly fashion. "Dear, if this is bigger than you, then why don't you try getting some help? I know that crash and Danny's death, God rest his soul, really shook you up."

Okay, maybe she didn't get it. Nan was playing a role, that was all. Saying what she thought needed to be said in circumstances like these. "I don't need therapy, Nan. I need a life. There must be some reason I wasn't on that plane, so maybe I need to be by myself and figure out what that is." And she needed to figure it out alone, without well-meaning people like Nan constantly bugging her.

The worst of it, the part she would never be able to talk about, was that if she had died alongside Danny on that plane, there would have been no one left behind to truly miss her. That part hurt as much as anything. She was alone in this world, and no one, except maybe Nan in her limited way, gave a rat's ass about her. Her friends she hardly saw anymore, her mom was dead and her absentee father was long gone to God knew where. Her colleagues, hell, they didn't give a shit about her outside of her job performance.

Nan eyed her curiously. That was okay. People wouldn't understand, because they weren't her and they hadn't been through what she'd been through. Courtney promptly excused herself from their dinner, promised to keep in touch, promised that if she got depressed or couldn't figure out what to do with herself, she would get help. It was all bullshit. Courtney planned to cut all her ties with her past, even to nice old Nan. Colleagues and friends all saw her as different now anyway, tainted somehow and either freakishly lucky or just plain freakish or fucked up. She didn't want to see herself in their eyes. Her self-imposed exile was the only way to accomplish that.

Courtney smiled now beneath her full-faced helmet, reveling in the wind buffeting against her leather-jacketed chest. She liked this feeling of the wind physically pounding her, because it reminded her that she was alive. She had jumped off a cliff, having left her former life behind, and this bike was her lifeline. Her lifeboat. For the first time since she was a kid, she had no responsibilities, no plans. And while at one time that would have scared the crap out of her, it didn't anymore. With each mile she put behind her she felt like she was shedding another layer of herself. Every mile was another inch of freedom.

Courtney throttled up a little more, watched the speedometer's needle creep up. Eighty. Eighty-five. Ninety. "Woohoo!" She passed a car that seemed like it was standing still, then another. She and the Indian were quick and invincible, like a laser beam shooting across the interstate. She was on the ground. Safe. Death couldn't catch her. No. Death had spared her for some reason. She had no clue yet what that was. Had no clue whether she would ever figure it out, either, but she could at least enjoy the ride and her newfound immortality.

Silently, Courtney continued to celebrate the bike and the road beneath her. Even more beauty awaited her as she gunned for Exit 231—Chuckanut Drive. She loved the name and the road, which was named for the mountains along the route. It was a beautiful, two-laned drive along the water, through small towns with views overlooking the bay, Samish Island and the San Juan Islands. She stopped the bike, mesmerized by the view of Samish Bay, where the setting sun was shimmering pink over the water. The allure of the sunset was like a magnet. She could not take her eyes off it for a very long time.

Courtney finally parked the bike and shut off its powerful engine, her rumbling stomach reminding her she hadn't eaten in hours. She would have dinner at The Oyster Bar, where she could gaze uninterrupted at what was left of the sinking sun. Removing her helmet, she pondered her sudden fascination with the sunset. It's not like she hadn't seen thousands of them, and beautiful ones too, living along the West Coast. But it was a thing of wonder, so peaceful and beautiful, with such a will of its own, setting every evening no matter what ugliness or horribleness had gone on during the hours before. It was one of the few things in this world, Courtney realized, that could be counted on. It astounded her that she'd hardly ever paid attention to it before.

Courtney took a seat at a small table by the window, shedding her leather jacket. The wood ceiling tapered to the giant windows overlooking the bay. It was quickly darkening as Courtney ordered from the menu, lights from the oil refinery beckoning from an island across the water. The lights twinkled, and Courtney's breath caught in her chest. A vision of that shiny, silver airliner, its wing lights winking as it backed away from the terminal, flashed before her. It was only an instant, but it was like she was right there again, pissed off and rushing around because she'd missed the damned thing by mere minutes. Sweat popped out on her forehead, and her breath tightened in her chest like a fist.

Courtney shook her head to clear it, then took a drink of the sour apple martini before her. Pleasure boats with their running lights, bobbing like candles flickering in the wind, slowly made their way along the shore. The alcohol was soothing, mercifully making that damned flashback fade. *Thank God.*

Her oysters arrived on a bed of sea salt, surrounding a dish of seasoned balsamic vinegar and oil. There were only a handful of them, and Courtney eagerly devoured them, dipping each one in the oil. The tiger prawns were equally satisfying, after she separated the soft flesh from the grilled shells to get at the tender, sumptuous meat inside.

She should have taken more time to enjoy this sort of thing before, she chastised herself. Celine had always wanted to take this drive up here and stay overnight at a bed-and-breakfast somewhere, explore the little towns and shop for antiques. But Courtney had been too busy or too tired or uninterested. All of that was history now, and the question of whether she and Celine would still be together if she had done those things was rhetorical. Celine was long gone, their relationship having crashed and burned like that goddamned plane.

Courtney moved from her table to the long wooden bar, where she ordered another drink. That probably meant she shouldn't drive her bike. She'd already had two drinks, surpassing her one-drink rule when it came to riding a motorcycle.

What the hell, she thought as the drink was placed in front of her. *You only live once, and when your number's up, your number's up.* Obviously hers wasn't.

"Hi."

Courtney hadn't noticed the young woman slide into the seat next to her. She had long brown hair, a shade or two darker than Courtney's sandy-colored hair, and her skin was clear and unlined. The girl's eyes were doe-like, the kind that hadn't seen much of the world yet.

Jesus, are you even legally allowed to drink? "Back at ya."

This was definitely a girl all right, proudly wearing her University of Washington T-shirt over braless breasts. It was hard not to notice those two orbs, jutting out like so many of the mountains Courtney had passed on her bike.

"What are you drinking?" The girl indicated Courtney's drink, her smile as bright and innocent as a toothpaste ad. "'Cause whatever it is, it looks divine."

Courtney blinked at the waitress, thankful for a mission. "A sour apple martini for the young lady."

The girl giggled, pleased, it seemed, to have won a drink so easily out of Courtney. "Thank you, um…what's your name?"

"C-Caitlin," Courtney lied.

The girl giggled again, her eyes nearly as big as her breasts. "That's so close to mine. I'm Katie."

Oh, my God, Courtney thought, then forced a fake smile. She couldn't keep her eyes from dropping down again to those young, fabulous breasts. It'd been a long time since she'd touched breasts like that, probably since she was a student herself and used to make out in the washrooms of campus bars or in a quiet corner in the library with her girlfriend of the day.

"See something you like?" Katie looked intently at Courtney, seductively licking the sugar from the rim of her glass.

Courtney swallowed against the dryness in her throat. She'd thought the girl simply wanted a drink out of her, nothing more. "Um." She stalled, taking a sip of her martini. "You a student at U. of W.?" *Brilliant one, Courtney.*

Katie laughed. "So that's all you were looking at? The logo on my shirt?"

Oh, for fuck's sake. What does she want me to say, that I was staring at her tits because I haven't been with a woman in months?

Courtney downed the rest of her drink, not wanting to play this little game anymore. "Look, Katie, it's been a slice, but I gotta go." She threw a twenty on the bar. "Treat yourself to another one."

Katie touched Courtney's arm as she rose. "Do you have to go so soon?"

"Yeah, I do actually."

The girl managed to look disappointed as Courtney gathered up her helmet and jacket, not feeling the least bit guilty. *There have to be plenty of fish in this kid's fishing pond. She can certainly afford to throw me back and cast her line again.*

Courtney steadied herself before starting the bike. She knew she'd drunk too much and shouldn't be driving. It was okay, she told herself. She'd go a mile or two up the road to a motel. Besides, she seemed to have her own personal guardian angel sitting on her shoulder these days, or perhaps it was that horseshoe up her ass, like her colleagues had suggested. Whatever it was, she was safe from harm.

Sure enough, there was a quaint little motel nestled in among the trees not far up the road. Courtney took a room. It was nothing like the lavish rooms she'd stayed in with all her travel for work. The Royal York in Toronto, the Hotel Meurice in Paris, the Regent Beverly Wilshire in L.A., the Fairmont in San Francisco, The Carlyle Hotel in New York City, The Drake in Chicago. This was a one-room job with a tiny bathroom, but it was fitting somehow, since all Courtney owned was now in the saddlebags of her bike. She had everything she needed.

She laid back on the double bed, her boots still on, and clutched the nickel-plated flask of brandy to her chest. All those fancy places with their gold bathroom fittings and marble fireplaces didn't mean shit to her anymore. Funny how one day they did and the next day they didn't. In practically the blink of an eye, her life had changed, even though it had taken her a few weeks to realize it. She'd been shaken to her roots, and now that she'd stripped away everything she'd come to value in her life, she had made sure her life would never be the same again. It was like gutting a house for a major reno but without a master plan. She was little more than a foundation and some two-by-fours, but by God, she was still standing.

Courtney took a swig of the brandy, the warmth of it coursing through her chest in a pleasurable wave. The alcohol and riding the Indian motorcycle were the only things giving her any pleasure at all these days. They kept the demons at bay. Selling off all her possessions had briefly made her feel good too, because it made her feel so unencumbered, unshackled, liberated.

34

But she was lonely. She wished now that she hadn't so abruptly dismissed that Katie or Kathy or whatever her name was.

Might have been nice to have someone around for a couple of hours. Someone to play with. Someone to make me feel alive.

Hell, it wasn't like she'd been trying to pay homage to the long-gone Celine by remaining so virtuous these last few months. It had just worked out that way since she wasn't one for quickies or transient relationships. Things were different now, she reminded herself. Her old habits and the way she'd lived her life all these years didn't mean a damned thing anymore. She could be dead tomorrow. It was a lesson she was learning well.

She took another long drink before setting the flask down on the nightstand. She unzipped her jeans. *I'll bet that Katie could do me real good. Oh yeah. Bet she knows exactly how to do it.* Courtney stuck her hand inside her pants. She was tired of being virtuous, tired of holding everything back. She was free now. *Free.*

CHAPTER FOUR

Gambling tip: Quit while you're ahead.

"Sam, I really don't need a babysitter. I'm not going to turn into the Wicked Witch and melt."

Sam hadn't left Ellen's side all evening. First they'd gone to a quiet piano bar on Vancouver's gay strip. Then Sam decided they needed something much more lively and dragged Ellen into Trax, a raucous gay and lesbian bar bursting with writhing bodies and loud dance music. Sam seemed reluctant to let Ellen out of her sight, much less arm's reach, as though Ellen might bolt. It was almost smothering. And definitely laughable.

"Don't worry," Sam shouted over Michael Jackson's *Don't Stop 'Til You Get Enough*. "I'm much more than your babysitter."

That was true. She was big sister, therapist and bodyguard all rolled into one. "I'm not a fragile flower, you know."

Sam's smile was slow and full of doubt. "No, but you're in a delicate stage right now. I don't want you wavering on the Susan thing. I want to get you over that hump for good."

Ellen rolled her eyes. She wasn't going to waver on the "Susan thing." About every six weeks she'd get an e-mail or phone call from her ex, wanting to reconcile. Ellen would alternately lose her temper or ignore the entreaties, but either way she was not getting back with Susan. There was too much hurt there, too much damage beyond repair. In her heart, Ellen had firmly closed the door on Susan and that part of her life. Maybe the reason Sam kept pushing her was because Sam needed assurance of that. Ellen could understand that, but she was in no hurry to do something silly or outrageous just to prove something to Sam.

Sam cast her eyes around the room like she was shopping for a specific brand in the soup aisle. Her discerning gaze fell on one woman, then another and another.

Ellen laughed. "Planning your next meal?"

"Maybe I am! A girl's gotta eat, you know."

"Thanks, but I don't want to hear about your menu plans."

"Actually, I'm checking them out for you."

"Oh, God. Give it a rest already."

Sam gave Ellen's soda water and lemon a look of disdain before taking a pointed gulp of her Molson Canadian. Sam's point was clear. She obviously thought Ellen a teetotaler and a prude.

"I told you," Ellen said defensively. "Two drinks are it for me, and I already had a glass of wine back at that piano bar."

"Well, let me know when you're ready to walk on the wild side and I'll order you another wine."

"You're not going to pick someone up tonight, are you? On my second night here?" She did *not* want to listen to her best friend getting it on in the next room with someone tonight. *Oh, my God. I did enough of that in college!*

Sam's grin was full of mischief. "Not unless you want me to."

"Do you have earplugs?"

"A whole drawer full of them."

37

Ellen pretended to give the idea serious thought. "Forget it. I don't want to have to make breakfast conversation with a stranger, thank you very much."

"I could kick her out before morning."

Ellen didn't doubt Sam could pick up almost any woman here. She kept herself fit, was handsome in a soft butch way and was a good conversationalist. She was funny too, with an edgy, dry sense of humor, her job as an ER nurse sharply honing her sarcasm.

"Sam? Do you ever get tired of this scene?"

"What scene?" Sam asked innocently.

Ellen shifted in her seat. She didn't want to seem judgmental, but she couldn't picture herself doing this every weekend. It seemed so contrived and reminded her of high school dances and all the juvenile little games that had gone with them. "You know, going to bars. Trying to meet women. Asking them out on dates."

"Are you asking me because you don't know how to get back out there in the dating world?"

"Well…maybe. I don't know. I'm not ready for all that. And even if I was, I don't really want to be looking for Ms. Right in a bar, you know?"

Sam could have chosen to take offense, but she didn't. "There's nothing wrong with looking for nice women at a bar. We're here, after all."

"True. Tell me something, though. Are you really looking for Ms. Right in a place like this? Or are you just looking for a good time?" Ellen couldn't even remember the last time she'd gone cruising in a bar. It must be thirteen years, around the time she got together with Susan. Come to think of it, she'd met Susan in a bar, and look what had come of that!

Sam pondered the question over a long sip of beer. "I'm always looking for Ms. Right. But sometimes a good time is all it's meant to be. I like to keep my options open, and you should too."

"It's just that, you know, we're not kids anymore. There's something adolescent about all this."

"Well, we're hardly ready for the nursing home either, at the ripe old age of forty. And it's not adolescent. It's people being people, trying to have a good time and make new friends, that's all."

Ellen took a good look around. There were plenty of women their age, and most of them looked nice. Normal, anyway. Dancing, laughing, flirting. Doing the things she supposed people did in bars when they wanted to have a good time, just like Sam said. She felt like an imposter though, sitting there with her soda water, having no intention of dancing or picking up women.

Sam leaned closer. "You know, you don't have to propose marriage to anyone here."

"Oh, thank God, 'cause I left my collection of engagement rings back at your place."

Sam laughed until she almost fell off her stool. "Okay, I guess I deserved that. But seriously. We're only here to have a little fun. No pressure."

Ellen's smile was her peace offering. "All right. No pressure."

"In that case, how about we get out there and dance?"

"Crap. I don't know."

"C'mon, it's Madonna. I know you love Madonna." Sam grabbed Ellen's hand and began pulling her from her seat.

"Wait, you know I don't dance much."

"You used to, way back when. It's Susan who didn't like to dance. Drink, yes. Dance, no. C'mon, shake a leg, Ellen baby."

It seemed like every conversation rolled around to Susan, and Ellen had had enough. To placate Sam, she let herself be tugged to the dance floor, because dancing would at least shut Sam up. She went through the motions, feeling stiff and awkward dancing to Madonna's *Ray of Light*. She envied the others on the floor, including Sam, who moved so effortlessly and unselfconsciously. Sam was right, there had been a time when she enjoyed dancing. It seemed lifetimes ago, though, and now Ellen couldn't seem to shed the weight of her sadness and sense of failure long enough to let loose and enjoy the moment. It was a damned shame.

Pathetic, really. There was zero sense of fun in her these days, and worst of all, she couldn't even decide when she'd lost that zest. All she knew was that it'd been a hell of a long time ago. Like the sand falling into the ocean a grain at a time, where it's years before you notice the landscape has changed.

"You okay?" Sam shouted.

Ellen nodded through the tears that had begun to collect in her eyes. "I think I could use that glass of wine about now."

Reclaiming her position at the bar, Ellen eyed the women on the dance floor. One in particular struck her immediately. She was dancing like she was the main attraction and everyone else merely the sideshow. She was good to look at too, but she acted like she knew it. Ellen guessed her to be close to her own age, maybe a bit younger. She had wavy, sandy hair that swooped over her forehead and just past her ears and over her shirt collar in a trendy cut with expensive highlights. She had a strong face, nice lines, Ellen thought. She couldn't see the woman's eyes, it was too dark, but Ellen knew without a doubt that they would be as appealing as the rest of her. That was the way the world worked, it seemed. Some people had all the luck, like this woman—good looking, obviously athletic by the way she danced, tall, money by the looks of her hair and clothes, and no shortage of women wanting to dance and flirt with her.

Ellen turned away and sipped her wine, fast losing interest in watching the little mating rituals on the dance floor. Even Sam seemed to be getting in on the act, chatting with a woman who didn't even look close to thirty. Never get involved with anyone more than a decade older or younger, Ellen's sage old aunt had told her a long time ago. She called it her ten-year rule, and she'd been on both sides of it. When Ellen asked her which side was better, her aunt had broken into a naughty grin and admitted it was a lot more fun being the older one. "Cougar" was the term now. Mildly amused, Ellen wondered what her aunt would have been called back then.

Well, Sam could be a cougar if she wanted, but Ellen had no such desire. Ellen had no desire to date, period. She didn't want to invest so much of herself again, only to get burned. Because sooner or later, that's exactly what would happen. The idea of a relationship lasting forever was a fallacy, and if it was only meant to be temporary, then what was the point?

Ellen was mid-sip when she felt a tap on her shoulder. Figuring it was Sam bugging her to get back onto the dance floor, Ellen flipped her off without turning around.

"You could just say no instead of giving me the bird."

Ellen nearly choked on her wine. *Oh, my God, that is not Sam's voice. Too deep. Too sexy too.* Ellen spun around. *Shit.*

The woman—the good-looking chick magnet from the dance floor—sat down uninvited. "I was only going to ask you to dance. For now." She winked slyly.

A flush rose in Ellen. Of course the woman had eyes to die for, pretty much as Ellen had figured. They were Caribbean green with a hint of smoky gray. Ellen, caught in the crosshairs, felt helpless for a moment before pulling herself together. "I don't really dance."

"Could have fooled me. I saw you out there a few minutes ago." She nodded at the bartender. "Bourbon, please. And make it a double."

So. She was a hard liquor drinker, just like Susan. Ellen felt her mood darkening. "Well, I only did it to humor my friend."

"Good. So she's only a friend." The woman's smile was at first apprehensive, then cocky as hell. "My name's Courtney, by the way."

Ellen nodded curtly. *Goddammit. Where the hell is Sam anyway?*

"Um, this is the part where you're supposed to tell me your name."

Ellen gave the woman the rudest look she dared. "Look. I'm not interested in dancing. Or chatting, for that matter." God, Sam was going to give it to her for being such a bitch about making new friends, but why should she bother? She was only in Vancouver a month—less if she got sick of it—and she certainly wasn't interested in dating. So this, this *Courtney*, was wasting her time, as far as Ellen could see. The darling of the dance floor with the eyes to die for and the smile suitable for rescuing swooning women would have to find some other prey.

Courtney leaned in, brushing against Ellen's arm. "Fine by me. We could skip all the preliminaries and go straight to bed."

Ellen felt her mouth drop and her eyes widen in mortification. She'd been off the market a long time, but... *Christ! Was that how it was done these days? Just come right out with it like that?*

"Well?"

Those gorgeous eyes were boring into her, and that lopsided, James Dean grin was almost too damned much, causing Ellen to mentally stumble for a moment. She swallowed hard and summoned her senses. "I should think not!"

The woman had the gall to laugh. "Are you a student of nineteenth-century English literature or something?"

Haughty and stammering, Ellen replied that as a matter of fact she was.

"Well then, madam, perhaps I should have gotten down on bended knee or something. Forgive me for being so boorish."

Ellen downed the rest of her wine and stood. She didn't need to be insulted this way. She glanced around and finally spotted Sam in a throng of people.

"Wait," Courtney implored after taking a healthy drink of her bourbon. "I didn't mean to—"

"Forget it." Ellen strode away without a glance back.

Sam was in no hurry to leave and happily ignored Ellen's protestations. Finally, Ellen stood up on her toes and shouted over Beyoncé what had happened at the bar.

Sam howled with laughter. "Is that *all?*"

Ellen was flabbergasted all over again. What had she expected from Sam anyway? Sam, for all Ellen knew, was probably every bit as outrageous as that Courtney woman when she was on the make. She dug in her heels. "Fine. I'll get a cab back if you want to stay."

"All right, all right. Let's go then."

Ellen glanced back at the bar one last time and saw

Courtney leaning against it, drink in one hand, her other resting provocatively on the thigh of a young woman. *Well, that didn't take long!*

It was surprisingly easy for Courtney to shrug off the rejection, to convince herself it was nothing. She could do that effortlessly now, ever since Chicago. That damned plane crash had taught her that it was easier—safer—to not allow herself to feel much of anything. She wore her indifference like armor, a way to protect herself. She didn't allow herself to feel hurt or insulted by the English lit woman—whatever her name was. Her newfound success with women would not be harmed by this aberration. There were plenty of other willing conquests to be had, Courtney was sure. In fact, she had drunk to that.

Goddamn! Was she really sitting in this bar hitting on nameless women as though she'd been doing it half her life? Had she really become this much of a slut, and so quickly? It was so out of character for her—or had been. But then, she reasoned, she no longer knew what was in character for her and what was not. All bets were off. The old Courtney didn't exist, and the new one was still a mystery to be unraveled. Like getting a gift and not knowing what lay inside.

It was then that she noticed the cute young blonde a couple of seats over, sitting alone and looking receptive as hell. She began to put the moves on her—Janis was her name, even spelled like the druggie rock diva of old—and Courtney was rewarded with all the right cues. The woman began to show more thigh, stuck her chest out a little more, smiled like she was being paid to, licked her lips seductively. *Oh, yeah, this was going to be so damned easy. Who knew?* Courtney had never picked up women like this before. It astounded her how easy it was. *Okay, that stuck-up one… that was merely a little detour. This one's about to lie down and spread her legs right here!*

Courtney couldn't fail now. She was irresistible. A winner.

A finisher. A sure thing. Indestructible. Women wanted her, obviously, and were willing to fall at her feet. Her heart beating a little faster, she led Janis into the ladies' room and into a stall. She kicked the door shut and pushed her up against the wall. She kissed her roughly, nipped at her neck, then her lips. Janis moaned her encouragement and ground herself against Courtney's thigh. There was no time, no need, for much foreplay. Janis was breathing hard, practically coming against her leg. Courtney shoved her hand up her dress, roughly pulled aside her underwear. The woman was wet, like melted butter, and Courtney thrust two fingers into her, hard and deep, giving her exactly what she wanted. She kept a demanding rhythm, pumping fast until Janis was squealing her delight. It didn't take long—a couple of minutes maybe—before Janis was gushing all over her hand, her body hiccupping in spasms.

"Oh, baby," Janis moaned breathlessly. "Jesus, that was something."

"Yeah." Courtney didn't want to kiss her again. Didn't even want to touch her anymore. She pulled her hand away as though she'd touched something hot.

Adjusting herself, Janis smiled cat-like. "We could go back to my place and, you know, try it again a little slower."

Courtney backed up, unlatched the stall door. "I don't think so, thanks."

Janis pouted. "Why not, baby? We could have a lot of fun. And I've got a bottle of Jack Daniels at my place."

The J.D. almost gave her pause. Almost. "Sorry. Got somewhere I need to be."

"How about a little more fun right here?"

"I think I've had about all the fun I can handle for the moment."

Janis raised a finely plucked eyebrow before pulling a tiny chrome vial from her purse. Methodically, she laid a line of coke down on the countertop, then began rolling up a ten dollar bill.

"Whoa, wait a second," Courtney said. "I'm not into that."

Janis smirked, as if to say *yeah right*, before bending over and quickly snorting the coke.

Courtney swallowed hard, willing her legs to get her the hell out of there. She'd done cocaine a couple of times early in her career, mostly because it was the thing to do for a young, hotshot computer guru with a big salary. She couldn't deny that she'd liked the way it had made her feel—uninhibited, energetic, confident, like she was the smartest person in the world, if only everyone would shut up and listen to her. It was like being God for thirty minutes or so. But she'd been afraid to fall into that trap of recreational drugs, afraid to risk her career and her sense of control over herself and her destiny, so she'd quit using long before it became habit forming.

Janis stepped up to her, raising the tip of her cocaine-dusted fingertip to Courtney's lips. Courtney opened her mouth, let Janis rub her gums with it. *Shit*. It felt good. Too good.

Courtney spun around and dashed out of the ladies' room as fast as she could, her heart pounding. She might be infallible these days, a born winner, but she would not go down this road. It was too dangerous.

She hopped on her bike, not caring that she was past her one-drink rule. Hell, if she'd had a three-drink rule, it would have been long gone. Not to mention that tiny taste of coke still numbing her mouth. She gunned the motor and headed to her hotel, the Westin, right on the harbor. She wasn't the least bit concerned about being intoxicated and driving her bike. She was a ghost, after all. Ghosts are already dead. They couldn't be harmed and they could do no wrong. It was a strangely liberating feeling, this newfound invincibility.

At the hotel, Courtney took a long shower, needing to wash Janis from her hands. *Jesus*. She'd never done anything like that before, fucking a stranger in a washroom. Even that night in Portland a few years back, when she was drunk and dancing like a crazy fool on a table, she'd not taken things any further. All these years, even as a kid, Courtney had been a good girl. Upstanding, reliable, sensible. She'd been the serious one, her mother the happy-go-lucky one who didn't worry much about where their next mortgage payment was going to come from.

While she knew that it would somehow materialize, Courtney fretted and worked extra shifts waitressing in her teen years to make sure they had a roof over their heads. *Well, things change, obviously.* She sure as hell wasn't that person anymore.

She let the blazing hot water course over her face, shoulders and chest. The hotter the better. The little needles of spray were almost painful. She needed to feel a little pain, because at least it would mean feeling something. Anything. Because since the crash, she'd felt only numbness.

Courtney wanted to cry, but she couldn't. Maybe, she mused, she'd forgotten how.

CHAPTER FIVE

Blackjack tip: The decisions you will make, whether to hit or stand, are based on the dealer's up card.

Sam ravenously tucked into her eggs. Her enthusiasm made Ellen chuckle.

"If you eat like that after a night alone, what are you like after a wild night of sex?"

"Well, if you'd like, we can go back to that bar on Davie Street again tonight. I can pick someone up so you can check out my appetite tomorrow."

"You'd like that, wouldn't you?"

"Actually, I was thinking more like it's something *you* should do."

Ellen's gaze drifted out the window of the café-style restaurant and settled on the big stone structure that was the Vancouver Art Gallery down the street. They were going to hit the gallery after breakfast. Ellen was looking forward to it. She loved the

Emily Carr paintings of British Columbia's spectacular scenery, along with the Indian carvings and the majestic totem poles. The gallery always had a large collection of Native North American art on display.

"Well?" Sam prodded, not particularly gently.

Ellen couldn't keep her annoyance in check. "You sound like a goddamned broken record."

"Maybe that's because I can't seem to get through to you."

"Look, if you think that me f—" Ellen almost said the word, then changed her mind. She lowered her voice. "*Sleeping* with someone is going to magically make everything all better in my life, then you're sadly mistaken."

"That's only part of it, Ellen. I know you're not going to start having one-night stands. Hell, I don't want you to do that crap. It's not who you are."

"Then why do you keep bugging me about it?"

Sam pushed her empty plate aside. "I just want to see you have a good time and to be happy for once. I want you to feel like women want you, because they do. I want to see you feel attractive and alive, the way you did before Susan."

"Screwing some stranger is not going to make me forget about Susan."

If anything, being at a bar only reminded her more of Susan. Being there made her wonder if that's what Susan had been doing to pick up women—if she'd acted like that Courtney woman, blatantly propositioning women. Jessica, the one she'd caught Susan with, was a bartender. They'd undoubtedly met at a bar during afternoons when Ellen was teaching, because Susan, a night shift postal worker, often had her days free. She could almost picture them flirting, Jessica leaning over the bar to intentionally show off her cleavage, maybe even giving Susan free drinks, giggling at Susan's jokes like a schoolgirl. The whole thing made her sick.

"You might have had a dance or a drink with that woman last night, that's all."

"I think she wanted a little more than that."

48

"So? Doesn't mean you have to. You could let her buy you a drink and enjoy the fact that she found you very attractive, you know. Have some fun flirting. And she was pretty hot looking, don't you think? Not that she's my type, but I'm just saying."

Ellen smiled in spite of her grumpiness. Yes, Courtney was hot. Eyes to die for and a smile that could curl your toes. Ellen even grudgingly admired the woman's cockiness and self-confidence. She'd never want to date someone like Courtney, but maybe Sam had a point. What harm would a little more flirting have done? It had flattered her a little, after all, though she wouldn't admit it.

"I'm not a total drag, you know." Ellen flashed a smile that she hoped looked a little daring. Maybe she would try to have some fun, to shed a little of the martyr syndrome she knew she'd acquired over Susan. Playing the role of the wronged wife was damned exhausting, and Ellen would love nothing more than to pick up her life and pitch herself forward. It wouldn't happen overnight, but maybe she could take some baby steps or even crawl. "You don't automatically get a lobotomy when you get married, you know. I still know how to have some fun."

"Good!" Sam grinned. "We're on the same page. So you'll trust me to find us a little fun?"

"We're going to the art gallery in a few minutes. That'll be fun."

Predictably, Sam grimaced. "I wouldn't exactly call that fun."

Ellen laughed. She knew Sam was only being a good host by agreeing to go with her. "When was the last time you went to the gallery anyway?"

"The last time you dragged me there. What was it, three years ago?"

"So in other words, it's only when you're with me that you get your culture fix."

"Lord knows what I would do without my culture fix from Ellen Turcotte! My life would be so incomplete." She sighed dramatically.

Ellen narrowed her eyes. "All right, all right. No need to be nasty."

Sam leaned over the table, an evil glint in her eyes. "So. I go to the gallery with you today, and tomorrow we go where *I* want to go."

Oh, no. Sam would for sure have something up her sleeve, and Ellen had a feeling she was going to regret it. On the other hand, if she were going to take a page out of Sam's book and try to have a little fun, be more unpredictable, then she'd have to agree and trust Sam. "All right, deal. But don't make me regret this!"

Sam's laughter filled the tiny café.

Courtney figured she must have run at least three miles by now, maybe four. She couldn't decide which part of Stanley Park she liked best—the seawall that followed the contours of the park along the water, the inland trails that cut through the majestic fir, cedar and hemlock trees or the wide-open grassy spaces. So she'd mixed it up, jogging along the seawall for a mile or so, then cutting inland.

She loved the feeling of her chest heaving for breath, the sweat dripping down her neck, back and chest and the quivering exhaustion in her legs. Driving her body like this reminded her she was alive, that her limits were boundless and that she could do anything she set her mind to. She commanded her body and it obeyed.

It was her mind that she could not beat into submission. Courtney had hoped the exhausting run this morning would clear her thoughts, ease her confusion, lighten the weight of the sadness she couldn't seem to shake. It was like quicksand, sucking at her from beneath, something she had to constantly try and stay above.

The mantra in her head played over and over. *Why me?* It had started after that newspaper reporter phoned her. A simple question. *Why me?* A thousand times a day her mind posed the question. She could be watching television, reading a book, riding her motorcycle, shopping for tampons. It didn't matter.

The question would rise up unexpectedly. There was no answer, but like a starving, insatiate beast, it kept demanding one.

"Why was I the chosen one?" Courtney muttered under her breath and looked to the sky. *Out of all those people booked for that flight, why did I have to miss it, when I've never missed a connecting flight in my life?* In the thousands of times she'd asked herself that, she could never come up with an answer, and yet there *had* to be one. It couldn't have been chance or shit luck. *Could it?* Had she been spared for some celestial reason? Was there something noble she should be doing with her life? Or was it her selfishness that had spared her? Courtney had always done what she wanted to do, whether it was work a kazillion hours a week, kill herself at the gym, get lost in a good book or lose a couple of grand in Vegas once a year. She had never even really let Celine or anyone else in, because Courtney did what Courtney pleased. And if she'd been a better person, she'd probably have been on that damned plane. Like Danny. Danny was a good guy, and he was dead now. It was like that old Billy Joel song, about only the good dying young. *Obviously I'm not good enough to die.*

The BlackBerry in her fanny pack rang. She'd forgotten to shut the damned thing off. The call display told her it was Nan. Courtney halted in front of the totem pole display and for a second considered ignoring the call, as she had the other two times Nan had called recently.

"Courtney Langford."

"Oh, thank goodness. I was getting worried. Are you okay?" Nan's concern was evident in her voice.

"I'm fine. Just out of breath."

"No, I mean…are you really doing okay Courtney? I've been worried, hon."

Courtney sighed impatiently. "I'm fine, Nan. There's no reason for you to worry. I never said I'd check in with you."

"I know, dear. It's…there's no one to look out for you, to keep tabs on you. I mean, do you even have someone you can talk to?"

"I don't *need* a babysitter, Nan. I can look after myself."

51

"I know you can, but you don't need to. Why don't you come back here and—"

"Look." Courtney's temper flared. "You're not my mother, Nan. Got it? My mother's dead."

Hearing her own words gave Courtney a little shock. She rarely spoke of her mother, who was dead like all those people on the plane were dead. Her mother's death hadn't been as dramatic and certainly not as newsworthy, but she was dead all the same. Ovarian cancer had killed her an inch at a time over a five-year period, almost a decade ago now. Courtney had looked after her mother's physical needs as much as she could and covered all of her financial needs. After her father's abrupt departure, she'd vowed to herself never to abandon her mother and she hadn't.

There was a sharp intake of breath on the other end, then stunned silence.

"I'm sorry," Courtney said quickly, not really meaning it. Anger came easily to her these days. So did sadness and guilt, but rarely remorse or joy or empathy. She felt oddly disconnected from the rest of the world and even from most of her own feelings. It was like watching her life unfold through a porthole. "Nan, you don't work for me anymore. You don't have to keep worrying about me, okay?"

Nan was silent for another long minute. Courtney could tell she was disappointed.

"All right," Nan finally offered, her voice deflated. "But if you need me, I'm always here."

"I'll remember that. Thank you." Courtney hit the disconnect button. She put the phone back in her pouch and resumed her running pace. She tried to let her mind float free, deciding that if running didn't give her the peace she needed, there was always that bar again tonight and its abundance of alcohol and women. She could be free there.

Later that night, Courtney indulged herself. She started with beer, finished with Jack Daniels—lots of it. She got into some heavy flirting with a couple of women, until one inexplicably dropped out of the bidding. That was fine with Courtney, as she turned her attention to the woman remaining. She wasn't even especially good-looking, though her body was more than adequate from what Courtney could tell through the haze of alcohol. Courtney had held out until well past midnight, hoping that hot-looking English lit woman from the previous night would show. The woman—Christ, she hadn't even offered her name—most definitely had a stick up her ass, but Courtney was pretty sure she could convince her to go a round with her, if given another chance. But hell, she hadn't shown, and Courtney simply got tired of waiting.

It wasn't a washroom stall this time, but the backseat of a sedan. Courtney didn't come. Wasn't even sure if she got this nameless woman off either. Didn't matter. She stumbled away afterward, at least having the sense this time to leave her bike and take a cab back to her hotel.

Lying in bed the next morning, her head mildly pounding, Courtney could not ignore the vortex of emptiness that consumed her very core. It wrapped itself fully around her, this nothingness that was now her life. No job, no friends, no future, and certainly, no love for herself. Courtney was existing. She was alive, after all, so it was her job to exist. But she wasn't happy about it. She wasn't happy about anything, as a matter of fact. Escaping her life in Seattle had been emancipating at first, but that freedom now smothered her. And the fun she was trying to carve out wasn't so fun anymore either. The booze was helping numb her a bit, but it wasn't wiping the slate of her feelings clean. And the women she was picking up? That was thrilling for all of about thirty seconds now, her liaisons only filling her with disgust, when she remembered them.

Courtney rolled onto her back. It was an accomplishment, she supposed, that she was still here on this earth. The plane crash hadn't killed her, and neither had the booze, the strange women or driving her motorcycle all over the place. *Well, that's something at least.* She'd passed whatever survival test God had thrown her way so far. Maybe it was time to test something else—the shit luck she seemed to have an abundance of.

CHAPTER SIX

*Definition of "house edge": The casino's built-in advantage,
usually gained by paying less than the odds.*

Ellen, a step behind, envied Sam's cool confidence as she
walked into the Red Rocket Casino. Sam had an air about her as
though she owned the place. It was in the way she held her head,
the way she glanced intently around, and most distinctly in the
purposeful way she walked. Ellen was like that too when she was
commanding a classroom, which was her domain. But certainly
not in a casino. A casino was a different planet to her—loud
and bright and busy. Machines constantly dinged and chimed.
Conversation was like a verbal jigsaw puzzle, with jagged bits
everywhere. Some of the groups at the tables were boisterous,
depending on which way the luck was going. "Disney World for
adults," Sam chuckled, giving Ellen a presumptuous wink.

"So this is your idea of fun, eh?"

"It's my little secret. I come here about once or twice a month to unwind, play a little poker or blackjack. And yeah, it's a hoot. Best place in the world to people watch."

Ellen snickered. "Don't you get enough of that at the hospital?"

"Yeah, but that's work. This is play. Come on." She tugged Ellen toward the gaming tables.

"Oh, no. Not on your life!"

Mildly protesting, Ellen let herself be pulled along as if caught in a wave, winding through a maze of craps tables, roulette and various card games. They stopped at a glass window to watch a group play Texas Hold 'Em. The hard-core poker games were played in separate rooms, Sam explained, before describing the rules of the game. The poker hands ranged from a royal flush, to straights, to pairs. The betting was complicated too—blind bets and all kinds of other bets. It was too much for Ellen to follow, especially when she had so little interest.

"Blackjack is much easier, I promise. C'mon."

Sam coaxed Ellen to the blackjack area, where signs announced ten-dollar minimum bets right up to fifty-dollar minimums. Most of the tables were full, with chips of various colors and heights either stacked neatly or piled in sloppy little mounds in front of the players. The tabletop was bright green felt, the cards a crazy pattern of red and gold. Hands deftly scooped up chips and dealt out cards. Players looked either bored or as if their very futures hinged on the next card. Ellen grew curious. It was a mathematical game, which was certainly not her forte, but still, how hard was it to count to twenty-one?

"Wanna try it?" Sam's enthusiasm was almost enough to pry Ellen's doubts away.

"I dunno, Sammy. I don't know the first thing about it."

"It's easy, I swear. I can teach you."

Casinos held no appeal for Ellen. It was her sister Jackie's fault. Jackie was adamant that casinos were some kind of scourge on mankind. She was bitter and negative about almost everything, always warning of some impending disaster. Twelve years older and far wiser in Ellen's youthful view, Jackie had sat Ellen down a long time ago and lectured her on the horrors of gambling and drinking. Her litany went on nonstop for about thirty minutes, scaring a teenaged Ellen nearly to death.

Of course, that was before Ellen realized that Jackie's husband was a drunk and a gambling addict. Jackie had finally gotten rid of the bum, but not her attitude that the world was one giant patch of quicksand lying in wait for unsuspecting victims. Jackie lived in Montreal now, and the sisters only contacted each other once a year, which was fine with her. She didn't want Jackie to know what had transpired between Susan and her. She didn't want the millions of I-told-you-so's and more lectures from her on how weak and hurtful and stupid people could be. Jackie thrived on people's misery and failures.

"Ellen?"

"Huh?"

"It won't kill you to try, you know. It's not going to turn you into an addict or make you have to sell all your jewelry at the nearest pawn shop. Play smart and you'll be okay."

Ellen laughed doubtfully. Sam knew all about Jackie and her paranoia and had probably guessed what Ellen was thinking. "Well," she ventured. "I suppose it couldn't hurt to at least watch *you* lose all your money."

Sam shook her head. "I'm telling you, it's a blast. C'mon."

The blackjack table was semicircular, with a bright blue felt top this time. The dealer, an attractive blonde in her late twenties, dealt cards almost as fast as throwing confetti. There were four players hunched over their cards and one open seat.

"A couple of things," Sam whispered, standing behind the empty chair. "Just bet the minimum to start. And never up the ante when you're losing. That's a surefire way to lose your money real quick. If you're on a good streak, then you can double your bet."

"Whoa, wait a minute. I'm not playing. I'm only watching, remember?"

Sam winked at her. "You'll be playing before the night is through, my friend."

Ellen swallowed. She needed a drink if she was even going to consider the possibility of playing blackjack. Trying new things made her instantly nervous, but since she had survived these last few months, she could surely survive an evening of gambling.

Sam laughed at Ellen as she downed a glass of white wine at the bar, then turned serious as she suggested that Ellen really shouldn't have more than one drink while she was playing. "The casinos would love you to get roaring drunk because you'll part with your money faster that way. But you need to keep your head about you, El."

"I always keep my head about me, you know that."

"True, but there are times when maybe you *should* lose your head a little bit." Sam winked. "If you know what I mean."

Ellen lightly pinched her best friend on the cheek, having no intention of indulging her in another conversation about women right now. "So are you going to teach me how to win millions or not? That is why we're here after all, isn't it?"

Sam grew more animated with each new piece of advice she offered. She explained when to double down, when to split, when to stay and when to take a hit. It didn't sound so hard, but Ellen wanted to watch the pro herself at work before giving it a try.

Sam was happy to oblige. Immediately she struck up a jovial conversation with the cute woman dealer and the other players next to her. Ellen wondered how Sam could be so casual about it as she placed her two five-dollar chips in her betting circle and accepted two cards. They were face up on the table so everyone could see them, and Ellen instantly did the math. Sam had an eight and a two, for a solid ten. The dealer had one card showing, the other face down. The card showing was a four. Sam placed a couple of five-dollar chips behind her first two to signal she was doubling her bet, and Ellen sucked in her breath.

"It's okay," Sam whispered. "With a four showing, odds are the dealer's going to bust and I can double my winnings this way."

The dealer, whose badge identified her as Zoe, gave the tiniest smirk. "Good job," she said to Sam, dealing her a third card. It was a ten. Sam now had a reliable twenty. The dealer turned up her hidden card, which was a ten. She had to deal to herself until she hit at least seventeen, so she took another card—another ten for a bust.

A cheer went up, the loudest from Sam, who raked her forty dollars in chips into her pile.

"That was a snap," Ellen enthused, impressed at how effortless it was.

"Don't be fooled. It doesn't always come that easy."

And it didn't. Sam won her next two rounds, but then the dealer got hot. First Zoe hit a blackjack, then hit for twenty, three times in a row. Sam sat out a hand, telling Ellen she would wait until the dealer cooled. Two rounds later and Sam was back in it, winning some, losing some, but still slightly ahead of the game.

Ellen had to admit it looked like fun, and it did not seem overly complicated, the way poker did.

"Are you ready to try, my little protegé?"

The chair beside Sam vacated and Ellen tentatively claimed it. Panic gripped her. Watching and doing were two completely different things. "Don't leave me," she quietly implored. She had to force herself to stay seated, when what she really wanted to do was bolt. *Damn, it would have been a hell of a lot less stressful if we'd just gone to a movie or something.*

"I won't leave you, my little duckling. I'll be right here."

With each card dealt to her, Ellen looked to Sam for advice. Sam, always the brave, cool one, didn't let her down. Gradually, Ellen relaxed. She didn't even cringe after losing a couple of ten-dollar bets. She was afraid to increase her bet or double down, but she played sensibly and conservatively, betting the minimum each time. Her winning stack of chips grew ever so slowly, and she smiled wider with each new round.

"See, I knew you'd like it! It gets your blood going, doesn't it?"

"Maybe," Ellen laughed. It did give her a thrill and sometimes heart palpitations too. She looked forward to each new card with nervous but excited tension, loved the feeling of adrenaline coursing through her. But she didn't let herself get carried away, remembering all of Sam's advice about when to feel confident with her bets and when to back down. It was moderation balanced with risk.

Pleased that she had won more than she'd lost, Ellen was beginning to believe that she might actually have a head for cards when she felt someone claim the empty seat on the other side of her. She glanced sideways, felt her heart stutter and turned her head enough to get a better sense of who it was. Her jaw slackened with recognition. *Holy shit!* It was the hot woman from the bar, the one who'd aggressively tried to pick her up the other night. *Courtney something, that was it.*

Ellen, her mouth suddenly dry, turned away slightly, hoping this Courtney woman wouldn't remember her. She hoped too that Sam hadn't recognized her.

No such luck. Courtney bumped her shoulder gently and gave her a slow, tantalizing wink that sent a tiny shock wave down to Ellen's toes. Ellen felt the blood desert her face as a wicked chuckle escaped from Sam on the other side of her. Ellen felt faint.

"Well, well," Sam whispered in her right ear. "This should be worth the price of admission!"

Courtney couldn't believe her luck. It was the English lit woman, the beauty with the dark hair and eyes who had given her a good verbal jousting in the bar the other night. It had to be part of Courtney's lucky streak that this woman was sitting next to her. Courtney had pretty much had it with the easy ones—the women who threw themselves at her or so willingly let themselves be conquered, the coke heads and the baby dykes too. Those women were the bar's roadkill. There was no challenge in them.

Courtney sighed. She still had no more answers to her burning questions than she'd had a week earlier, but she was pretty sure she hadn't survived a doomed flight just so she could become the world's biggest slut. She was making progress, at least, in cleaning up her act. If she didn't exactly know what she wanted in life, she was fast learning what she didn't want.

Courtney was inexplicably drawn to the woman next to her, whatever her name was. She wanted to get to know her, and not, this time, because she was sexy and had a gorgeous body under all that piety. She was intelligent and obviously didn't suffer fools gladly. And, best of all, she didn't know a damn thing about Courtney or what she'd been going through.

"Do you think," Courtney said, "that I might at least get your name out of you this time?"

She got nothing in response, until the woman's friend leaned behind her and offered her hand in a friendly gesture. She flashed Courtney a conspiratorial grin as they shook hands. "I'm Sam Calloway, and this shy one is my friend, Ellen Turcotte."

Ellen gave a horrified little squeak and Courtney smiled before shaking Sam's hand. "Courtney Langford. It's nice to meet you both."

Ellen nodded curtly, then proceeded to ignore Courtney, placing her bet and studying the cards like there was going to be a quiz afterward. If it were anyone but this intriguing woman, Courtney would have walked away, because she sure as hell didn't need anyone treating her like crap or acting like she didn't exist. She was doing a fine job of treating herself like crap, thank you very much.

Courtney hit for blackjack and whooped her pleasure. When it happened again the next round, the rest of the table congratulated her. The others were winning too, with Courtney leading the way, and pretty soon they were murmuring excitedly about her being their lucky charm. Courtney shook her head, scooped up her winnings and played on. It was all going her way today. The cards, the reappearance of Ellen. She felt like celebrating with a drink but quickly decided against it. Ellen would sneer at her or maybe even give her some lip about it, and right now, Courtney didn't want anything to upset the dynamics of the table or compromise her lucky streak with the indomitable Ellen Turcotte.

"Are you always this lucky?" Ellen grudgingly asked, before hastily adding, "Never mind. Of course you are."

Courtney threw a twenty-five-dollar chip on the table for a new bet. Yes, she was blessed. Christ, she'd narrowly missed being on a plane that had sailed straight into the ocean. How much luckier could you get? But the rest of it—her job, the fancy cars she drove for years and her swanky Seattle condo—had all resulted from hard work and drive. Same with the money she was throwing around the blackjack table. Not everything had come to her easily, but Ellen certainly seemed to have a chip on her shoulder about it.

"What would you know about luck, Ms. Turcotte?" Courtney asked quietly, no judgment in her tone.

Ellen let out a frustrated sigh as her hand went bust. "Not a hell of a lot, unfortunately." She looked pointedly at Courtney, her expression hard to read. "But you do, don't you?"

"Because I win at cards?" It was true Courtney had always been good with cards, but her winning streak this afternoon was a bit over the top, even for her. Still, she wasn't about to turn her nose up at it. She was going to ride this lucky streak for as long as she could.

"Yes. But it's more than that, isn't it?" Ellen's eyes bore into Courtney's, as if reading her very soul.

Courtney shook her off with a dismissive smile. "Not really. I've always had good instinct with cards."

"Well, in my experience, people who are always really lucky in certain aspects of their life are very unlucky in others. The law of extremes."

That made a certain sense to Courtney, who'd done very well in the most visible areas of her life but had never been lucky when it came to love. Maybe Ellen, who seemed to be on such an even keel all the time, was perfectly happy in her love life. Maybe that was why she'd rejected Courtney's advances the other night.

"So what are you, Ellen, lucky or just the average Jill?"

Ellen laughed bitterly. "I'm afraid I'm a bit unlucky of late. And yes, I am the average Jill in most regards."

"No, she's not," Sam piped up. "This woman is anything but average. She's smart, funny, gorgeous and—"

Ellen must have given Sam a pinch or a smack under the table, because Sam yelped and shut right up.

"Well, you don't have to convince me," Courtney said, raking her eyes appreciatively over Ellen. This was most definitely a woman of substance, one who neither displayed nor especially tried to hide her natural beauty. She was earthy and genuine in her appearance. *But she could stand to be a little friendlier and a little less cynical. It's that damned stick up her ass.*

"I'm not a set of encyclopedias up for sale, so please ignore my friend Sam's inappropriateness."

Courtney laughed. "Too bad. I could really use a set of encyclopedias about now."

Ellen gave Courtney a scolding laugh. "You don't give up do you?"

"Should I?"

"No," Sam replied. "You definitely should not."

"Well, in that case, can I buy you ladies a drink at the bar with all these winnings?"

"I don't think so," Ellen answered quickly. "Thanks, though."

"C'mon, I have all this money to spend now. It's good karma to share your winnings."

Sam was shooting all kinds of indecipherable looks at her friend, but Ellen was doing a good job of ignoring her.

"Maybe another time." Ellen smiled and seemed to mean it for once. "I hope your winning streak keeps up."

"Me too." Courtney watched the women exchange their chips and walk away. She felt far more disappointed than she had a right to. It would have been nice to have made a couple of friends here in this city of strangers, but she wasn't about to hustle after them and beg.

She turned her attention back to the table as a new dealer was replacing Zoe.

"Hey." He was short and muscular, about thirty maybe, with black hair slicked back and a twinkle in his dark eyes. "I'm Jeff. How you doing today?"

"Hey, Jeff. Can't you tell by the chips in front of me?"

He laughed deeply. "Of course I can tell by that stack of chips in front of you. Problem is, you look like you lost your best friend, and usually people with that many chips in front of them look a little bit happier."

He had a lilt in his voice, or perhaps it was his intonation, but Jeff was every bit the homo Courtney was. She grinned at him. "See? I'm happy as a clam now. Is that better?"

His teeth gleamed back at her. "That's much more like it, girlfriend." He dealt the cards out like an automaton.

Courtney turned at the light tap on her shoulder. It was Sam, a bundle of nerves and excitement. "I'm sorry about my friend. She's a bit down right now and could use a little fun in her life, and I could use a favor."

Courtney raised her eyebrows questioningly. "You're not looking for a threesome, I hope."

Sam's quick and boisterous laughter startled Courtney. "No, unfortunately, but the idea does have its appeal."

"Well, I, ah—"

"Don't worry, that's not my intention. It's just that, you see, Ellen is here visiting me for a month and I have to go back to work in a few days. I don't want her kicking around by herself all the time, and she doesn't know anyone else in the city. Would you, you know, maybe show her around or something?"

"I'd love to, but for one thing I'm visiting the city myself, and for another, I think maybe she'd prefer someone else as her tour guide."

"Maybe the two of you could sort of discover the city together?" Sam looked hopefully, almost desperately, at Courtney.

Another winning hand for Courtney, and she tipped Jeff with a five-dollar chip. "Look, Sam. Ellen and I got off to a bad start at the bar the other night and I don't quite think she's forgiven me for it, okay? I am not a masochist and I'm not going to try to force someone to spend time with me."

"Well, for what it's worth, I think Ellen would love to spend time with someone who knows how to have a bit of fun. She just doesn't know it yet. How about you give me your cell phone number, and if she calls you, then she calls you, and if she doesn't, then she doesn't. Okay?"

Against her better judgment, Courtney scrawled her number on a slip of paper and handed it to Sam, who quickly thanked her and turned away.

"Getting hooked up?" Jeff asked with a wink.

"I seriously doubt it. But tell me something, Jeff. Do you guys play these same high school games the way women do?"

Jeff laughed and shook his head. "Yes, but the gamesmanship usually comes afterward, not before."

CHAPTER SEVEN

Definition of "busted": The loss of all of one's chips;
can also refer to going over twenty-one

Courtney's head pounded. She downed a couple of Advil with her morning coffee and stared at the scrambled eggs she'd ordered from room service. Today wasn't going to be a good day. *Dammit.* She'd thought it would be, because yesterday had been one of her better ones. An afternoon and evening at the casino, a nice buzz from winning and from running into Ellen Turcotte and finally putting a name to the lovely face. She'd even behaved herself with the booze. A couple of beers and a couple of martinis over the course of a few hours, in bed well before midnight with a lorazepam to settle her down. No night terrors or tossing and turning in bed.

She took a tentative bite, the chewing motion rattling her head. She'd been blaming her headaches on alcohol, but she couldn't this time because she hadn't consumed enough. *Crap.*

She settled back on the couch. She'd almost never had days like this before that stupid plane crash, days where she could barely get off the couch. She'd always been a bundle of energy. But lately this lethargy crept in every few days, and when it happened she tried to force herself to push past it, to keep moving, to ignore the symptoms as best she could. Today she was not sure she wanted to. Or even could. A run was most definitely out of the question.

She wouldn't think, that was it. She would lie around, watch TV, do nothing. Courtney ate as much of her breakfast as she could manage, had a long leisurely shower and felt her headache mercifully fade to a dull roar. Wearing cotton boxers and a T-shirt, she flipped on the *Ellen* show and sat mindlessly watching, forcing herself to focus on the host's antics. She didn't want to think about anything important. Thinking ultimately led to questioning what was happening to her, why this ridiculous plane crash had shaken her to her very roots, why it had even happened at all and most of all, why it had happened to *her* and to Danny. Ultimately there were no answers, so the whole exercise was futile and frustrating. Distracting herself worked for a while. Numbing herself with booze or lorazepam helped for a while too. Now she would try not thinking.

The *Ellen* show over, Courtney flipped through the channels. English football. *Boring!* There was *Dr. Phil.* Nope, that wouldn't work. Soap operas. *Please!* CNN was next, a Ken doll talking about weather across North America. *This* she could do. Courtney was somewhat of a weather junkie from way back. She loved looking at weather radar or satellite pictures and almost always had the forecast memorized a week in advance. Weather was a safe topic.

Courtney began to doze off as weather segued into the markets and the latest oil prices. Moments later she awoke with a start, sitting bolt upright as the newscaster announced breaking news. A twelve-seater commuter jet had crashed in South Carolina, possibly carrying an unnamed rock band.

The voice and words began to fade, replaced by the sound of her pounding heart. It filled her head. Her ears burned, her throat constricted painfully. She was helplessly near tears. This crash had absolutely nothing to do with her, so why was she suddenly feeling like her world was coming apart? Why this sense of foreboding in her bones, like something really bad had happened to her or was about to? Why was she feeling immobilized suddenly, like her heart might stop? Her stomach spasmed a couple of times. *This is not good.*

Courtney reached for the remote and shut the television off. She was breathing rapidly. Dizziness closed in on her like walls compressing. This was ridiculous. Maybe Nan was right. Maybe she needed help. *Help.* A shrink, Nan meant. *Hell.* What good would talking to a shrink for a hundred and fifty bucks a pop do? Someone to tell her to pick herself up by her bootstraps and get on with it? Or perhaps encourage her to sit there and cry, to "let it all out," as though being an emotional wreck was going to make everything all better.

Well, they could save it, because no one was going to understand what was happening to her. Christ, *she* didn't even understand what was happening anymore, so how could some stranger possibly get inside her head?

Courtney popped a couple more Advil and washed them down with cold water. She washed her face and threw some clothes on, determined to go for a long walk. And if that long walk ended at a bar, then so be it.

Courtney walked for blocks. People, cars, trucks all blended into a riot of noise and blurred colors and movement. She walked in a daze but purposely headed for the gay neighborhood—Davie Street. She could at least feel a little less alien there, have a drink with like-minded people. She would not pick anyone up today, that was a certainty. Sex with strangers might be a momentary distraction, a cheap way to convince herself that she was living in the now, that she was alive, but it didn't make her feel better. It only made her feel more like shit. Like she was being a shit. Like she deserved to be treated like shit too.

The bar, Nelson's, was quiet. At two in the afternoon, it was far too early for cocktail hour. Courtney took a seat at the long, leather-covered bar and ordered a beer, determined to behave herself and nurse it all afternoon. She flipped through a tourism magazine sitting in front of her.

"You know, you really should try visiting some of those places around here if you haven't already."

Courtney turned toward the deep voice behind her and broke into a spontaneous smile. It was Jeff, the dealer from the casino. He had one of those infectious smiles, and those damned twinkling dark eyes were an instant mood-lifter.

"How did you know I'm not from around here?"

Jeff laughed and sat down beside her, ordering a beer. "The way you play blackjack. You didn't get that good overnight, so I'd have seen you at the casino before if you lived around here."

"You're quite a student of human behavior, aren't you?"

"In my line of work, you can't help it."

"Do you like it?"

"What, dealing cards at the casino?"

"Well, yeah. Do you?"

Jeff's eyes lit up. "Love it."

He had to be only a few years younger than Courtney. Old enough that it shouldn't be a transition job or a way of putting himself through college. "Can I ask how long you've been doing it?"

"Four years and counting."

Courtney sipped her beer, contemplating how to phrase her next question. She didn't want to insult him, but it was hard to relate. Dealing cards for a living was considerably beneath someone like herself, but obviously it wasn't for him. "You don't... You're happy doing it, right? I mean, is it something you see yourself doing five years from now?"

Jeff laughed, but there was a sharpness to his tone. "Did my father put you up to this?"

"Huh?"

"Never mind, I was kidding. Look, I know what you're trying to ask me, and as far as I'm concerned, what I'm doing is not underachieving or living out some childish fantasy or anything like that. It's not most people's dream career, but I love people, I love cards, I love the atmosphere. End of story."

Courtney seriously doubted that. Nobody's story was ever that simple and complete. "No regrets then?"

"None." Jeff's eyes grew serious. He scrutinized her, but not in an unfriendly way. "What's the deal with you?"

Courtney shook her head lightly. "Nope, no regrets."

"That wasn't what I meant."

"Come again?"

Jeff sipped his beer contemplatively. When he spoke next, it was in a no-bullshit way. "Who or what are you so angry at?"

"Angry?" Courtney laughed derisively. "Are you kidding me?" She wasn't angry. Hell, she was on top of the world. She was lucky, the charmed one, the indestructible one, spared for some greater purpose. The world was her oyster, all laid out there ready for her to pick and choose what she wanted. So what the hell was Jeff talking about?

"It's written all over you," he answered softly. "You do know that the root of anger is fear, right? Fear eventually makes us angry, especially when it can't be directed at the source of the threat. So my real question," he said in a calm, steady voice, "is what are you afraid of?"

"What are you, the author of some dime-store psychology book or something?" Courtney scoffed.

"No, but I know a thing or two about both fear and psychology."

"Let me guess, you take psychology courses in your spare time or something."

"As a matter of fact I do. At U.B.C. I'm halfway to my degree."

"Well, good for you, Jeff. But I don't want to be your term paper, thank you very much."

Jeff laughed appreciatively. "You're safe. School's out for the summer."

Courtney drained her beer and ordered another one, a little pissed at Jeff and at herself for succumbing to another drink. She could blow him off so easily. Just get up and walk the hell out of here. She hardly knew him, after all. She didn't have to be nice to him. She didn't have to humor him or hang out with him or be his friend or answer his damned questions. She sulked in the suds of her fresh beer, felt his gaze resting patiently on her. In seconds, he was wearing her down. "Okay, wait. Who said I was afraid of something? Or angry for that matter?" *What the hell does he know anyway?*

"I can tell. It's in the way you drink. It's in the way you play blackjack. It's even in your eyes, Courtney."

Courtney wanted him to look like a smug bastard so she could tear his head off, but he didn't. There was no pity or judgment in his face, only concern. "What do you mean it's in the way I play blackjack?" she asked.

Jeff shrugged. "You're intense about it, but not like the others who are playing to win. You do it to prove something. I don't know, it's hard to explain. Maybe you could explain it to me."

Courtney slowly shook her head. "Whatever I do, whether it's work or recreation, I try to do my best, that's all."

Jeff wasn't buying it. "There's a controlled recklessness when you play cards. Like you're daring something or someone to knock you off your horse."

Courtney's patience was beginning to wear thin. She gulped her beer to keep her mouth occupied, because she was this close to telling Jeff where to get off. "Being analyzed like I'm some bug under a pin is really not what I'm interested in at the moment."

Jeff wasn't fazed. "All right. I get it. I guess I thought maybe you could use a friend. Where are you from, anyway?"

"Seattle, and yes, I could use a friend." She decided in that instant that Jeff would be her friend. He was smart, had a sense of humor and didn't have an ulterior motive. She had nothing to prove to him. And while she didn't have to spill her guts to him about her past, there was no need to be secretive either. He could be trusted, as far as she could tell, and Courtney had always been a pretty good judge of character.

"Good. As your friend, I think you could also use a little fun and a healthy way to blow off some steam."

Courtney was instantly curious. "What'd you have in mind?"

"You free tomorrow afternoon?"

Courtney reached for her BlackBerry and pretended to check the calendar feature. "Hmm, well, I could cancel my appointment with the Prime Minister of Canada and slot you in. How's that?"

Jeff grinned. "Perfect."

The bartender, a beefy guy with hairy arms and a feminine mouth, set two more beers in front of them. "Jesus, awful news about that rock band, eh?"

"What rock band?" Jeff asked.

The bartender punched a remote control and the television came to life. CNN was showing smoky bits of twisted and charred metal, a crumpled wheel in a field. Courtney went cold.

"You know, that crash today down in the States. Killed the members of that group Slater and their entourage. Damned shame. Man, I liked their music."

Courtney's stomach roiled, threatening to empty its contents of beer and the pickled sausage she'd begun to munch. She leaped up from her chair. "Excuse me," she mumbled and ran as fast as she could to the washroom.

"God, I love this place," Ellen enthused as she and Sam stepped off the small boat taxi and onto Granville Island. It was a small island in the hub of Vancouver's downtown, its gritty industrial past transformed into trendy galleries and shops, restaurants and a fabulous public market that rivaled Toronto's St. Lawrence Market. Ellen always made a point to spend at least a day on the island whenever she visited Sam.

"I know, I know. You've told me a hundred times about your dream to open a little gallery here."

Ellen sighed. Any dreams she'd had of early retirement were up in smoke now, thanks to Susan's departure. They hadn't put their two-bedroom Cabbagetown town condo up for sale yet. In fact Ellen had yet to decide if she wanted to sell or buy Susan out. She made more money than Susan by about forty thousand a year, and so she would also have to either give her a settlement or pay her alimony. *Christ, what a nightmare.* A legal marriage such as theirs came with a lot of financial benefits, such as pension sharing and filing joint income tax. But the flip side of the coin—divorce—meant someone would be out a good chunk of money, and in this case it was Ellen.

Ellen couldn't hide her disappointment. It would be years before her finances recovered. "I guess I won't be boring you with any more of those plans."

"Aw, Ellen." Sam put her arm around Ellen's shoulders. "You're going to be okay, I promise. And you're going to have dreams again, and you're going to fulfill those dreams!"

Ellen laughed bitterly. "You know, I'm beginning to think I'd be a lot better off being more like you. Not getting married or living with anyone. Date eventually, I suppose but nothing serious. God! I never want another serious relationship again!"

There was no sassy comeback from Sam, and Ellen looked at her friend curiously. She was struck by the sadness in Sam's eyes and the hard line of her mouth. "Are you okay?"

Sam smiled, but it failed to reach her eyes. "Couldn't be better. C'mon, let's check out our favorite pottery store."

Ellen let it drop and followed Sam into the pottery shop they usually spent gobs of money at whenever they stopped in.

"Samantha Calloway, I can't believe it!" The woman was small and cute, with dancing gray eyes and blond highlights in her shoulder-length hair. She was young, thirty at most, and was clearly smitten with Sam.

"Looks like it's your lucky day," Ellen whispered, smothering a laugh.

Sam gave her a dirty look, then smiled sheepishly at the younger woman. "Julie, I didn't know you worked here."

"If you did you would have come in sooner, right?" She winked hopefully at Sam.

"Sure," Sam replied, playing it cool. Ellen knew her best friend and knew Sam wasn't playing it cool as in "hard-to-get." She was playing it cool as in "not interested."

"You never did give me your phone number," Julie persisted. "And I've even got a piece of paper and pen this time."

"Actually, um, Julie, I'm in the process of getting a new cell phone, so I don't really have a phone number right now."

Ellen's mouth slid open at Sam's bald-faced lie. She turned and pretended to examine a set of pottery mugs. Studied them, in fact, like they were famous works of art.

"Okay, I'll give you mine then." There was a faint rustling of paper. "I only wanted to thank you for rescuing Buster. Maybe take you out for a drink or lunch or something."

"It was no biggie, and you don't have to do anything to thank me. Buster would have come back once he realized he was never going to catch that squirrel." Sam laughed but it sounded hollow to Ellen's ears.

"Well, in any case—"

"Oh, Sam!" Ellen interrupted. "This would make the perfect soup bowl set for my mom for her birthday! Don't you think? The colors would be perfect for her kitchen."

Sam joined in on Ellen's timely enthusiasm, and Ellen quickly made the purchase.

"Thank you." Sam gave her a hug outside.

"I did it enough times for you in college when someone was after you."

"Remember the codes we used to have?"

"Oh, God, like I could forget them?"

"Remember flipping the little welcome sign on our dorm door when one of us didn't want the other to come in?"

Ellen rolled her eyes. "Oh, I remember all right. It was a long walk back down the stairs and to the library to kill time while you finished getting lucky."

"Hey, now. You flipped that ol' sign a few times yourself."

"Yeah, well, none that were as memorable as yours, I'm sure."

Sam steered them into the market. "I need to pick up some salmon and some of that delicate Japanese eggplant for dinner later. But how about a coffee on the dock first?"

"Okay, but only if we can share one of those giant chocolate éclairs." Ellen pointed to the bakery.

Coffees and an éclair in hand, Sam and Ellen made their way to a sun-drenched bench on the massive wood-planked dock. Gulls called in the distance, swooping down on their prey in the water or circling overhead. The breeze carried a faint smell of salt, and Ellen inhaled deeply. It was a blunt reminder that she was no longer around the Great Lakes.

"The worst thing you ever did was that time at the campus pub when that really ugly woman with all the face piercings was trying to pick you up," Ellen joked. "Remember that?"

"Oh, God, how could I forget? And clearly you haven't let me off the hook yet."

"Like I'd ever forget you told her you had to leave with me because you had to help me change my colostomy bag? Christ, you're lucky I still speak to you."

Sam laughed deeply. "You have to admit, it was a pretty good one."

"Yeah, you were good at ditching women then. Much better than you are now."

"What do you mean?"

"That Julie woman in the pottery shop. She's cute and she clearly has the hots for you."

"Oh, hell, I was at the park one day a month ago or something, and she was playing Frisbee with her black Lab. He took off after a squirrel and I went and corralled him for her, that's all."

"Oh, c'mon, it's much more than that."

"Not for me."

Ellen took a huge bite of the éclair, eliciting a protest from Sam. "Why not?"

Sam shrugged and took her own generous bite. "I don't know. Not interested."

"That's not the Sam Calloway I know."

"Maybe I'm getting old."

"You'll never be *that* old. But come to think of it, I've been here almost a week now and you've done nothing more than make a show out of looking at other women."

"What? No way!"

"Yes, way! You seem to be all talk and no action these days, and that's not like you."

"What, like I'm going to pick someone up and bring them home while you're staying with me? Or stay over at someone else's place and leave you alone? I'd be a pretty shitty host if I did that."

Ellen considered Sam's response, which was certainly plausible. And yet there was something different about Sam. On the outside she was the same good-time girl, horny as hell and fun loving. But her heart didn't seem to be in it the way it used to.

"Is everything okay with you, Sam?"

"Of course, why wouldn't it be?"

"We seem to spend all our time talking about my problems. I wanted to make sure nothing was going on with you, that's all."

Sam patted her knee reassuringly. "Everything's fine with me."

"You sure?" A dreadful thought occurred to Ellen. What if Sam had developed a crush on her, now that Susan was out of the picture? Could her best friend be in love with her? Is that what was different about Sam?

Oh, God. The pastry in Ellen's stomach felt heavy and cloying. She stared at Sam, panic in her throat. *Please don't have a crush on me, please don't have a crush on me!* They had decided very early on in their friendship, on a college winter break trip in Florida together, that there was no chance of a romance between them and they were both more than fine with that. It was refreshing to have a totally platonic best friend, something Ellen had perhaps been too casually taking for granted all this time.

Sam looked mildly startled. "What? I'm fine. Jeez!"

Ellen wasn't so sure.

CHAPTER EIGHT

*Gambling tip: A number is never "due" to come up, but the odds
are that it will sooner or later.*

Courtney checked the message indicator on her BlackBerry.
Lately she had found herself checking it every couple of hours,
knowing it was stupid to think Ellen Turcotte would actually
phone her. Ellen had been cordial to her at the casino, but it was
really nothing more than superficial politeness, and even then it
had been a minimal effort. Still, Courtney couldn't stop hoping
she would phone, and that fact alone annoyed her. Was she really
so desperate for a woman's friendship that she couldn't wait for
someone only lukewarm toward her to give her the time of day?

Jeff smiled smugly from the driver's seat. "She still hasn't
called you, eh?"

"First of all, I don't know what you're talking about, and
secondly, do you Canadians have to say 'eh,' like, all the time? Is

it the first word you learn when you're a baby? Christ, most of us learn 'mama' or 'dada' first."

Jeff laughed, not the least bit insulted. "You really are in a mood today, aren't you?"

"I would be less in a *mood* if you'd tell me where the hell we're going."

"Courtney, darling, you're a treasure."

Courtney sulked, shielding her eyes from the brilliant sunshine. "Guess that means you're not telling me. But since we're heading north on Highway Ninety-Nine, I'm going to take a wild guess and say that you're taking me to Whistler."

"All I'm going to tell you is that the mood you're in is perfect for what we're going to do."

"What, hunt bears?"

Jeff burst out laughing, his voice high like a girl's, and it made Courtney do a double take. He was muscular and square-jawed with a fashionable five-o'clock shadow. His giggle was totally at odds with his appearance, yet it augmented his appeal. Jeff didn't try to hide who he truly was, and Courtney admired him for that.

"Can I ask you something Jeff?"

"Sure."

"You must have no shortage of boyfriends. So what are you doing being a dyke hag, spending the day with me?"

"Wait a minute. You're the fag hag hanging with me, not the other way around!"

Courtney shook her head, but she was smiling. "All right, whatever. But it's nice to make a friend here, so thank you for inviting me today."

Jeff patted her knee. "Hey, I can use new friends too. And lesbians are perfect."

"Oh, yeah? Why is that?"

"Because I don't have to worry about you ever trying to get into my pants."

Courtney laughed. "Touché! That works both ways, buster."

As they drew closer to Whistler, Courtney noticed all the signs pointing the way to the various 2010 Winter Olympic venues. She'd watched some of the events on television, in particular the downhill skiing. It was cool to think how a few months ago, the world's best athletes had converged here, all with dreams of gold medals and record-breaking performances. She would have loved to have made the drive up from Seattle to stand out in the cold and watch the skiers fly past her in a blur, but as usual, there'd been no time in her life then. Now, she had nothing but time.

"Did you go to any of the Olympic events?" she asked Jeff.

"Are you kidding me? It was a zoo around here. Besides, I got lots of overtime at the casino and made some damn good tips with all the foreign big shots here." He grinned knowingly but remained silent.

"What? Okay, Mister, how many world-class jocks did you bag? And don't play innocent with me! You look like the cat that ate the canary."

"You're way too smart for your own good, do you know that?"

"Yeah, well, I'm not feeling overly smart these days. But anyway, spill it."

"Two, that's it, but man, they were so worth it!"

"So what was their sport? Besides sex!"

Jeff laughed. "Oh, no, you're not getting that information out of me! One of them happens to be very closeted and very well-known."

"Fine, I'll have to guess. Let's see. They were both figure skaters!"

Jeff's mouth fell open in mock disgust. "Please! Do you have to stereotype us as badly as straight people do?"

"All right, all right. I was messin' with you."

She could tell by his grin that he couldn't totally contain himself. "One was a bobsled driver and the other was a hockey player."

"Ah, hit the jackpot with the hockey player, did you?"

"Don't tell me you've never hit the sheets with anyone famous."

Courtney thought back to her mostly boring life. In college

she'd had a nice season-long tryst with a basketball player who later went on to play a couple of years in the WNBA. Charlene was her name, and at six-foot-three, she'd towered over Courtney's five feet, eight inches. Charlene had been as close to sleeping with a celebrity as Courtney'd ever gotten. "Not really, no, but somehow I think I'll survive."

Jeff's face sagged, his look of pride and vanity collapsing. "It has its upside, but honestly, the downside outweighs it."

"Like what?"

"Like not being able to tell anyone who you're sleeping with. Like being very, very careful to avoid attention when you go out anywhere. Or not go out at all. And knowing you'll never have a normal relationship with someone like that. In other words, honey, it's not all it's cracked up to be."

"I'll take your word for it." Courtney had no intention of dating a celebrity. In fact, at the rate things were going, she might never end up dating anyone ever again. Period. "This Porsche makes you look like a celebrity or that you're at least sleeping with one." Courtney chuckled. "Is the hockey player paying for this?"

Jeff shot her a look of mock indignation. "I'll have you know he is not! But it's not exactly my own hard-earned money either. It's all compliments of Daddy and his stubborn persistence."

Courtney pushed her sunglasses up on her head to get a better look at Jeff. She liked his honesty. It was downright refreshing. "What is he trying to convince you to do?"

"Same thing he has for the last fifteen years. Join the family business."

"Let me guess, it's not the casino business?"

Jeff laughed hollowly. "Nope. Pharmaceuticals. Legal ones, by the way. My dad and his brother own a very successful company that lucked out with a blood thinner drug twenty-one years ago."

"Sounds lucrative."

"Very."

"So why not go for it?"

"Are you kidding me?" Jeff asked in disgust. "I am not made from the same mold as him and could never be like him. Please!"

"But isn't it kind of noble, developing drugs for the sick?" It was more impressive than developing computer games, something Courtney was no longer proud of.

"Noble? Are you kidding me?" Jeff shook his head, his face reddening. "It's an industry that makes gobs of money on the backs on insurance companies and sick people who will pay anything for something they think will help them. And don't even get me started on AIDS in Third World countries and how there's no money to be made selling drugs there, so these drug companies refuse to. They'd rather stockpile them here and lose money than send them there and give them away or sell them at cost."

"Sorry, I didn't mean to—"

Jeff took a deep breath and blew it out slowly. His smile was slow to return. "No worries. I didn't mean to jump all over you. It's a sore point with me and has been for years. Drug companies are greedy sons of bitches."

Courtney wanted to press him for more on his family and their business but decided to leave it alone. She was private and didn't like it when people tried to pump her for personal details, at least not until there was a lot of trust and loyalty.

As they entered the grounds of the Whistler resort, Courtney marveled at its European-style buildings and chalets. She would love to see it in the winter, full of skiers strutting around with the latest equipment and clothes, dripping money and athleticism and energy. She was pretty good at ripping up the hills herself, but unfortunately it was the wrong time of year.

"So what exactly does one do at Whistler-Blackcomb in early summer?"

Jeff's exuberance was palpable. He was practically dancing. "Oh, my God, woman, you are going to love this."

"Love what? Look, I've been good, haven't I? Why don't you spill it already." Courtney had been damned patient. It was time he confessed his plans.

Jeff silently parked the little Porsche, stubbornly not giving in to her. As they walked toward a kiosk, he pointed to a sign announcing mountain biking.

Courtney's blood surged in her veins. Mountain biking down Whistler-Blackcomb. What a blast this was going to be! She hadn't gone mountain biking in years but remembered the thrill it gave her, tearing down trails, flying over rocks, zipping around trees, splashing through puddles. She grinned at her new friend. "How did you know I would go for something like this?"

Jeff winked at her. "You look athletic, and that motorcycle of yours tells me you're into courting danger."

"How did you know I had a bike?"

"Saw you retrieve your helmet from the coat check at the casino. I'm good at observing people, remember?"

"All right, all right. But just because I ride a motorcycle doesn't mean I'm into hurling myself off a mountain on a bicycle." She didn't really want him thinking he'd pegged her so perfectly.

"There's nothing like a little controlled danger to suck the world's worries out of your mind. Trust me. It's the best stress-reliever in the world that's not illegal or immoral."

Courtney did need a healthier outlet for her stress than sleeping with strangers and drinking herself silly most nights. Maybe Jeff's idea would work and she could finally start feeling normal again. The last few weeks it was so hard to feel much of anything. At first it was relief over missing the crash, and then it was insecurity, anger, guilt, helplessness. It was a vicious cocktail that had turned her into some sort of apparition moving through her life one-dimensionally. There but not really there. It was as though she were floating sometimes, and when someone said something to her or asked a question, it often took a few seconds for it to register. She was a shadow, out of sync with the world, a step behind everyone else.

On top of the mountain, Courtney straddled her bike and looked down. Maybe this was her chance to feel at one with something or at least a part of something else. The bike felt light yet solid between her legs—more than adequate for the job. The trail ahead was wide at the start before narrowing at the opening of a thick patch of trees. She'd have to get her speed down before entering the chute or she'd find herself wrapped around one of those trees.

"Man, look at this, eh?" Jeff motioned to the scenery around them.

Courtney's eyes followed his hand, and for a long moment she drank in the breathtaking beauty before her—the distant snow-capped mountains jutting into an azure sky, the cedar and pine trees and their intoxicating scent. The village below was tiny, like a child's miniature play town. The air was fresh and cool, and Courtney took as deep a breath as she could at six thousand feet. This mountain, these trees, did not know that she'd cheated death less than two months ago. Neither did any of these people here, including Jeff. It felt like a beginning. Or maybe an end. She hoped it was both.

"Ready?" A trio had taken off before them. They were a couple of hundred feet ahead, about the right amount of space to follow safely.

"After you."

Courtney adjusted her helmet again to make sure it was tight, then pushed herself off. She gained speed quickly and stood up on the pedals, using the strength in her legs to brace herself for the bumps. She braked gently before the chute through the trees. She heard Jeff howl in delight behind her and she whooped back, loving the speed and thrill of it, the hint of danger, and the cool, crisp mountain air.

Courtney sat down on the bike and hugged it tightly as a sharp curve approached. Bearing down, she gave herself as wide a berth as she could to make the turn safely. As she did so, Jeff suddenly shot ahead of her, taking a tight angle through the turn and brushing the trees as he passed.

"You crazy son of a bitch," Courtney muttered, laughing.

The trail wound down and around, then up again, and Courtney pedaled until her legs burned. She splashed through a huge puddle, the water at pedal level, and pushed on. Her lungs burned, and the cool breeze on her face was heavenly.

This was what it was like to truly be alive, and for the moment at least, she was ridiculously thrilled with her existence in a way she hadn't been in such a long time. If only this would last, oh, about fifty more years, but what the hell, she would take it for what it was—a moment. And really, what could she count on beyond this moment anyway? The plane crash had at least taught her that much, and it was a hard lesson for her. Most of her life, she had figured that if she worked hard enough, was a little smarter and more determined than everyone else, things would fall into place for her. That life would bend and capitulate to her wishes. And mostly it had, giving Courtney a sense of omnipotence. She was a survivor and a conqueror through hard work and determination. Missing that plane, however, had been mere luck. Luck had never factored into her equations before. Luck was fickle, and Courtney hated fickle. Fickle was for losers who couldn't plan their lives.

Courtney rounded a bend. Another cyclist had stopped cold right in the middle of the trail. Before she could take evasive action or even think of taking any evasive action, she crashed into the woman, clipping her bike's back wheel. Courtney careened through the air, heard a scream she was pretty sure wasn't hers. She tried to get into some kind of a tuck and landed with a painful thud that knocked the wind out of her. *Jesus Christ!* She gasped for air, then took mental stock of her body. Everything seemed to be in one piece, but what about the other cyclist? They'd collided pretty hard.

Courtney hobbled to the other woman, who sat on the ground a few feet away looking stunned. No bones were jutting out anywhere, no puddles of blood.

"You okay?" Courtney was almost afraid of the answer.

Blue eyes lifted tentatively up at her. "I, ah, I think so."

"Here, let me help you up." Courtney extended her hand, and the woman, about Courtney's age, took it gingerly and pulled herself up. "You sure you're not hurt?"

The woman touched a small bump on her forehead below

her helmet. "Other than a couple of bumps and bruises, I think I'm okay. Are you okay?"

"Yeah, I'm fine." Courtney wasn't entirely sure that was true, but she wasn't about to act like a wimp in front of a stranger, especially a nice-looking one. "I'm sorry about the crash." It wasn't really her fault, actually, and there was a time she would have jumped down this woman's throat for stopping in the middle of a trail. That she was able to keep her temper in check surprised her a little.

"No, I'm sorry. I should have pulled off the trail. A twig or something got caught in my wheel and I was trying to pull it out." She extended her hand. "Chris Hatt. Sorry we had to meet under these circumstances."

"Courtney Langford, and don't worry about it."

Jeff, who had been well ahead of Courtney, was hauling his bike back up to their position. "Everybody okay?"

"A few bumps and bruises, that's all," Courtney replied.

Chris stepped forward, the look of interest in her eyes unmistakable. "It's nothing that a drink over dinner wouldn't cure. Are you two interested in grabbing a bite at the bottom?"

"Sorry, can't." Courtney didn't dare look at Jeff right now. "We have plans."

Chris shrugged before smiling warmly. She'd taken Courtney's hasty rejection in stride. "Okay, then. See you around."

"Jeez, Courtney," Jeff hissed after Chris rode off. "I could have made myself disappear for a while if you wanted a quiet drink with her."

"Thank you, but I don't."

"Oh, I get it. You're holding out for that woman at the casino. The one who's supposed to call you. Ellen, right?"

"I'm not holding out for anyone." Courtney's tone was a little sharper than she'd intended, and to avoid an apology or worse—an explanation—she hopped on her bike and sped off without looking back. She really wasn't holding out for anyone, and while Chris seemed nice and seemed willing to spend time with Courtney, Courtney no longer wanted the company of a stranger. It wasn't because she was stuck on Ellen and it certainly wasn't because she was too prudish to strike something up with Chris. She had no real reason, other than she didn't feel like it, but so what. It was her business and Jeff could think what he wanted about her and Ellen.

Ellen. Courtney's spirits heightened instantly at the thought of Ellen. She was quite sure Ellen would never take any of her brooding crap, her stoicism, her adolescent bravado, her evasive tactics. Ellen could pretty much see through any act that Courtney could dish out, and Courtney took some comfort in that. She hadn't been around a woman like that in a long time, and she missed it. Yes, Ellen would more than keep her on her toes, keep her honest. It was too bad she hadn't cared to give Courtney more than the time of day. They'd probably never see one another again. Courtney's spirits sank with that thought and she was instantly lonely again. She had so few honest, unaffected people in her life. Jeff was one. Ellen could have been another.

"Wait up already!" Jeff yelled from somewhere behind. But the end of the trail was in sight and Courtney pedaled on to the finish as though the devil himself were chasing her. Nothing could catch her!

"Oh, my God, that was awesome!" Courtney yelled, pumping a fist into the air from the exhilaration of it. She ripped off her helmet and shook her sweaty hair free.

"I knew you'd love it! Now let's go toast the fact that we came out of it in one piece, though you nearly didn't."

Courtney had a couple of scratches and bruises from her collision with Chris, but she was proud of her little battle scars. "You're just jealous."

"No, I'm not. But if it'd been a cute guy instead of a cute girl you ran into, I definitely would be."

Over burgers, fries and light beer, they got to know each other a little better, though neither volunteered anything about the hard parts of their lives. They were skirting the personal stuff. It was like being on the bikes and trying to catch air over tiny potholes. It was getting exhausting. Courtney found that she wanted to be real with him. She needed someone to talk to.

"I imagine it's been hard for you to rebuff your father's wishes to join the family business," Courtney said gently. "Does your family still speak to you, or have they written you off?" It was bad enough he wasn't interested in the family business but probably even worse that he was gay.

Jeff smiled. "Do you mean am I the family black sheep? Yes, absolutely, and I wouldn't have it any other way."

"So you're a rebel without the disguise?"

"You could say that." For the first time, Courtney noticed the fine lines around his eyes, which seemed more pronounced now. It was a tough subject for him. "Since I was a kid, I never fit in with their plans in any way, shape or form. I tried for a while. I enrolled in business at the University of Toronto right out of high school, but that was just for show. I hated it and spent most of my time drinking and doing drugs. And *not* the legal kind. I dropped out in second year, lived off of friends' couches for a couple of years. Worked odd jobs. Finally came back here about eight years ago and slowly started getting my shit together. For years, they didn't talk to me or even acknowledge I was alive."

"Wow, that must have hurt."

Jeff shrugged. "It's about what I expected from them."

It was a rare person who walked away from family fortune because he didn't want to be something he wasn't, and Courtney respected that. "Are you on good terms now?"

"I wouldn't say it was good, but it's okay. We talk once a month or so. Usually one of my parents tries halfheartedly to convince me to join the business. At least they don't try to get me to date women anymore." Jeff shook his head. "It got so bad that I used to try to rub their noses in me being queer. I'd bring a guy home and kiss him in front of them or grab his ass or something. They were predictably mortified, which of course would make my frigging week."

"So you enjoyed torturing your parents a little, huh?"

"It's not like they didn't deserve it."

"Did your family experiences make you want to be a psychologist?"

"Well, it seemed to me that if I could figure them out, I could figure anyone out." Jeff grinned between bites of his burger. "So yeah, they prepared me well. But I like what I'm doing at the casino too and taking part-time classes, letting my parents buy me that car because they feel guilty or manipulative or whatever the hell it is they wanna feel." He looked like he should feel bad, but clearly he didn't. "I guess I'm not anxious to grow up."

Courtney tilted her bottle of beer in his direction. "Here's to being comfortable in your own skin and living the way you want to live."

Jeff clinked bottles with her. "Like the Bon Jovi song, 'it's my life.'" He took a long drink from the bottle. "And speaking of which, you don't seem to be letting life hold you back. What's your story?"

He couldn't have described her situation more perfectly. There was absolutely nothing holding her back from anything right now, nothing putting any constraints on her, but it certainly hadn't always been that way. Her home life had forced her to grow up at a young age, and her career aspirations continued to fuel her drive. "I guess I chose to be rebellious now instead of in my teens or twenties. You know, basically sticking my middle finger to the world." Midlife crisis might be a more accurate description of where she was at, Courtney supposed, because she was probably in the middle of her life and apparently in some kind of crisis.

"It's all right, you know. You can shed your skin, or change who you want to be, or have an identity crisis at any age. There's no expiry date on that kind of thing."

"Darn, because I'm about ready for it to expire. I've about had all the fun I can manage these last few weeks."

"C'mon, having fun doesn't have a shelf life. Why stop now?"

Whoring around and drinking wasn't as fun as people like Hemingway and other celebrities made it seem, that was for sure. Or maybe the point was that you had to be a rock star or a famous novelist to appreciate the torture of it all. "Really, it's not particularly glamorous. I decided to leave a good job and travel a bit and sow a couple of wild oats in the process, that's all."

"Ah. Having the quintessential midlife crisis. Leaving it all behind and searching for what's important."

Okay, so a spade was a spade. "Believe me, I wasn't expecting to fall into this rabbit hole." That was exactly the crux of it. She'd woken up one morning and suddenly nothing made sense anymore. All she could think to do was to run away, find a different landscape, because then at least it was okay for everything to seem strange and different and confusing.

Jeff looked at her so intently that it caused her to squirm a little. She should have known there'd be no hiding anything from him. "And what made you fall down that rabbit hole in the first place?"

"Nothing in particular."

He seized on her abrupt answer. "Bullshit. Most people don't decide one day to change their entire lives. It's usually more subtle than that, unless something happened to you to speed up the process. Something big."

"Researching that term paper again, are you?"

"I'm not joking. Something did happen to you."

"Well, if it did, it doesn't mean I want to talk about it."

"Fair enough. But I saw the way you reacted to that plane crash on the TV at the bar yesterday."

"So? People got killed in it. It was upsetting."

"Lots of things are, but not enough to make you run off to the bathroom, pale as a ghost, and looking like you wanted to puke."

Courtney could lie to him, but really, what was the point? He seemed to genuinely care, and he was her friend. She didn't have to confess absolutely everything. It might be nice to talk about it a little. "It…those images on the TV yesterday brought back memories of something that really…you know."

"I don't know, actually." His voice was kind. "Will you tell me?"

Goddamn, this wasn't easy. She pursed her lips and tried to decide how much to tell him. Slowly, she raised her eyes. Her mouth quivered a little and she spoke quietly. "I narrowly missed being on a plane that crashed, okay?"

Her words had the barest effect on him. His eyebrows twitched a little, but his face remained impassive. It was damned disconcerting. Courtney didn't know what kind of reaction she expected from him, but a big fat nothing sure wasn't it.

"Well?" she persisted. "Didn't you hear what I said?"

"Of course I heard what you said. You missed being on a plane that crashed. It's what you *didn't* tell me that I'm waiting on."

"What the hell do you mean? Christ, Jeff, this is the biggest thing that's ever happened in my stupid, boring, comformist, small-r republican, lapsed Catholic life!"

Jeff laughed—*laughed*!—at her. "Well, it's about time something shook your ass up then!"

Courtney felt her jaw slacken in surprise. She would have left him right then if it wasn't such a long way back to Vancouver. Decking him might be a good alternative. Dammit, there was nothing funny about any of this. How could he laugh? "Are you finished making fun of me?"

Jeff recoiled. He looked mortified and that gave Courtney a measure of satisfaction. "Good God, girl, I'm not laughing at you. I'm sorry, I was trying to lighten the mood a bit, that's all."

"Well, there is no way to lighten anything about this, okay?"

"All right, all right. I want to know why this event has thrown your world off its axis so much. Can you tell me that?"

Frustration rose in her. "Why do you think? If I hadn't slept in that morning, I would have died in that crash. It's just…" There was no way Courtney could make him understand what she was feeling. No way was she going to confess how guilty she still felt that Danny had died and she hadn't. "Okay, look. I was damned lucky to have missed that plane. The problem is, sometimes it feels like I did get on that plane and that I died like all the rest of them. Does that make any sense?"

"Of course it does."

"It does?"

"Sure. You weren't physically on that plane, but you lost a part of yourself with it. It was true, what I said about shedding your skin and becoming someone else. Hell, I've shed my skin a couple of times over. That's what you're doing now. You lost a big part of yourself, and now you're reinventing yourself."

Without warning, tears welled in her eyes—powerful tears that could explode any minute if she wasn't careful. "But…" Courtney mentally pulled at the fragments of herself, near panic. "What if I don't recognize myself in this new skin? What if I don't like myself?"

Jeff smiled reassuringly and squeezed her hand across the wood laminate table. "You might not at first, but you will eventually. You'll still be you, only a different you that's stronger, faster, better." He winked, and his smile was the rare kind that said everything was going to be fine. The tension had been broken. "You'll be the *Bionic Woman*."

Tears ran freely down Courtney's cheeks, disguised as laughter. "I used to watch reruns of that show when I was kid. Oh, my God, I had the biggest crush on Lindsay Wagner."

"If I was old like you I would have had one on Lee Majors. But since I'm *much* younger, my big childhood television crush was MacGyver. Some of that show was even filmed here, did you know that?"

"I didn't, but I'll be sure to remember that next time I'm playing a trivia game. That's what us *old* folks like to do, you know."

"You know where to find me if any questions about the show come up." His eyes glinted anew with mischief.

"Oh, my God, don't tell me you slept with that actor!"

"No! I was only, like, fourteen or fifteen years old! Have you no shame, woman?"

Courtney's smile leaked out slowly. "None whatsoever. So, stud, did you?"

Jeff looked disappointed but totally busted. "No, but I gave a hand job to one of the crewmen," Jeff blurted out. "My first brush with fame!"

Courtney laughed and shook her head. "Started young, huh?" She hadn't been nearly as brave at that age. Hell, she hadn't even kissed a girl until her last year of high school.

"Yeah, but it's not about when you start, my dear. It's all in how you finish."

Courtney drained the last of her beer. "Funny, I thought it was all about the ride in getting there."

CHAPTER NINE

Definition of "progressive betting": The size of the player's wager increases after a winning round.

Ellen yawned as she poured another cup of coffee for herself and swung the carafe toward Sam. Sam snatched her cup away.

"I'd love to, but if I'm going to get to work on time, I need to leave here in about ten minutes."

"Crap, is it that late already?"

Sam, in pale blue scrubs at the kitchen table, sighed deeply. "Unfortunately, yes. God. My first twelve-hour shift in a week. It's going to be brutal. I suppose every nut job in the city will have waited until today to come into the ER, looking for Nurse Sam to make them all better."

Ellen smothered a laugh at Sam's crankiness. "Well, with that kind of attitude, how can they resist you?"

"That's what I'm afraid of."

"At least you'll have a nice dinner to look forward to. Don't forget, I'm cooking tonight."

Sam rose and took her plate and mug to the sink. "I promise you, that's the only thing that will get me through the day today."

Ellen enjoyed cooking and looked forward to kicking around the house with nothing to do but menu plan. A glance at Sam's face, however, told her Sam had a different agenda for her.

"Hey, why don't you call that Courtney woman and go out and do something fun with her instead of sitting around here all day?" Sam tried to sell it as a thought that had just occurred to her, but Ellen knew different. Sam was a lousy actor.

"I'm perfectly happy to sit around here all day cooking up a storm."

"I look forward to the fruits of your labor, but I'm just saying—"

"Christ, Sam!" The verbal explosion was so uncharacteristic of Ellen that she instantly regretted it. At the look of shock on Sam's face, she tried to dial back her outrage. "Look, I don't understand why you keep trying to hook me up with that woman."

"I'm not trying to hook you up. I want you to meet people and have a little fun, that's all. We've been over this. There would be absolutely nothing wrong with you spending a couple of hours with her. In broad daylight even!"

Ellen couldn't pull herself out of her defensive posture. "Do you want me out of your hair? Is that it? Are you trying to pawn me off on someone else?"

"Oh, for God's sake! That's not it at all."

"Well… Are you sure I'm not being a complete pain in the ass?" She undoubtedly was, and she hated being so needy and so…un-fun. *Dammit!*

"Honey, you're a nice little pinch in my ass." Sam's smile was warm and innocent and not the least bit lecherous. "I don't expect you to come out here after your breakup and be the life of the party or to entertain me with laughs every two minutes, okay?"

"All right." Ellen's mood lifted considerably, but it was short-lived. She was still unsure if Sam's feelings toward her had shifted into romantic territory, and the uncertainty made her nervous. It would be a shock if Sam had a crush on her after all this time, but it was not unheard of for lesbians to suddenly find their hearts leaping and their loins pulsing in the presence of their best friend. Ellen had seen it happen before, and if it was happening to Sam, she needed to address it and get it the hell out of Sam's mind. The idea of a fling with Sam was outrageous, not to mention a complication she did not want or need. It would be incestuous after all these years. "Um, Sam?"

"Yes?"

"You don't…um…you know…" Ellen picked at a piece of lint on her button-down, cable-knit sweater. There was no way to soften the question. It had to be asked. "…Have some kind of crush on me, do you?"

The silence was like hitting a wall suddenly. Ellen began a mental dance, trying to think how she could back out of this, because she knew instantly she'd made a mistake. How could she unask the question or at least make Sam think she'd been kidding? Before she could take a new tack, Sam began giggling. Soon she was roaring with laughter.

"I wasn't trying to be funny, you know," Ellen grumbled, alternately amused and annoyed.

"Oh, my God!" Sam blurted out between fits of laughter. "You're not serious, are you?" If she could stop laughing long enough, she might actually look horrified, Ellen supposed.

Heat crawled up Ellen's neck. *Crap.* She'd picked up all the wrong signals from Sam, who obviously had no more of a crush on her than the old lady at the end of the street did. She was glad Sam's feelings toward her hadn't changed, even if she did feel like a fool now. "I thought, I don't know. I don't know anything anymore, okay? Other than the fact that I am probably going slowly crazy these days." That's if she didn't die of embarrassment first.

"Oh, Ellen." Sam sobered up and wrapped her in a bear hug. "You know I love you with all my heart. And I think you're gorgeous and smart and funny and sexy, but I don't want to sleep with you, okay?"

"You don't?" Ellen asked, slightly—but only slightly—hurt.

"Maybe it's crazy of me, but I value our friendship and the years together just the way they are."

"Thank God. Me too!" Ellen quickly kissed her friend on the cheek. It was time to get back to normal, to stop looking around every corner for things that weren't there. She didn't need any more trouble or stress in her life. "Glad we got that one out of the way."

Sam eyed her curiously. "What made you suddenly wonder if I had some kind of crush on you, anyway?"

"I thought I was getting a weird vibe from you, I don't know," Ellen answered sheepishly.

"What, like I was staring at your ass or something?" Sam grinned lasciviously.

Ellen laughed. It was wonderful to laugh again with Sam. "All right, no. But you don't seem like the old Sam I know and love."

"What? C'mon, I'm still the same ol' Sam."

"Well, what happened to the Casanova in you? How come you're not dating anyone or even much trying to date anyone?"

Sam looked intently at her watch, and Ellen could tell the effort was exaggerated for her benefit. "Crap, I gotta get going or I'm going to be late."

Ellen touched Sam on the arm before she could slide past her. "You're not seeing anyone, right? I mean, you would have told me if you were, wouldn't you?"

Sam smiled benignly. "Of course I would tell you. But there's nothing to tell, so stop worrying, okay? Jeez!"

"Okay." Ellen would never stop worrying about her friend, but she let it go. "Don't forget, I'm cooking us a nice dinner tonight."

"I look forward to having my own little housewife waiting at home for me." Sam grinned from the front door.

Ellen narrowed her eyes menacingly. "Oh, you're going to get it for that one, Calloway."

Sam laughed all the way down the front sidewalk.

It was a gorgeous early summer day in Vancouver, which meant, surprisingly, no rain. The sun shimmered on the freshly sprung leaves and a pleasantly cool breeze descended from the mountains, bringing with it the tiniest scent of fresh cedar. Ellen had decided against hanging around Sam's house all day cooking after all. She could throw together a lasagna later, and in the meantime, there were all those wonderful high-end shops she could browse through on Robson Street. Instant window-shopping therapy.

Ellen took her time, sauntering from store to store. As she passed some, she merely studied their window displays of mannequins in their gorgeous clothes. Other stores she strolled through, pretending to be interested in making a purchase, but not enough to require a sales clerk's help. The jewelry store she stumbled upon was a small slice of heaven. She paused over the display cases of beautiful Swiss watches, admiring the ones that were bold, yet fashionable and obviously expensive. The array of diamond earrings was adorable, and she had no trouble at all imagining them adorning her ears. She practically drooled over a black opal necklace, but quickly moved on to another display when she saw the $1,600 pricetag. Ellen had never really treated herself to good jewelry, and Lord knew that Susan never had either—not on her modest postal salary that she managed to mostly drink away. Now Ellen wished that at some point, she'd said, "Screw it, I'm going to buy myself something beautiful and expensive." Something that had no practical use, but would have made her feel like a million bucks. If she had, though, Susan would have bitched about it and ridden her ass for wasting money until Ellen felt like crap. So she'd never done it.

Ellen walked out of the store in an angry daze, her heart heavy. She'd spent the last few months blaming everything wrong with her life on her ex. Every little thing Ellen had done or not done that had made her unhappy or regretful over the years, she had laid at Susan's feet. It was Susan's fault she'd never felt like she should buy herself nice jewelry. It was Susan's fault she would now have to give up at least a year's salary as a divorce settlement. It was Susan's fault they'd never traveled much—because Susan would rather sit at home or at her favorite bar on weekends off, drinking. It was Susan's fault that Ellen had gone to countless social events on her own because she was too embarrassed to bring Susan along. Susan the drunk. Susan the ogre. Susan the slut. Susan the thief who had sucked away Ellen's best years.

Ellen walked on, unaware of how many blocks her anger was carrying her. She stopped eventually at a bench on the sidewalk and sat down, her fury finally exhausted.

The truth was, it couldn't possibly have been all Susan's fault. It was an easy out to heap it all on Susan the philanderer, Susan the boozehound. But if Ellen's life sucked, well, she had to take some responsibility for that herself. *She* had settled for Susan escaping into booze. *She* had not demanded more for herself over the years, because at some point, she must have decided she'd rather be with Susan, despite her faults, than be alone. She had loved Susan, had even married her. So, unless she'd totally lost her mind these last few years, she had long ago accepted her life with Susan. If Susan had not ended up in the arms of that Jessica woman and whoever else she'd been fucking around with, Ellen would probably still be with her, sleepwalking through her life. The infidelity was the deal breaker though, the mountain between them that could not be scaled.

She didn't feel particularly rested, but she needed to move on. Looking around, trying to determine where she was, she spotted a bookstore. She got up and trudged toward it, happy to have found not only a diversion but also one that she could actually afford. Inside, she purposely zigzagged around the self-help section—she'd done enough introspection lately to last at least a few years—and made for the fiction area. As long as it wasn't lesbian fiction, she decided. Dyke drama was *not* what she needed right now. She pulled out an Amy Tan book. *Nah, too intense.* Same with the classics, which she'd read many times. Chick lit might do the trick. There was Nora Roberts, Emily

Giffin, Jodi Picoult, Nicholas Sparks. Pedestrian as hell but stuff she could easily get lost in. She reached for *American Wife* by Curtis Sittenfeld. As she touched its spine to pull it out for a closer look, she felt someone at her shoulder.

"Hey, you," a woman's voice, warm and deep, whispered close to her ear, sending an inadvertent shiver up and down her spine.

Ellen turned and instinctively smiled. She really didn't want to smile at Courtney Langford, but those green eyes, warm like a Caribbean seascape, loosened something in her. Like toes wanting to spread out in warm sand. "Hi."

Courtney's eyes scanned the book behind Ellen. "*American Wife*, huh? Was that my cue to appear or something?"

Ellen felt herself blushing furiously. Courtney certainly had a knack for popping up when she least expected her to. "I, ah—"

"You're not looking for one, are you?"

Ellen swallowed nervously. "What?"

"An American wife." Courtney grinned provocatively, and the look was damned appealing on her.

If it were possible for Ellen's face to grow any redder, surely it was now. Gamely, she said, "I already have a Canadian one. Technically, at least, though not for much longer. Perhaps the American variety might suit me better."

Courtney's laughter was like warm, thick honey. "Well, I've got the American part down, but I don't think I'm very good wife material."

There were plenty of Americans in Vancouver with the border being so close, so Ellen wasn't surprised Courtney was an American. Neither was she surprised at the admission that she wasn't good wife material. *Just like Susan.* "Some people should never get married. At least you already know you shouldn't, so you're one up on my ex."

"Yes, well, it does take the mystery out of it a little." In spite of the lightness in her tone, Courtney managed to look slightly aggrieved, and it gave Ellen pause. It was Courtney who'd steered the conversation this way and said she wasn't the marrying kind, and yet she looked somehow upset about it, like maybe she regretted it. Well, you're lucky, Ellen thought. *Marriage is no bed of roses.*

When Courtney asked her to join her for coffee, Ellen surprised herself by quickly accepting. Maybe the enigmatic Courtney Langford would share with her how she managed to look like such a party girl one minute, then disappointed about not being the marrying kind the next. Ellen sensed there was much to learn about this woman. And besides, it might be more interesting than shopping for things she couldn't afford.

"I have a book I need to purchase first," Courtney said. "How about I meet you outside?"

"All right."

"Not going to run away on me, are you?"

"What would ever give you that idea?"

Courtney laughed and walked away, lightly shaking her head.

Outside, Ellen was thinking about Courtney's contradictions. She was a gambler, a drinker, but also a reader? Of course, Courtney could be thinking the same about her, considering where they had run into each other. Courtney seemed so sure of herself, and yet there was something very insecure about her. Something very sensitive, or perhaps painful just beneath the surface. She was self-deprecating, and yet it seemed to be a cover for something else.

"Ready?" Courtney clutched a bag containing her newly purchased book.

They began walking. "Do you actually like books or were you in there looking for women to pick up?" Ellen asked carefully.

Courtney's expression was indecipherable. "Because I said I wasn't the marrying kind, you question my motives? Why, you cynic, you!" Courtney burst into laughter. She had an easy, genuine laugh that was pure and contagious. "You said that to needle me, I assume."

"Well." Ellen smiled helplessly. "You are an easy target sometimes."

"Yes, I know there's a bull's-eye painted on my butt. But it's worth it if it gets the pretty girls teasing me."

Ellen felt herself blush. *Damn.* How could this stranger have that effect on her when they hardly knew each other? "Is that your way of getting out of answering the question?"

"Ah, yes, the question of do I like to read or am I some horny Neanderthal who goes into bookstores to pick up intelligent girls. I did actually buy a book, in case you didn't notice."

"I did notice. Guess it's not a book on wedding planning, right?"

Courtney looked at her with astonishment before bursting into a peal of laughter. "You surprise me sometimes, Ellen. I like that about you."

"There you go again. Evading."

"Evading what?"

"The question about what book you bought."

"It's just a picture book...since I don't know how to read."

"Yeah, right. I was kinda serious, you know. I like knowing what people read, since I'm an English professor."

"All right, as a matter of fact, I do love to read, Professor Turcotte. I have a decent collection of classics, but mostly I like contemporary stuff. I'll read pretty much anything, actually. Romances, mysteries, biographies. Queer stuff, straight stuff. However, I'll bet your reading list is much more impressive than mine."

"Not really. You did notice the chick lit section I was in?"

"Actually, I did notice that. But you're on vacation, right? An English prof is allowed to slum it once in a while, you know."

Ellen smiled. She liked Courtney's humor. "How did you know I was on vacation?"

"Your friend Sam asked me to show you around the city. At the casino."

Ellen rolled her eyes. "Oh, that's right. And I was supposed to call you, according to Sam's big plan."

They stopped in front of a Starbucks. "So, why didn't you call? Or are you going to tell me you were just about to before I ran into you?"

"Here?" Ellen indicated the coffee shop.

101

"Too busy. Let's keep going."

"Actually I probably wouldn't have called you."

"Guess I need to go back to charm school, huh?"

"I...I don't know." Ellen couldn't look at Courtney. "I didn't feel like being hit on mercilessly."

"Well, you don't have to worry about that anymore. We can spend hours talking about books now!"

Ellen laughed. It felt easy to laugh with Courtney. She was much more charming and funny than Ellen had guessed. "Where are we going by the way? We've only passed about a gazillion coffee shops."

Courtney abruptly stopped in front of a little shop with tinted glass windows. In its display area were handmade wooden humidors of various shapes, sizes and colors. "La Casa del Habanos." Her face lit up with unexpected joy. "Anything Cuban is forbidden for us Americans, and I'm dying to try some Cuban coffee. You game?"

"But it's a cigar shop."

"With coffee." Courtney pointed to a small sign over the door advertising it as a cigar and coffee shop. "It's perfect because it will be nice and quiet inside. And..." Her eyebrows rose in a challenge. "We can be extra naughty and try a Cuban cigar too."

"You're not afraid of turning into a Communist if you go in there, are you?"

"Well, it would be my country's loss if I did and decided to stay here in socialist Canada. Or, hell, if I moved to Cuba!"

Inside, the place smelled of polished wood and moist tobacco of the expensive variety. Courtney asked the proprietor if she could check out the walk-in humidor, and he happily obliged. Ellen followed behind. She was not schooled in fine cigars and had no idea what she was looking at. They all looked the same, but the smell was wonderful. Moist Spanish cedar and hand-rolled, expensive tobacco.

"Do you smoke these things?" It smelled so surprisingly good in here, Ellen began considering the idea of buying a cigar herself. She'd never smoked one in her life, and it occurred to her that maybe she should have. It wasn't typical for her to try things new and different, at least not without a little kicking and screaming. But the sky surely wouldn't fall in, nor would she turn into a lung cancer patient with one cigar. Sometimes she hated how unadventurous she could be.

"I've only smoked a Cuban cigar a couple of times, but I like to smoke a good Dominican or Honduran about once a month or so. Do you ever smoke cigars?"

"Nope, never."

"Why not?"

Ellen shrugged. "I always thought they were stinky and unhealthy and...I don't know, kinda butch maybe." She couldn't even remember the last time someone had offered her one. Maybe in college, one of those cheap, wine-tipped Old Ports that seemed to go with beer.

Courtney laughed. "I don't think you have to worry about the butch part." She carefully selected a Bolivar petite corona from an open box. "Would you like one too? My treat."

Ellen declined, worried she would make a fool of herself. She had no idea how to smoke one. She'd probably cough and hack and spit out little brown bits of tobacco all over the place or get them stuck in her teeth.

After ordering Cuban coffee, they settled into a private, glassed-in room with soft, deep, leather wingback chairs that hissed when they sat down. Courtney was still sniffing her unlit cigar when she looked at Ellen. "You don't like to live dangerously, do you? Or is the casino about as crazy as you get?"

Ellen wondered for a moment if Courtney was trying to insult her, but there was no condemnation in her eyes or in her voice. "I guess I'm about as boring as they come. I barely drink, I don't do drugs and I'm not promiscuous." She wasn't going to apologize, but she did feel like being honest.

Courtney's eyebrows shot up, prefacing a grin. "Okay, but that's not what I asked."

Ellen had nothing to prove to this friendly, attractive stranger, and furthermore, she didn't care if Courtney thought she was boring. Boring had its upside, and frankly, living on the wild side didn't seem to be doing wonders for Courtney. There were dark circles under her eyes and she looked tired.

Courtney slowly lit her cigar with a wooden match. After the flame licked its way around the tip of the cigar, she extinguished the match, then softly blew on the cigar tip until it glowed red. "You want to make sure it's evenly lit, see?" She took a gentle puff, exhaling quickly, her nose twitching at the aroma that Ellen had to admit smelled divine—earthy but sort of like coffee and chocolate too. "You don't inhale cigars when you smoke them, did you know that? Here, try it."

Ellen gingerly accepted the proffered cigar. It looked dry but was slightly moist to the touch. She was intrigued and feeling a little naughty, sitting in a Cuban cigar and coffee shop with an American stranger. A good looking American stranger who appealed to the daring side Ellen didn't even really know she had.

"Go on. I don't have germs, I promise."

Ellen closed her eyes and took a puff, blowing the smoke out quickly, as though it might turn around and chase her if she didn't. She took another puff and let her mind empty with each inhalation and exhalation. After a moment she handed it back to Courtney. "That was actually a lot better than I thought it would be."

"There's something therapeutic about it. And Cuban tobacco is supposed to be the best in the world." Courtney took a puff. "It's so damned smooth. And it has the allure of being illicit for us Americans, so that always makes it better of course."

The proprietor, a short, bald man who looked like he should have retired years ago, shuffled in balancing two cups of coffee on a tray, along with cream and sugar and two tiny spoons. Ellen leapt up to help him set the tray down on the table in front of them before it teetered and fell to smithereens.

"Thank you," Ellen responded.

"Anything else I can get for you ladies?" He smiled at Courtney. "How about a box of those Bolivars?"

Courtney hedged. "A whole box might be a bit much, but how about a couple more?"

"Of course. I'll have them waiting at the front when you're done."

Ellen waited for him to leave. "You don't strike me as the kind of woman who worries about overindulging. I'm surprised you're not taking the box."

Courtney grimaced as she reached for her cup of coffee. She kept it black and simple. There was something veiled in her eyes when she raised them to Ellen. "I don't normally overindulge in things, you know."

Ellen wasn't sure she could buy the fact that Courtney's drinking, gambling, promiscuity and god-knows-what-else was an aberration. "Well, I get the distinct feeling you're certainly not as boring as I am."

"You are not boring, trust me." Courtney sipped her coffee and licked her lips in delight. "Now *this* is coffee."

Ellen carefully stirred in cream and sugar before she took a sip. "Oh, this is strong."

"Cubans don't water things down. They seem to do everything boldly. That's why I like their coffee and cigars."

"Their rum too?" Ellen couldn't keep the trace of derision from her voice. Courtney's drinking reminded her of Susan, unfairly or not. Courtney might be a very lovely woman, but if she was an alcoholic, Ellen wanted little to do with her.

"Look," Courtney said levelly, deliberately setting her coffee down and, elbows on her knees, leaning closer to Ellen. "I know I made an ass out of myself with you at that bar a few nights ago. The person you saw…" Courtney swallowed visibly, the frown between her eyes deepening. "That wasn't really me. I'm not normally that much of a dickhead, okay?"

There was something utterly genuine in Courtney's voice and in her distressed look. Ellen believed her. She had to stop thinking every woman with a drink in her hand was like Susan. Courtney was her own woman, with her own set of faults and attributes. "Okay. Thank you for telling me that. Is there a particular reason you have not been yourself?" People didn't normally go off on a booze or sex binge all of a sudden for no reason. Behavior shouldn't change with the weather.

Courtney settled back in her chair and took a long puff from her cigar, a look of deliberation on her face. "Yes, there was a reason, and I'm working through it right now. I don't like to talk about it. In fact, I'd much rather talk about you."

"Oh no, you're not going to turn this around!"

"Yes, I am, because you keep telling me you're boring and I think you are anything but. I bet you've got at least one or a dozen rip-roaring stories about yourself."

Ellen wasn't falling for it. She sipped the strong coffee and tried to figure out how to turn this back on Courtney again. Courtney the enigma. Courtney the American drifter who seemed to have no agenda. She had money, though. Seemed educated, smart, capable. Something was up with her. "I bet my stories aren't half as interesting as yours."

"Another puff?"

Ellen accepted the cigar from Courtney and took a long, satisfying drag. It didn't seem at all odd to be trading saliva with a woman she hardly knew. Truth was, it was unifying in a way that went beyond sharing a drink. "You don't like to talk about yourself because you're hiding something, is that it?"

If Courtney was surprised by Ellen's blunt question, she didn't show it. In fact, she smiled mischievously. "Well, let's see. You know I like books. I'm good at blackjack and poker. Not that I spend a lot of time at cards, but it seems to come natural. I like old Blondie music, Depeche Mode, modern stuff like Beyoncé, Usher, Kanye West, Alicia Keys, Nelly Furtado."

Crap. Ellen couldn't keep up with that. Madonna was as exciting as she got, with her tastes more along the lines of Diana Krall, Feist, old Rosemary Clooney and Ella Fitzgerald. It was her mother's fault, always playing those old crooning songs. And as for cards, Ellen was obviously a novice.

"Well?" Courtney looked smug, as though she had thoroughly figured out Ellen's nerdiness.

"Are you as forthcoming on other things too?"

"Like?"

"Like what you're doing in Vancouver."

"I'll answer the question if you do."

Ellen wanted to wipe that know-it-all, self-righteous look off Courtney's face. Instead she met her cockiness head-on. "I'm here trying to expand my musical and book-reading repertoire. Same as you, I expect."

After a moment, Courtney emitted a long, appreciative laugh. "Exactly."

The cigar was spent, their coffees drunk. As Courtney rose, her smile said she had genuinely enjoyed their little exchange.

On the way out, Courtney handed Ellen one of the wrapped Bolivar cigars.

"Are you sure? You don't have to."

"I want to. Maybe you'll smoke it while you're reading outside or something."

"I will. Thank you."

There was uncharacteristic tension in Courtney's voice when she said, "You have my number. I hope you'll call me sometime."

"You never know. I might need to ask you how to light this cigar properly."

"You'll be fine. I already had him clip the end for you. But if you'd like someone to smoke it with, I'd love to."

"Okay, I'll remember that." Ellen was not about to make promises.

As she walked away, she reflected on the fact that Courtney never had divulged what book she'd bought. Clearly, there was a lot more to Courtney Langford than she was willing to admit.

CHAPTER TEN

Gambling tip: No betting system can convert a sub-fair game into a profitable enterprise.

Ellen couldn't remember the last time she had felt this good, this relaxed. As she assembled the lasagna, she let her mind drift to nothingness. It was like hitting the mute button on the television. She didn't have to solve her life right now. In fact, she didn't have to solve anything, other than the fact that she didn't have a baguette to make garlic bread. She felt freer, more unencumbered than she had in a long time. It was finally beginning to feel like she'd turned a fresh corner in her life, like starting a new semester at school where a future full of possibilities lay ahead.

She threw the lasagna in the oven, took money from her wallet and stashed it in her pocket. There was a little grocery store a couple of blocks away that she could walk to and back from before Sam got home.

She still felt a little wired from the Cuban coffee earlier.

Maybe it was the caffeine giving her the ridiculous urge to whistle as she walked. Ellen never whistled, rarely skipped as she walked or danced a spontaneous jig, and yet she had the impulse to do all of those things now. Maybe there was something in that cigar. Or maybe it was the banter with Courtney. Or the danger and adventure and spontaneity Courtney seemed to exude. Sam had always told her she needed to be a little more like that, so maybe that was what attracted her to Courtney. The whole "opposites attract" thing. And yet Courtney was also intelligent, quick-witted, sensitive, well read. They weren't complete opposites.

Oh, well. It was a harmless, fleeting attraction, because Ellen would probably never see her again. She was only in town for three more weeks, and unless Courtney really was stalking her, the odds of running into her again were pretty slim. She most certainly had no intention of calling her and making it seem like she was interested in seeing her, because she was not.

Ellen purchased a fresh baguette and was on her way back to Sam's when she was sure she spotted Sam's car idling at the curb.

As she got closer, sure enough, she could see Sam's profile in the driver's seat. She smiled, thinking she would rap on the window, ride the rest of the way back with her. She could tell Sam how she'd run into Courtney and smoked a cigar for the first time in her life. Wouldn't Sam be shocked!

But Sam was not alone. There was a woman in the passenger seat. They were facing one another, their heads close together, talking. Ellen stepped behind a tree for cover. She wanted to stare without being noticed. Okay, she wanted to spy on her best friend and the mystery woman, since Sam seemed to be so virginal these days.

The tree was rough and cool to the touch, especially when she put her cheek to it. Ellen closed her eyes for a moment, reminded of playing hide-and-go-seek as a kid in their leafy, suburban neighborhood. She wasn't a good tree climber, so she would settle for making herself as skinny as possible tucked up against a tree trunk. Her ploy only ever worked for about twenty seconds.

When she opened her eyes, Sam and Mystery Woman were kissing. Not friendly see-you-later kissing, but really kissing. As in trying-to-swallow-each-other's-tongues kissing! Emotions crashed down on Ellen like a landslide. She was happy Sam had a girlfriend and it made sense now why Sam hadn't been trying to pick anyone up lately. But why hadn't Sam introduced Ellen to her or even mentioned her? Why had Sam been so coy about the subject of women lately? What was she trying to hide, anyway?

Ellen thought the make-out session was never going to end. Finally, the woman emerged and scurried to an empty car parked across the street. She looked tiny, like a fine bird, with quick but graceful movements. She didn't wave at Sam as they each sped away.

Ellen took her time on the walk back. She needed to think. Should she come right out and confront Sam with what she'd seen? Not that "confront" was quite the right attitude. She wasn't pissed at Sam for having a girlfriend, but she was pissed that Sam had been keeping it from her. She wanted to know why, but she didn't want Sam to get defensive and close up on her, or worse, deny whatever it was that was going on.

Ellen played it cool back at the house, asking Sam about her day and getting a play-by-play of kids with runny noses, two women with whiplash from fender benders, an older guy with acute appendicitis. Ellen didn't mention running into Courtney or sharing a cigar with her; she wanted to keep the focus on Sam.

Dinner was a big hit with Sam, who wasn't much of a cook. Kraft dinner with broiled wieners on top was gourmet for her, so she ravenously ate Ellen's lasagna.

"Sam?" Their dinner was devoured, the plates practically licked clean, their wineglasses still half full. It was as good a time as any to bring up the mystery woman in the car. Ellen knew there was no way she would be able to sleep tonight without finding out what was going on. "I saw you today. Right before you got home from work."

"Oh?" There was a nervous lilt to Sam's voice.

"You were in your car with a woman."

"Oh, that." Sam's laughter was fake and hollow. It was so unlike her. "That was Rebecca. She works at the hospital. We ride to work together sometimes."

It was shocking that Sam would lie to her like this. Sam, her best friend of twenty-one years. Sam, who shared everything with her—every zit, every date both good and bad, every big life decision. Nothing was too inconsequential for a phone call or an e-mail between them. "Is making out with Rebecca part of your carpool arrangement?"

Sam visibly stiffened. Whatever this was, thought Ellen, it was not going to be good.

"Drop it, okay?"

"What do you mean, drop it?" Ellen had never dropped any subject between them, ever, and she wasn't about to now.

"As in, I don't want to discuss it."

This was definitely a new and different Sam. She'd never shut up about anything in her life before as far as Ellen knew. Sam was such an open book, a foghorn sometimes with her opinions, and she had lots and lots of opinions on pretty much everything. "All right, who are you and what have you done with my friend Sam Calloway?"

Sam's chair squeaked roughly on the tile floor as she hurriedly pushed it back and stood. She gathered the plates in jerking motions and began fussing at the sink. "There's nothing to tell, that's all."

"Nothing to tell?" Ellen went and stood at the kitchen counter next to Sam so she didn't have to speak to her back. "Honey, why haven't you told me you're involved with someone? What's going on?"

Sam couldn't seem to look at Ellen. This mendacious, cagey Sam was a stranger to her.

"Ellen, this is something I'm going through on my own, okay?"

"What's that supposed mean? What are you going through? And why can't you share it with me?" Ellen's anger and impatience surged. "Everything I've been through the last few months,

I couldn't have gotten through them without you. We share everything important about our lives. That's what best friends are for. Why won't you let me in about this?"

Sam shook her head, her face tighter than Fort Knox. "I can't."

"Yes, you can. You have to, because I love you, and something's wrong. If it wasn't, you wouldn't be this unhappy and secretive about it."

Sam took the wine bottle from the counter and filled her glass. She downed half of it in one gulp. "Trust me, you'd hate me if I told you."

"That's ridiculous." Ellen topped up her own glass and took a sip. "I didn't hate you that time you started dating my ex in college. What was her name again?"

"Beth."

"Oh yeah, Beth. God, remember that tattoo she had on her butt of Brad Pitt?"

Sam smiled. "That should have told us she was only experimenting with girls and wasn't really a dyke."

"Oh, I don't know." Ellen took another sip of wine, feeling the edges of her sobriety begin to fray. "I might even do Brad Pitt, and I'm a dyke."

"This isn't about college and me dating your leftovers."

"Oh, good. Because for a minute there I thought you were going to tell me you're dating Susan now."

Sam made a face. "I'm being serious."

"C'mon." Ellen led the way back to the kitchen table. "Sit down and talk to me. I can handle whatever it is that's going on with you. I promise. And I love you no matter what."

"I know you do." Sam sat, looking miserable. It made Ellen's heart skip a beat. She was afraid of what Sam was going to tell her.

"Please, Sam. Tell me."

Sam took another bolstering drink of wine. "All right. Rebecca and I first met about eight years ago. She was a pharmacist at the hospital." Sam smiled tentatively, as though she didn't want to look too happy. "We started seeing a lot of each other, spending a lot of time together. It got serious."

"Wait. I don't remember you mentioning anyone named Rebecca back then."

"I didn't. I didn't tell anyone about her because she was married."

"Married?" Ellen was confused. Sam had dated a married woman eight years ago?

"Yes, married. She was younger than me, just out of college, and had married her high school sweetheart, like, two months before we met. I didn't know at first. I mean, her husband was working temporarily in Ontario in construction, so he wasn't around."

"Wait a minute. You dated a woman who was straight and married, but she didn't tell you she was straight and married?" *Oh, God, Sam, how could you be so stupid?*

"It wasn't like that. We became friends. Good friends very quickly. And there was this huge chemistry between us. We spent time together and we began falling in love."

"And that's when she laid it on you that she was married? And straight?"

"Yes. Once she realized the direction things were going between us, she told me it couldn't go any further."

"Jesus Christ. Why didn't you tell me any of this before?"

"Because I was embarrassed. Because I hated myself for finally meeting the love of my life, only to find she wasn't available and that it wasn't going to go anywhere. I felt like a fool."

"Oh, Sam." Ellen reached across the table to squeeze Sam's hand. "I'm so sorry. But I still wish you'd told me. I could have been there for you."

"Oh hell, that's when you were still madly in love with Susan and sharing domestic bliss with her, and I...I didn't want to be some weak, needy, blubbering idiot bothering you with my shit."

"Bothering me with your shit? Are you kidding me? Besides, what do you think I've been doing to you these last few months? God! I thought we loved each other. We're best friends."

"Crap, of course we are. But..." She released her hand from

Ellen's to take another drink of wine. "I think the problem was that I hated myself for being in love with her. I guess I wanted to punish myself by wallowing in my own misery. I mean, I couldn't believe how stupid I was being, and I didn't need anyone else thinking I was stupid."

"Okay, wait. This was eight years ago. Why are you kissing her now?"

"Eight years ago, right after she told me she was married and that we couldn't be involved, she got pregnant when her husband came home for a visit. I knew for sure then there was no chance for us, that she wouldn't leave Rick. They moved to Ontario right before the baby was born, and I didn't hear from her for years."

"Looks like she found you again."

"Yes, she did." Sam looked alternately miserable and ecstatic. "They moved back here ten months ago. She started working at the hospital again. Her daughter is seven now."

"Are you telling me she's still married?"

"Yes."

"And judging by that kiss in the car, I'd say you're involved with her for real this time."

"I've been secretly seeing her for a few months."

"Oh, my God." Ellen's stomach protested its recent contents. Her best friend was involved with a married woman. Her best friend, who had wanted to tie Susan to the back of her car and drag her about twenty blocks, was involved with a married woman. Sneaking around, lying, keeping secrets. Sam was every bit as despicable as Susan, fucking whoever she wanted, without moral consideration. Why did no one seem to care about monogamy anymore? Was it only boring people like herself that did?

"What the hell happened to you? You'd kill anyone who did that to you! You wanted to kill Susan for doing that to me! And don't give me some bullshit about her being married to a man and how that's not as sacred or something. Christ! You're sleeping with someone who isn't yours, Sam! And that's wrong."

Tears slid down Samantha's face. Ellen couldn't even remember the last time she'd seen Sam cry. In fact, she wasn't sure she'd ever seen her cry. She was making up for it now. Her tears cascaded down her cheeks, and if Ellen weren't so pissed at her, she'd have gone to her and hugged her and whispered soothing words to her. She couldn't bring herself to offer comfort, though, not when she wanted to shake the living crap out of her.

"I didn't mean for it to happen." Sam sobbed into her hands. Her slumped shoulders shuddered; her hands shook. This was a side of her friend Ellen had never seen before, and it scared her. Unflappable, tough, sarcastic and generous to a fault—that was the Sam she'd always known and loved. This Sam was a mess.

"Of course you didn't mean it to happen. But no one ever wins in a situation like this. You've got to stop it."

Sam was shaking her head. "She loves me too, Ellen. You don't understand. We *are* going to be together."

"Don't be stupid. You can't go on like this. This is killing you."

Sam stood abruptly and gathered up her glass and the wine bottle. "I wish you would drop the whole thing. There's no point in talking about it."

"Sam, don't."

"No, *you* don't. Don't tell me how to live my life. I'm not you and I'm not Susan."

The words were like a slap. Stunned, Ellen let Sam disappear upstairs with her wine and her tears and her wounded dignity.

For a long time Ellen sat at the table, spinning her empty glass around. Sam was in love, but she was in love with absolutely the wrong person. And she *knew* better. That was the thing that bugged her. Sam was not stupid, nor was she the type to morally compromise. Sam certainly had her wild days of transient relationships, but never had she involved herself with someone who wasn't single. Sam wasn't like that.

Was there anything in Ellen's life the last few months that wasn't fucked up? Was everyone, from Susan to Sam, not who they seemed? Was Ellen the only person stuck in some kind of outdated, old-fashioned view of the world and what she wanted?

After a long time, long after darkness had fallen, Ellen took her cell phone from her bag. Without further hesitation, she dialed Courtney's number. She had no idea if Courtney was as complicated and screwed up as everyone else in her life seemed to be, whether she ascribed to Ellen's obviously antiquated morals or not or whether she'd even understand any of this. But she connected with Courtney in an honest, unaffected way that she didn't seem to have with anyone else at the moment. With her, Ellen was in the present. She was herself. And right now, that was exactly what she needed.

CHAPTER ELEVEN

Definition of "chasing": Betting larger and larger sums to win back what you've lost.

Courtney tingled where Ellen's hands clung to her leather-clad waist from behind—the kind of touch that almost made you shiver, but not quite. Mild surprise had flickered across Ellen's face when Courtney had pulled up on the Indian motorcycle, but she'd gamely donned the spare helmet and hopped on the back, not even seeming to care where Courtney was taking her on this gorgeous afternoon. Her only comment was a simple, "Nice bike."

Courtney had been completely surprised when Ellen called her late the night before. She'd been reading the book on post-traumatic stress disorder she'd bought at the bookstore when the phone rang. In spite of their easy connection over coffee and a cigar, Courtney would have bet money she'd never hear from Ellen again. She didn't seem the type to give in to her impulses and do something as wild as meet with a stranger again and on purpose this time. Yet there she was on the phone, asking Courtney to take her somewhere fun, a place where she didn't have to think about anything. "And not the casino," Ellen warned, her laughter low and throaty over the line. "It can't be anywhere that I have to think, and playing blackjack requires a lot of my brain power."

Courtney knew the place to take her; she'd discovered it in a tourism brochure. It would be a surprise, and Ellen would either think it the coolest thing ever or the craziest. *So far so good.* Courtney carefully threaded her way through the streets of the lower mainland, Ellen clutched to her like a hand in a glove.

Courtney quietly worried whether her plan would be too much for Ellen. She did not seem to be the fearless adventurer type. On the other hand, she did not seem to be a wilting flower either. She was one of the sensible ones who liked to play it safe, who made plans and fully expected those plans to reach fruition, and who didn't take well to spontaneity. Courtney knew the type well. After all she had been mostly that way herself. Until six weeks ago, when God or whoever had decided to show her who was *really* in charge.

Courtney held tighter to the bike's handlebar grips. It wasn't supposed to be this way, her dangling over the edge of a cliff with nothing beneath her. She had a healthy bank account and this bike, her new friends Jeff and Ellen, but that was about it. Her career was nonexistent, and the few other friends she had were scattered between Seattle and San Francisco, living the kind of lives Courtney once had. A week ago she thought this pared-back version of her life was a good thing. Now, she wondered what it might be like if this woman on the back of her bike were her lover and the two of them were out for a fun day of romance and adventure together, on a small vacation before returning to their life of order and stability. Well, she'd had order and stability in her life before, but not romance and happiness. Not someone she was in love with to come home to at the end of the day.

"Are we there yet?" Ellen yelled over the wind and the engine.

Courtney smiled. "Where?"

"Wherever it is we're going!"

She felt a smack on her shoulder, which only made her laugh. "I never would have pegged you as the impatient type."

If there was a response, Courtney didn't hear one. She was pretty sure she'd get a good earful in a couple more minutes.

The signs for Grouse Mountain didn't make it immediately apparent what Courtney had in mind for them. There were plenty of touristy things to do here. Skiing was obviously out, but there was hiking, scenic chairlift rides, an aerial tram system, a restaurant at the top of the mountain, and best of all, ziplining.

Courtney parked the bike, letting Ellen hop off first.

"I'm still not sure what you have in mind for me," Ellen said innocently, shaking that luscious dark hair free from her helmet. It was thick, shiny and wavy—definitely a blessing from her genes. Courtney had to fuss with hers and spend good money to make it look passable. "Should I be scared?"

"I promised you an afternoon of adventure, and that's what you're getting."

"That's what I'm afraid of!"

Courtney could see that Ellen wasn't truly afraid, only curious. There was a gleam in her eyes and energy in her movement. It was apparent that she was ready to try something a little daring. She was much more sensible about her life than Courtney was. Ellen was prepared to push her limits, but in a controlled, measured way, and not recklessly, the way Courtney had been doing lately.

Courtney admired Ellen's self-control and her intelligence. She couldn't blame Ellen for blowing her off the first couple of times they'd met. She'd been right to keep her distance, given Courtney's danger and unpredictability. Now, though, Courtney wanted to prove to Ellen that she could be trusted, that she wasn't the crazed, promiscuous barfly she was when they first met.

"Can I ask you something, Ellen?"

"Let me guess. You want me to sign a waiver so I won't try to sue you for whatever it is you're about to make me do."

Courtney grinned. She loved Ellen's dry sense of humor,

119

which still managed to surprise her. "Don't worry about it. It's okay. But the waiver is probably a good idea."

Ellen settled serious eyes on Courtney. "Courtney, I'm sorry. You were being serious, weren't you?"

"It's okay. I like when you joke around with me."

"Except you were about to ask me something that wasn't a joke, and I made a joke about it."

"No, look. Forget it. It's too nice a day for anything serious, okay? We're here to have fun."

Ellen touched Courtney's arm, and once again her skin tingled beneath the leather. "We are going to have fun, but I wish you'd ask me whatever you were going to ask me."

"I just…" Courtney was not a shy person, but expressing her feelings and fear were all new to her. Ellen—smart, kind, pragmatic Ellen—made her feel safe somehow, as though she would listen without judgment, tell her the truth without being hurtful. She took a deep breath and started over again. "You're different with me now. What made you change your mind?"

If the question surprised her, Ellen didn't show it. She simply shrugged one shoulder and smiled softly. "I realized, when I ran into you at the bookstore and then when we had coffee together, that I hadn't really been fair to you. I'd made up my mind about you without giving you a chance. I've actually surprised myself a little here, because I'm not always so free about giving second chances."

Ellen's tone and the firmness of her jaw seemed to confirm how rare this was. "Then I won't blow it. And I'm glad you didn't hold that night at the bar against me, because I could use a friend these days."

Relief swept across Ellen's face. "So could I. And I feel so much better knowing that you only want to be my friend and nothing more."

Okay, but I never really said that. She'd laid off the predator act with Ellen, because her friendship was more important and far more rewarding to her than any one-night stand ever would be. But she hadn't exactly turned off the attraction switch. She was enjoying Ellen's companionship, but she still found herself wondering what it would be like to kiss her, to pull her close, to feel her pressed up against her body.

Stop it, Courtney. If she could read your mind right now, she'd turn around and get the hell out of here as fast as she could.

Courtney gave Ellen a reassuring smile. "You are perfectly safe with me and I promise to be nothing but a gentlewoman."

"Thank you. But I'm still a little worried about what we're doing here. Are you *sure* I'm safe with you?"

"Perfectly. C'mon."

Ellen's face fell a little when she saw that Courtney was leading her to the zipline kiosk. She tightened and grabbed Courtney's arm. "You can't be serious! Ziplining? I can't do that!"

"You just rode all over town on the back of my bike. Ziplining should be the least of your worries."

Ellen wasn't seeing the humor in it; in fact she looked terrified. "No way."

Half-heartedly trying to smother a smile, Courtney said she was totally serious. "It'll be awesome, I promise. The speed, the views. You'll thank me when we're done."

"Don't be so sure."

Ellen was quiet on the ride up the mountain in the large gondola. Not exactly pouting, she sat squeezed into a corner with her gaze everywhere but on Courtney. That was okay, Courtney figured. At least she hadn't run off and hailed a cab. She would forgive Courtney for this—eventually.

After more silence at the top, Ellen finally said, with a trace of contempt, "So I take it you're some kind of ziplining expert?"

"Actually, I've never done it before."

Ellen looked surprised. "Really?"

"Yes, really. Sorry to disappoint you. I know you think I'm some kind of crazy daredevil woman—"

"You mean you're not?"

Sheepishly, Courtney replied, "Okay, I've gone skydiving a handful of times and bungee jumping twice."

Ellen beamed, looking relieved. "I knew it! I knew you

weren't the bookish type. Still I thought maybe you had a few more stunts up your sleeve than that."

"Why, because I ride a motorcycle, get drunk at bars and win a crapload of money at cards?"

Ellen looked puzzled, as though she couldn't decide if Courtney was kidding.

"You don't have to answer that." Courtney winked to show she was joking and was rewarded with a smile. "And for the record, I'm more than okay with you thinking I really am the bookish, nerdy type."

Ellen laughed. "Actually, I like multifaceted women."

Courtney's heart raced. Was that a compliment from Ellen? Was she flirting? The possibility both thrilled and scared the crap out of her. Ellen had made it clear she only wanted to be friends, but Courtney was still undeniably attracted to Ellen—drawn to her physically and emotionally. "Well, we'll see if you still like me after this."

After being strapped into harnesses and helmets that made them look like fighter pilots or high-rise window washers, they silently stood in line like cattle being led to slaughter. Most of the other cattle looked thrilled and excited to be nearing their turn. A few others, however, looked as solemn as Ellen did, their jumpy eyes hinting at their fear. Each time someone ahead of them screamed on takeoff, Ellen flinched but kept staring straight ahead. Courtney looked sideways at her. *Probably contemplating the many ways she wants to kill me!*

Their turn approached.

"Do you want to go first or do you want me to?" Courtney asked dutifully. Now that she'd led Ellen here, the least she could do was let her choose how she wanted to handle things.

"I'll go first." Ellen's tone was unequivocal. Her offer came as a shock to Courtney and it must have shown on her face. "What?"

"Nothing." Courtney played it cool, not wanting to spook Ellen now that she was primed and ready.

"Look, I like to get…unpleasant things over with as quickly as possible."

"You know, it's really not like going to the dentist. You're going to like it, I promise."

Ellen shot her a *yeah, right* look. She stepped forward, listened to the brief instructions, and signaled that she was ready.

Courtney held her breath as she watched Ellen lower herself into a sitting position on a sling attached to a thick overhead wire. The guide reached up and attached her harness to a large hook on the wire too. Ellen was as safe as she could be as long as this man-made contraption held.

Ellen was launched from the platform. She gave a loud gasp, and then she was gone, receding quickly away from Courtney. Little black specks dotted Courtney's vision. She reeled a little, light-headed, heart pounding. *Shit.*

"Are you okay, ma'am?" The guide looked skeptically at her.

"Y-yes." Courtney took a deep breath and tried to calm down. She'd never before had such little faith in man-made things—things that were supposed to be perfectly safe but sometimes weren't. Sometimes they failed and failed badly. But not always, a voice in her head told her. She'd been feeling so indestructible after the plane crash, riding her bike like a maniac, daring the gods. She was obviously losing some of that overconfidence now. She hoped that was a good thing. "I'm fine. I'm ready."

Courtney held her breath again and gave the thumbs-up. She took off with a whoosh, picking up speed instantaneously. *Oh yeah!* She loved the speed, loved zooming over treetops that were seemingly only inches beneath her. The air was cool and fresh and tickled her throat and lungs. She closed her eyes against the sun for a moment, letting it warm her face. It was exhilarating. The only noise was the sound of the wind rushing past her. She looked below as the trees gave way to a deep canyon, a river snaking its way through the middle of it. She dipped closer to it, could see the rocky bottom of the deep green water, the bright pebbles nestled in the riverbed as if God had flung handfuls of them at the river. Her line jerked a little, suspending her momentarily over the water, before she picked up speed again.

The ride only lasted six or seven minutes, but Courtney

123

figured she'd probably traveled a couple of miles easily. She unhitched herself on the landing pad, still a little breathless from the excitement of it all. She cast around for Ellen and spotted her standing off to the side, grinning like mad.

"You're smiling. That's a good sign." *God, I want to kiss her.* The thought struck her like a thunderclap. It was the adrenaline of the ride, Courtney reasoned, and seeing how much Ellen had enjoyed it too. It had her all fired up and turned on.

"Honestly, I thought I'd be throwing up by now. Or extremely pissed off at you."

"Well, Ms. Turcotte, it seems that you're neither."

Ellen laughed, her cheeks rosy and her hair windswept. "That was the most fun I've had in years! Flying along like that over that canyon, and those trees right under us, it was amazing!"

"It was pretty cool, wasn't it?"

"I can't believe I really did it!"

They brushed knuckles like athletes after a victory. "You were awesome, Ellen!"

"Oh, my God, I can't wait to tell S—" Her mouth became a hard line as she bit off Sam's name.

"Has Sam ever done this?"

"I don't know." The joy in Ellen disappeared like the snuffing of a candle.

"Why don't you ask her to come join us for dinner on top of the mountain later? I mean, if you'd like to have dinner with me."

"Sure, but Sam's working and I doubt she could make it here in time anyway."

Something seemed clearly amiss between Ellen and Sam, a fact made even more obvious because Ellen was changing the subject now and burbling about the zipline ride again. Courtney wanted to talk about what was wrong, but not now, when Ellen was so happy and excited again.

"Do you want to go back up the mountain? I hear you can take a horse and wagon ride around up there."

"Okay. And then dinner like you promised me? I think I've worked up an appetite."

Courtney smiled. "Most definitely dinner." She'd worked up an appetite too, but she was also strangely sated. There was a calmness, a completeness in her body when she was around Ellen. The excitement of the ziplining had been a blast, but she was sure she could sit with this woman in a restaurant for hours now and be perfectly content. In fact, it was all she wanted.

The wagon ride was relaxing. It wasn't a buggy, but rather a farm wagon with rubber tires, bench seats and six other people crowded onto it. As they rode around the resort, Courtney imagined the scene in winter, picturing a thick blanket of snow jeweled by brightly clothed skiers congregating on the flat areas or slicing down the runs.

"Still hungry?" Courtney asked.

"Even more hungry now. You'd think I hadn't eaten in months!"

"Maybe you just haven't been enjoying food for months."

There was sadness in Ellen's voice. "It's true. I haven't been in a very good place the last few months. I haven't been enjoying food or much of anything else."

"I know exactly what you mean."

The restaurant was cozy, romantic, with floor-to-ceiling windows overlooking the coastline and the city of Vancouver four thousand feet below. Lights were beginning to twinkle on, the sun's last rays shimmering off the distant water. A single candle burned on the white tablecloth. Courtney suddenly worried it might seem too romantic and send the wrong message.

Ellen sat down, ignoring the candle and fixing her gaze on the scene below. "Wow, this is gorgeous from up here!"

"Isn't it? The city looks like a kid's toy set."

"Like we're up in an airplane!"

Courtney's breath caught in her throat. Her chest hurt as though someone had her clutched in a big bear hug. *Dammit! This has got to stop!* This physical reaction to any mention of airplanes or flying or crashes was getting ridiculous. What was worse was that it was completely beyond her control. It was an instant physical reaction, the same as if something smelled bad or something burned her. She was damned sick of being this crazy person who nearly had a coronary over things that normal people barely gave a thought to.

"Are you okay?"

"Yeah, sure. I'm fine." Courtney took a drink of water to cool herself and buy some time. She was surprised Ellen had picked up on her reaction, because she thought she'd done a good job of hiding it. "Why do you ask?"

"You seemed upset or something. You really tensed up."

Courtney studied Ellen. She didn't look judgmental or critical. In fact, she looked concerned. Her eyes exuded a soft warmth, like an easy embrace. Courtney began to weaken. Would it be so bad to tell this woman what had happened to her? To share her pain, fear, confusion? To show her weakness? She'd already confided in Jeff, though not everything, and only because he'd chipped away at her, chiseling it out of her. It had been more of a confession with him than confiding. With Ellen, however, she wanted to confide. Ellen had no hidden agenda, no past history with her to trip over, nothing on her mind but friendship.

It was hard to start, though, to dive right in and spill it. She was out of practice with this kind of thing—and had never been much good at it in the first place. The last time was over coffee with her friend Josie a few years back when she'd blurted out how Celine had broached the subject the night before about the two of them having a baby. Josie had laughed her ass off. Before she knew it, Courtney was laughing too, and that was that. The last of any personal warm and fuzzy sharing sessions with anyone.

"Courtney?" Ellen pressed gently. "What's wrong? You look pale and you're wound up tighter than I was before we went ziplining."

Courtney caved like a flimsy deck of cards. Words tumbled out of her so rapidly, she barely understood what she was saying. Chicago...missed connection...Boston...plane crash... dead...horrible...the airport...newspaper reporter. She was like a volcano erupting, her words thick and disorderly, at least to her own ears. But Ellen nodded as mild expressions of surprise, concern and finally understanding flickered in her eyes. Courtney knew instantly she'd made the right choice in trusting Ellen.

The waiter homed in on them at this awkward moment to ask them what they wanted to drink. Courtney was annoyed at first. *Jesus, they must learn in waiter school how to pop up at the worst possible moment!* She cleared her throat and chuckled with false amusement. Maybe the interruption was a good thing, because it had probably saved her from crying. "I could use about a pail of red wine right now, but a glass will do."

Ellen ordered the same. "Wow. That's an incredible story, Courtney. I don't honestly know what to say, except that I'm so sorry that happened to you."

"I was the lucky one, remember? Nothing to be sorry about."

"That's not true. You're still a victim."

Victim. Courtney hated that word, had never planned on being one, in fact had taken great pains to avoid it, starting with her father's abandonment. The word was like a choker around her neck, cutting off her air. It didn't fit because it wasn't her, and yet here she was, a victim who'd not chosen to be a victim. She told Ellen how she felt.

"Most people don't choose to be victims, you know."

That was true. Her mom hadn't. Danny hadn't. "But a lot do, Ellen. Like people who choose to have kids with some loser who knocks them around or people who go wandering around downtown by themselves in the middle of the night or hitchhike."

"Or drive their motorcycles after they've had too much to drink?"

It wasn't said maliciously, but Ellen's words were sharp, like a pin pricking her. Ellen was right. She had been doing some stupid things that could have made her a victim all over again. "You're right. I was behaving really, really stupidly for a while. I was asking for trouble."

Ellen's eyes were kind. "The important thing now is that you're realizing what's happening to you. Are you okay now?"

"Sometimes yes, sometimes not so much. It's like…" Finding the right words was like trying to pick up matchsticks in the dark. "You know when you're driving through a long tunnel or something? And then you come out of it, but there's a gap where your radio still isn't picking up a signal yet and your eyes haven't readjusted to the daylight? I think that's where I am. I think I'm coming out of the dark now but I haven't adjusted to the light."

"You're still adjusting."

"Yes." The wine arrived and Courtney took a long sip. "It's like the landscape has changed. It's like I'm a bit lost."

"Which explains why you were acting like a drunken sex-starved maniac at the bar that night."

Courtney couldn't help but laugh. "No, I *was* a drunken sex-starved maniac that night. I wasn't just acting like one. I was being stupid."

Ellen laughed too. "So you're not a stupid sex-starved maniac now, right?"

"Oh, God, no. I couldn't keep up with that pace of life. I'm not exactly twenty years old anymore, and besides, it's not who I am anyway. I think I…went a little crazy for a while."

After they ordered—Ellen penne-a-la-vodka and Courtney bruschetta and a side salad—Courtney explained how'd she quit her job after the crash, sold everything and hit the open road. She explained how free, how unencumbered it felt for a while. "But it catches up to you no matter how hard you try to outrun it. That's the part I wasn't figuring on."

"So what are you doing, taking things a day at a time?"

"Yes. An hour at a time if necessary. I was at a library this morning checking out books on surviving traumatic things and stuff. The book I bought yesterday when I was with you? It's about PTSD. I've started reading about it. At least I figure that's the first step in doing something positive."

Ellen nodded with more than a passing curiosity. She listened intently. A little too intently. Ellen was a kindred spirit.

"Ellen, you know something about coming out of the dark, don't you?" She'd dropped enough hints about a failed relationship, and she'd said herself she hadn't been in a very good place the last few months.

Their food arrived and they silently tucked into it for a while, Courtney's earlier question still unanswered. She knew Ellen would answer in her own good time, and she did.

"I guess I'm finally finding my way out of the dark too." Ellen talked about her thirteen-year relationship with a woman named Susan and about Susan's betrayal. She spoke in a formal way that was totally devoid of emotion. It was like she was reading a news story out loud, and Courtney could understand that. Sometimes the only way to express something hurtful was to strip all of the emotion out of it. Both of them had merely laid out the foundation and framework of what their lives had been like the last little while. With luck, there would be time to fill it in later with one another.

After dinner and dessert coffees, they rode the Indian back to the city. At a stoplight, Courtney asked Ellen if she was ready to go back to Sam's.

"Not especially."

"Okay." The reason didn't matter. Courtney wasn't ready for the night to end either. She steered the bike in the direction of her hotel.

It had to be an expensive suite, maybe close to three-hundred dollars a night, Ellen figured. The bedroom and living room were separate, there was a small kitchenette and two bathrooms. What on earth would one person need two bathrooms for anyway, she wondered.

Courtney had money, obviously, and she seemed in no hurry to move on or move back to Seattle.

"How long are you going to stay here?"

"You mean in this hotel or this city?" Courtney sat on the sofa beside Ellen with two glasses of red wine. She handed one to Ellen.

"Either. Both, I guess."

"Don't know."

"Really?"

"Really. I guess I'm not in a hurry to figure it all out. I needed a place where I could do whatever the hell I want and nobody would give a rat's ass. And besides, I like it here."

Ellen sipped her wine, a California Cabernet-Merlot that tasted of money. "I guess I'm doing the same, in a way."

"You played it a little safer, staying with your friend Sam."

She'd never thought of it as playing it safe. Escaping for a while maybe, but compared to Courtney, who had struck out on her own without a parachute or a best friend to prop her up, well, then yes, maybe she had played it safe. It wasn't in her to blindly jump off into the unknown, not after thirteen years in the same house, in the same job, in the same relationship. Sure, she was stuck in a rut, but what was wrong with getting out of it one wheel at a time?

"I guess I'm not one to jump off cliffs, no matter how tempting it might be sometimes."

"I can tell you it's not all it's cracked up to be. A best friend at the other end of it wouldn't be such a bad thing."

Ellen thought of Sam, and her heart sank. She missed her. They'd barely spoken this morning, their disagreement a big Road Closed sign hanging over their path. She was sad for Sam too, because Sam was clearly unhappy. "I'm not sure Sam and I are best friends. Not at the moment anyway," she said quietly, not looking at Courtney.

"You had a fight?"

Ellen sipped her wine thoughtfully, unsure how to describe what had happened between them. She didn't want to diss Sam, but she was angry at her. "I guess you could call it a fight. We're not very happy with each other at the moment."

"I'm sorry. Is it…you know, reparable?"

"I hope so. I don't know." Tears began to well unexpectedly. It was all Ellen could do to tamp them back down. She didn't do such a good job of keeping them out of her voice, however. "I'm angry with her right now, and I'm sad for her too, and I'm pissed off at myself for being so mad at her."

Courtney moved a little closer on the couch, their knees almost touching. "What happened?"

"She, um…" Ellen took a deep, shuddering breath as she recalled their conversation. "She told me she's been having an affair with a woman who's married."

Courtney's eyebrows rose, but she didn't say anything.

"And, um, I got pretty upset with her about it."

"Because of what Susan did to you?"

"Yes, because of Susan!" Ellen's anger was sharp and sudden and bitter in her mouth. "Sam was with me every step of the way after I caught Susan fucking around. Sam knew how devastated I was. Hell, Sam was devastated. She wanted to kill Susan!" Ellen swatted a stray tear from her cheek. "And now she's with someone who's fucking around on her spouse. She's with someone exactly like Susan, and in my book, that makes all of them alike."

Courtney's hand, warm and soft, was suddenly entwined with Ellen's, and the simple, caring act shattered Ellen's anger into tiny pieces. More tears were swiped away as sadness filled the place Ellen's anger had occupied.

"I'm so sorry, Ellen. I know how much that must hurt you."

"I feel betrayed, and even if I'm not being fair, I still feel betrayed. It's like Sam's been lying to me all this time or something. It's like I don't even know who Sam is anymore."

"Maybe you two need to talk about it some more and work this out. Try to see things from her side."

"Instead of judging her. Isn't that what you really mean?"

"No, look—"

"Go ahead, you can tell me if you think I'm being too hard on her." Ellen was prickly and knew the conversation was about to go downhill fast, but she couldn't quite pull herself back from the edge. She had to be angry at someone right now. "You've probably been in Sam's or Susan's shoes yourself a few times, right? You probably think it's amusing I'm so worked up about this. You probably think I'm some tight-ass, self-righteous bitch who got what I deserved from my ex."

Ellen expected Courtney to really let her have it. Or laugh at her. But Courtney looked horrified. "I would never think that! And no, I've never screwed around while I was in a relationship or knowingly ever screwed someone else who was in one either. Why would you assume that about me?"

Ellen drained her glass of wine, her nasty streak still fueled. "Well, you have to admit you didn't exactly come across as a nun at that bar last week."

Courtney was adamantly shaking her head, looking thoroughly pissed. "Oh, so now I'm an immoral ass too, like everyone else in the world, huh? I thought I already apologized to you for my behavior that night!"

Courtney, red-faced with indignity, looked so incredibly hot that it took Ellen's breath away. Her button-down, rich white cotton shirt hung open to just above her cleavage—*how come I never noticed that before?*—and her strong denimed thighs were shoulder-width apart on the sofa, hard and enticing. Ellen slowly raised her gaze. Courtney's eyes were smoky and dark, her lips full and a little pouty, her jaw clenched tight. In her anger she was sexy as hell.

Oh, my God, Ellen thought as she realized how wet she was. She couldn't stop this speeding train she was on. Her libido was fully in charge now. It had been years since she'd been this turned on, and it shocked the hell out of her.

In one swift move, Ellen straddled Courtney. Her mind had mercifully left her, thank God, because if it hadn't she would have been mortified by her action. Her hands, her mouth, her twitching clit were alive and desperate for contact. She kissed Courtney hard, like a woman on a mission. If Courtney was surprised, it was short-lived, because she was quickly giving back as good as she was getting, her hands roughly in Ellen's hair, keeping Ellen's mouth on hers.

Ellen squeezed her eyes shut and devoured Courtney's mouth. There was nothing soft and sweet and seductive about the kiss. This was pure animal urge. She needed Courtney's mouth colliding with hers. She craved this racing of her own heart and the accompanying breathlessness. She was dying for Courtney's hands to touch her. Anywhere. Everywhere.

Ellen began rocking softly against Courtney, her hips demanding something from her, even the tiniest attention. She wanted a hand right there, cupping her, so she could press into it. She wanted Courtney to feel her hardness and wetness right in the palm of her hand. Right through her clothes.

Lightly, Courtney's hand brushed Ellen's hip, teasing her, as if she were reading Ellen's mind. Ellen moaned gently. She pulled her mouth from Courtney's and mumbled into her cheek. "Oh, God, Courtney."

"Look at me," Courtney whispered.

Ellen didn't want to. She didn't want to see her own hunger mirrored in Courtney's eyes. She just wanted to kiss and be kissed back, to touch and be touched back, to keep feeling so alive and so wanted. There was no thought to where it all might lead. There was no thought about anything. Only raw need.

Courtney again asked her to look at her, and Ellen did this time. Courtney's eyes were aflame with desire, and Ellen knew in that instant that they would be in bed within minutes.

"I want you," Courtney whispered, nipping suddenly at Ellen's lower lip. "Stay with me."

Ellen swallowed hard against the sense and caution that were intrusively beginning to assert themselves in her consciousness. *Dammit*. It was like the first pricks of consciousness when waking from a great dream. "I want you too."

Courtney tugged her hard against her and kissed her thoroughly. Her lips were soft but demanding and easily showed Ellen who was in the driver's seat. Ellen closed her eyes again and tried to fall back into that abyss of sexual yearning. She wanted a good tumble, mentally and physically, but it was getting harder and harder. Ellen Turcotte was no slut, no easy lay. As turned on as she was—hell, she was dripping wet—this wasn't who she was, this sexually charged woman in the room of an almost stranger, ready to roll over and pull her own clothes off and demand to be fucked. She'd been in a relationship so long, and while her body was ready to make love with Courtney, she wasn't there yet emotionally.

Ellen slowly pulled away, kissed Courtney quickly on the tip of her nose, then collapsed on the couch beside her.

"What's wrong?" Courtney was still breathless from their kissing.

"Nothing, I'm fine. I, you know, should go now."

There was no mistaking Courtney's disappointment. "We don't have to…you know…go to bed."

"I know."

"Did I scare you?"

Ellen shook her head and rose from the couch. "No, Courtney, you didn't. I started it, remember?"

"But you're sure nothing's wrong?"

Ellen leaned down and kissed Courtney on the lips one last time. She wanted this woman with a ferocity that shocked her. But it was all too much, too fast. The old Ellen would need at least a month to think about this before acting on it. Even the new Ellen would need at least half that much time. "Everything's fine. Can you call me a cab?"

Courtney reached for her cell phone and did as she was asked. Afterward, as Ellen pulled on her jacket, Courtney asked if they could see one another again.

"I'll call you, okay?"

Courtney looked as though she didn't quite believe Ellen.

After locking the door, Courtney collapsed against it, her breath coming in quick bursts. *Holy God, what happened?*

Had someone invaded Ellen's body? Because that sure as hell couldn't have been Ellen Turcotte throwing herself at her like that, practically demanding to be made love to. That wasn't the calm, cool, conservative Ellen who had made it clear she only wanted friendship. No. This woman had been raw and ready, oozing passion and desire. It *was* heavenly, though, if not heart attack-inducing. Courtney had barely restrained herself from throwing Ellen down on the couch or floor, tearing her clothes off and showing her the greatest ecstasy of her life. *She's absolutely aching to be loved and I am absolutely the woman for the job!*

But as tempting as the idea was, it wasn't their time. Ellen clearly wasn't over the hurt from her ex, and Courtney was still fucked up from the plane crash. She grudgingly had to admit that she was a little grateful Ellen had brought them to their senses before things had truly gotten out of control, because if not for that, they would have ended up in bed. Courtney wanted Ellen, was still wet and turned on for Ellen, but this was no one-nighter she'd picked up in a bar. This, Courtney didn't even begin to know what to do with.

At the coffee table, Courtney poured herself another glass of wine and downed half of it in one gulp. She needed to tread carefully with Ellen. She didn't want to lose her. A woman like Ellen wasn't worth losing over a quick fuck. *Or an all-night-long fuck. Whatever.*

The point was, she wanted Ellen's friendship. She wanted to look at her smile, wanted to see her try new and exciting things again, like ziplining, wanted to drown in her laughter and in the intelligence of her eyes, to talk books or blackjack or anything at all. There was something special about Ellen, Courtney thought as she sat and stared unblinking at the blackness outside that was the water. There was something special about the way they connected too. Like fitting a final piece into a puzzle and making it complete. She'd never had that feeling with Celine or any of the other women she'd dated or been interested in or even been friends with. It had all been jagged little pieces with them and not something that came together to make a greater picture.

Hours later, Courtney awoke in a cold sweat. She'd been dreaming she was trapped in a room that was quickly filling with smoke. She couldn't see the way out and had begun coughing and choking on the thick smoke until she grew frantic. She was sure she was going to die in this room that seemed to have no way out, and then a hand appeared, reaching out through the heavy fog. She grasped it, let it tug her out of that room.

It was Ellen's hand.

Courtney sat up and brought her hands to her cheeks. Ellen wasn't her savior. No one could be. But maybe Ellen had been placed in her life at this moment to be her guide, to show her how to start living again. And maybe, just maybe, it worked both ways.

CHAPTER TWELVE

Gambling tip: Every spin of the roulette wheel and every toss in craps is independent of all past events.

There was at least one positive from the fact that Ellen and Sam weren't really talking. It meant they wouldn't be having a big tell-all conversation about what Ellen had been up to last night with Courtney.

At the kitchen counter, Sam eyed Ellen in that smirky, suspicious way that said I-know-something's-up-so-don't-even-try-to-pretend-it's-not. Ellen knew that without meaning to she was giving out exactly the kind of signals that said she was trying to hide something. *So what.* They could both have their little secrets. She was still pissed at Sam for keeping a secret from her all these years.

"Are you going to be here for dinner tonight?" Sam asked carefully.

"Sure, of course." Ellen matched her tone. "Are you?"

"Yes. I can bring home Thai."

It was a peace offering and Ellen took it. "Okay. I'll throw a bottle of wine in the fridge."

"Good. Maybe, um, we can talk a bit."

Ellen knew they should, but she'd have to get a handle on her emotions if she wanted it to go better than their last conversation. And she did. Thankfully, she'd have all day to try to calm down, turn herself around on this issue and at least try to see things Sam's way without getting so worked up. "Okay."

With Sam off to work, Ellen lingered over her coffee. Twice she reached for her phone and almost called Courtney. Except she had absolutely no idea what to say. She felt a gush of wetness thinking of how she'd straddled Courtney and kissed her—the first real kiss she'd had with a woman in a long time. She was not even sure now how long it had lasted, whether it was ten seconds or ten minutes, but the world had stopped. She knew that much. And when Courtney's hand had pressed firmly against the small of her back, pulling her closer, her heart had pounded so loudly she was sure Courtney must have heard it too.

Ellen could have so easily gone to bed with Courtney. It was a thought that both horrified and thrilled her. Courtney was probably a very skilled lover, and she, well, she had been totally ready to surrender her body to her like she'd never done with anyone before. Sex with Susan, when they'd bothered to have any the last few years, had become very mechanical and boring. But the power and fierceness of her desire for Courtney had rocked her off her axis. The intensity of it was like nothing she'd ever known, not even when she'd been young and single in college and had slept with her share of women. She'd never been as sexually aggressive with anyone the way she'd been with Courtney last night. *Christ!* Was it all a dream? Had she been the star of her own little porn flick in her head or something? It was crazy. Scary. She hadn't even recognized herself.

For lunch, Ellen walked to a tiny café a few blocks away. She ate a grilled cheese sandwich while reading the newspaper, taking her time over it with a couple of cups of tea. Three times she glanced at her phone on the table beside her, a little annoyed that Courtney hadn't called. Of course, Courtney might or might not have her number. She may not have kept it from when Ellen had called her yesterday. Still, it was Courtney who'd asked her to stay last night. Shouldn't she call her now, to ask if she was okay? Maybe even to ask for another date? Something, because Ellen felt like she had been doing all the chasing and all the calling.

Oh, crap. Ellen sighed in disgust. Courtney was probably mortified at how Ellen had thrown herself at her after giving such mixed signals. It was probably the last thing Courtney'd ever expected from uptight, goody-two-shoes Ellen. Courtney probably wouldn't even know what to say to her now, unless it was to make fun of her clumsy, confused advances. She deserved whatever Courtney might throw at her.

Ellen sulked a few more minutes, then reached for her phone. She swallowed her pride and insecurities and dialed Courtney's number. She didn't even know what she wanted to say, only that she wanted to hear her voice. If Courtney was mad at her, or disappointed, or even if she laughed at her…well, Ellen would deal with it. There was no going back, especially now that the phone was ringing. Even if she could undial Courtney's number, she didn't want to. She was a bit lonely if she were honest with herself. Sam was like a stranger to her right now, and she was in this city with not another soul to hang out with or talk plainly with.

Courtney answered on the third ring, and Ellen's heart lurched a little at the sexy timbre of her voice.

"Hi. It's Ellen."

The pause was excruciating. Ellen's hand shook a little. *Crap.* It was like she was calling Courtney for a prom date or something, except she wasn't calling for any kind of date. Her body might have had a mind of its own last night, but Ellen really just wanted to talk to her as a friend. It was time to put an end to the ramped up hormones and crazy kissing of last night. They were both too old and jaded for that adolescent crap or at least Ellen was. It was time to set the record straight and go back to being friends.

"Hey, I was just thinking about you."

"Thinking about what a fool I made of myself last night you mean?" *Might as well get it out in the open.*

"Hardly." Courtney took a deep breath, which resonated through the phone and deep into Ellen's bones, making her quiver a little. It reminded her of Courtney's breath against her throat last night. "I was thinking quite the opposite, actually."

Relief swept through Ellen. Friendship aside, she wanted Courtney to want her and to want to plumb those crazy depths of desire in her again. Even though it was never going to happen a second time, Ellen hoped Courtney at least wanted it to.

"Must have been something in that wine." Ellen laughed for effect. "I, um, didn't mean for that to happen last night."

"Sometimes the best things in life happen when we don't mean them to."

Ellen searched for another subject. She didn't want this conversation with Courtney right now. "Sam and I are going to talk tonight."

"Good. You two have to clear this up and get back to being best friends again."

"I know, but it's not going to be easy."

"You're sitting there fretting about it, aren't you?"

"Among other things, yes."

"Do you want me to meet you?"

"No!" *Shit.* Ellen hadn't meant to practically yell at Courtney. "I'm fine, really. Thanks."

"All right, so we'll talk about you and Sam for a few minutes, and then we'll talk about what else you're fretting about."

The business executive must be coming out in Courtney, Ellen thought with amusement. Either that or she was secretly a movie director or something, lining things up in exactly the order she wanted them, setting an agenda. Ellen wanted to chuckle at the bossy attitude, except that it pleased her. The take-charge, confident direction was exactly what she wanted to hear from Courtney right now. She was right to force her to talk about these things.

"I'm not sure I can forgive her for what she's doing."

"Except that she's not *doing* anything to you. She's living her life, and you don't seem to approve of the way in which she's living it."

"But she betrayed me. She lied to me and acted so pissed off over what Susan did to me. And the whole time she's been doing exactly the same thing as Susan." Anger and hurt bubbled up anew in her.

"Okay, wait. It's true that she was holding back from you, that she wasn't being totally honest."

"That's an understatement."

"Maybe she has good reasons for that. Maybe she was trying to avoid exactly what ended up happening between you two. Maybe she just…I don't know, needed some little corner of her life that was totally her own, you know?"

"Yeah, her own little cheatin' corner, you mean." The silence that followed was ominous. Ellen could tell Courtney wasn't about to mince words. It was the calm before the storm.

"Ellen, you've got to stop being so hard on Sam. You guys have, like, loved each other forever by the sounds of it. She is in your corner and I'm sure she wasn't acting all pissed off over what Susan did to you. She *was* pissed off. Give her a chance to explain without judging her. She loves you. I can see that in her clear as day."

Ellen let out a long breath. Of course Sam loved her. But how could she do this? How could she have an affair with a married woman and then keep it from her? It made Sam a double cheater in Ellen's books.

"Ellen, Sam is not Susan, okay? That's the bottom line here. You've got to stop thinking every woman who cares about you is a cheating, lying, hurtful bitch."

The starkness of Courtney's statement sent a wave of shock through Ellen. Was it really that simple? Was she really transferring her feelings for Susan to the people closest to her? She'd certainly failed to give Courtney the benefit of the doubt initially, having pegged her for a slightly younger and better looking carbon copy of Susan with her promiscuous, boozing ways. And as for Sam, well, it was true, she'd decided that Sam was pretty much as bad as Susan in the morals department. She was jumping to these conclusions because she was blinded by her own hurt and rage. She was getting damned tired of it.

"Oh, God." Ellen felt suddenly drained. "You're right. I'm sorry. I'm being a bitch when I have no right to be."

"Don't be sorry. Do something about it. Have your talk with Sam tonight and then come see me."

"What? No!"

"Why not?"

Ellen didn't really know why not, only that it wouldn't be appropriate. She couldn't trust herself around Courtney anymore, it seemed. The wild beast in her might burst out of its cage again, for she seemed to have no control over it. Or at least she didn't know if she still had control over it, and she didn't want to test it.

"I, ah, you know, it might go on all evening between Sam and I." Ellen's heart beat faster.

"That's fine. I'll be here, no matter how late it is."

Ellen signed off, Courtney wishing her luck in her talk with Sam and Ellen making no promises about anything. She sat a while longer at her table, feeling a little hollowed out inside after letting her emotions fly with Courtney. She was calmer now, in a much better place from which to open up with Sam. Her anger was spent, though her emotions were still a little raw. She did want to go to Courtney later tonight, have a drink with her, talk about how things went with Sam, feel Courtney's hand slip into hers on the sofa again.

No, dammit. She would *not* go to Courtney's tonight.

Courtney jogged through Stanley Park, paying no attention to how far she'd run or how long she'd been running. Sweat was dripping down her face and neck, and her legs had begun to burn.

So far so good with wearing out her body, at least. Her mind was still as clogged as ever and going a mile a minute.

With no effort at all, she could recall the feel of Ellen's soft lips on hers, the curve of her firm ass in her lap, the heat of her skin beneath her clothing. Thinking about it made her sweat more and her legs burn more. Ellen's actions last night had confused her mind, but certainly not her body. Her body knew *exactly* what it wanted to do with Ellen. But Courtney couldn't afford to run around anymore letting her body rule her life. She'd been doing that the last couple of weeks and, frankly, it sucked. It was dangerous and totally unfulfilling, though Ellen didn't seem to be either of those things. Oh no. Taking her to bed would be tremendously fulfilling, that much was clear. And it scared the hell out of her.

Courtney stopped at a bench and began to stretch. First her calf muscles, then her hamstrings. She stretched her shoulders and arms too, then her neck. The burning subsided and her lungs began to settle. The calming was exactly how she felt when she was around Ellen. All the churning and turbulence in her body and mind ground to a gentle halt when they were together. Ellen had the surprising ability to still Courtney's soul. It was akin to pulling into the driveway of what was once her family home, which of course she couldn't do and hadn't done for a long time, her mom having been gone for ten years and her father even longer than that. But if she *could* pull into the family drive again and get out of her car and walk toward the familiar big red door with the stained glass panels, it would feel the way it did when Ellen walked into a room. *Like home.*

Courtney sat down and draped her arm lazily over the back of the bench, turned her face up to the light rain that was more like a Scotch mist. There was something about Ellen, something that made Courtney want to take care of her. She wanted to wipe away her pain, for one, and make her forget the betrayal that had made her so bitter, for another. She wanted to make Ellen happy. She wanted a fresh start for both of them. Courtney wanted to be happy too. And maybe that was the key, she thought. *She* needed to be happy. She needed to take care of herself before she could even begin to think of taking care of someone else.

She thought of Celine and was immediately embarrassed by her selfishness over the three years they were together. She'd been so wrapped up in her career, and the bit of room in her life that was left over, she'd kept for herself as well. She'd been selfish and horrible when Celine had tested the waters with her about having a baby. *God. How could Celine have been so stupid to want to have a baby with me, though? I was a shitty partner. How could she have expected me to be a good parent?*

She hadn't really listened to Celine. Hadn't wanted to have any deep discussions with her. Celine was right to have left her. They were going nowhere as a couple, mostly because Courtney wasn't capable of it. Courtney wanted to be capable now. And not because she was lonely and still lost, or because she wanted to be saved or be a savior. She wanted to be a better person, and when she could get to be that better person, *if* she could get to be that better person, she wanted to share it with someone. Someone like Ellen, perhaps.

Courtney took her cell phone out of her fanny pack and punched in Jeff's number. He was at first shocked, then over-the-moon pleased when she asked him for the number of a good therapist.

If she wanted to become a better person—and she did—she was going to need a little help.

CHAPTER THIRTEEN

Gambling tip: When you win a hand, increase your next bet by fifty percent.

Sam and Ellen picked at their Thai takeout food, intentionally avoiding the verbal minefield they knew awaited them. Ellen was in no hurry to finish eating and get to the big conversation that would either be a breakthrough or a smackdown in their friendship.

It wasn't like them to dance around the tough stuff. Finally Sam set her fork and knife down with a clatter. "I hate this. I hate feeling like we're mad at each other."

"Me too. I don't like being mad at you, Sam."

"I don't like being mad at you either."

"You're mad at me?" What had *she* done wrong? Well, besides act like a judgmental bitch?

"Look, you're holding me up to some sort of standard that's not fair."

"What, being in a monogamous relationship is not a fair standard?"

"No, of course it is. And Rebecca and I are monogamous."

"What?" Ellen couldn't believe what she was hearing. "I thought you said she's married to some guy named Rick."

"She is."

"Oh, come on, you don't really believe she's being faithful to you while she's still married to him?"

Sam's annoyance over being challenged looked about to spill over. She exhaled loudly, the muscles along her jaw tight, like a rope. "They're not together. I mean, other than in name only right now."

"Oh, for God's sake, you're not falling for that crap, are you?"

"Ellen, don't," Sam pleaded quietly.

"Don't what?"

"Don't try to compare what I'm doing or what Rebecca's doing to what Susan did. It isn't like that."

"Well, I'm sorry, but I'm having a hard time believing that. It seems awfully alike to me." Ellen was trying hard not to sound bitter, judgmental again, but she was failing. The whole subject hit way too close to home, made her doubt people's intentions and loyalties all over again. It infuriated her, actually. She knew she was sounding an awful lot like her sister Jackie, pointing out everyone's mistakes and acting like the bastards were always gunning for you. But these days, she felt like Jackie—a bitter victim.

"It's not the same situation," Sam said carefully, perhaps sensing the emotional precipice Ellen was on. "No one's doing anything behind anyone's back."

Ellen took a calming breath. She was not anything like her sister and she would never be like her sister. She would not live her life as some miserable hag, stuck in her own lousy past. It was exactly why Jackie had no close relationships, and it was a hell of a way to live. "Okay, I'm listening. I promise."

"Rebecca and I have a plan to be together, but we're a few months away from it. Rick has been laid off from work, so she's supporting the family right now. They're putting their house up for sale in a couple of weeks, and they still have to figure out custody and support arrangements and all that. It's not as simple as her walking out and being with me. She has her daughter to think about and financial obligations to work through. We're trying to go slow and do things right."

Ellen certainly knew from experience that ending a relationship wasn't tidy. She still had to deal with the logistics of legally divorcing Susan when she returned to Toronto. She'd been too emotionally exhausted to take those steps before, but she was much closer to being ready now. "And you're sure she's not stringing you along?"

Sam looked her straight in the eye, deadly serious. "Yes, I'm sure. She loves me and she's going to be with me. Her husband has known for a long time that their marriage is over, but out of respect for him and their daughter, we've been keeping things quiet until everything is in place for her to move out. He's actually been pretty supportive of her coming out. There have been absolutely no secrets where he's concerned."

Ellen's thoughts swirled. So Sam really did have a grip on things. She had a plan and seemed to know what she was doing, even if the whole thing was rather unorthodox. "Wow. I'm sorry, Sam. I'm sorry I came on so strong and doubted you. I just—" *Jumped to the conclusion that you were no better than Susan.*

"I know." Sam reached for her hand. "It's my fault for not telling you sooner and explaining things better. I was scared to. I was so scared you would think I was a fool. For a while, *I* thought I was a fool."

"Well, I should have remembered that I know you better than anyone. I should have had more faith in you. I'm sorry."

"Believe me, there were plenty of times when I didn't have much faith in me and my relationship with Rebecca either. It's been so damned hard sometimes." Tears pooled in Sam's eyes. "It's been horrible, not being able to go out and do normal couple things, not being able to start our life together. And all those dark moments when you start to worry that maybe she never really will leave her husband, that it's all for nothing. It's not a nice place to be. Some days, it was all I could do to put one foot in front of the other."

"I'm sorry I wasn't there for you."

"I'm sorry for not giving you that chance."

"So you're happy with Rebecca?"

A smile bloomed on Sam's lips, and it was the most joyous smile Ellen had ever seen radiating from her friend. It was positively angelic. "Yes. I've been waiting for her all my life."

Sam's joy was hard to resist and Ellen's apprehension dissolved in a smile. "Then I can't wait until we can celebrate."

Sam laughingly rolled her eyes as they clinked glasses. "Honey, you got that right. I can't wait to share it all with the whole damned world!"

After more discussion about Rebecca and their plans, Sam finally got around to asking about Courtney. "Are you seeing her?" There was no teasing behind the question.

Ellen didn't quite know how to answer. She went for playing dumb. "You mean, have I seen her over the last couple of days? Yes. I ran into her downtown two days ago and yesterday she took me ziplining at Grouse Mountain."

Sam laughed skeptically. "*You* went ziplining?"

"Yes, I did, and it was amazing!" Ellen was proud and a touch indignant the Sam doubted her.

"Lots of things are amazing if you give them a whirl, El." A familiar, mischievous gleam danced in Sam's eyes. "I'm glad you tried something new, but what I meant was, are you *seeing* her?"

A nervous lump about the size of Texas formed in Ellen's throat. Had the ziplining and dinner afterward been a date? She didn't think so, but the evening had sure ended like one. Making out the way they had, only a minute or two away from the point of no return. It sure as hell had all the hallmarks of a date, and Ellen didn't honestly know how she felt about the prospect of dating Courtney. She wasn't ready to date, and yet with Courtney, it was so easy, so right, so natural…

Her thoughts must have been written all over her face

because Sam was grinning crazily. "Well, for the record, I think it would be awesome if you were seeing her. You deserve a little happiness, even if it is just for two or three weeks. She seems like a fun person to be around."

Ellen shrugged, then rose and busied herself in the kitchen washing dishes. If she was dating Courtney, she'd be happy to share the news with Sam, but she wasn't exactly. She didn't even really know Courtney very well, didn't know if they'd keep in touch after she headed back to Toronto or if they'd ever see each other again. Weeks ago, hell, days ago, all the uncertainty about her life would have driven Ellen nuts. Now she was beginning to accept that it was okay to think about today, about right now, and nothing more. Answers and plans and predictions could all go up in smoke anyway, the way Susan had incinerated their life together or the way Courtney's life had changed when that airplane fell from the sky and smashed to bits. Maybe having a plan in life wasn't such a hot idea after all.

Ellen threw her towel on the counter. She didn't know much of anything right now, except that she wanted to be with Courtney.

Courtney had just drawn a blackjack when a knock at her door startled her. She played blackjack on her own sometimes with a couple of tattered old decks of cards she carried around in her backpack. It helped pass the time if she was bored or was trying to work something through in her mind. There was most definitely plenty on her mind these days.

She quickly gathered the cards into a pile and went to the door, expecting it to be hotel staff or maybe Jeff stopping by on his way home from the casino. When she opened the door, her heart stilled and her breath stalled in her chest. It was Ellen, looking gorgeous in a button-down light cotton blouse and cream-colored jeans.

"Is it okay?" Ellen smiled but it did nothing to mask her

obvious nervousness. Her eyes were jumpy and the corners of her lips twitched. It was adorable and made Courtney want to take her in her arms and hug her anxiety away.

"More than okay. Come in."

Courtney pushed the door open wider to let Ellen pass. A subtle waft of her perfume, or maybe it was lotion, passed with her, and Courtney recognized it as Estee Lauder, Beautiful Love. It was the same scent from yesterday, and she breathed it in like a swimmer coming up for air. It was sexy, beautiful, lovely. It was Ellen.

"Sorry, I should have called."

"You don't need to call. It was an open invitation." It was Courtney's turn to grow nervous. "Would you like a glass of wine with me?" She hadn't had a drink yet today, a small victory she was beginning to build on, but she wanted one now.

"I must look like I could use one."

"Could you?"

Ellen cocked her head thoughtfully. "Yes, but I'd be okay without one."

In that instant, Courtney knew she was okay without one too. "I've got this killer sparkling raspberry stuff that looks like champagne."

"Sounds perfect."

"Please, have a seat." Ellen did, and if she was still nervous, she no longer showed it. In fact, she looked positively serene, taking up a corner of the sofa and casually spreading her arm across the back of it.

Drinks in hand, Courtney returned to the sofa and set them down on the coffee table. She'd even poured the sparkling liquid into champagne flutes. Ellen admired the effect, picking hers up and studying the bubbles before sniffing it.

"Oh, this looks wonderful!" She sipped, and her face lit up. "Oh, my God, this is so good!"

"Told you it was."

"So I should always take you at your word?"

Courtney laughed. "I wouldn't have it any other way."

"If you sit down, I promise I won't...you know." Ellen's cheeks glowed adorably.

Courtney sat down, smothering a smile, and kept a respectable distance between them. She wanted to tell Ellen that she could go ahead and jump her any time, but it was obviously a moment where she was expected to play by the rules and respect Ellen's cautious nature. Courtney understood that relationships were a balancing act. It's just that she never gave a shit before.

"I trust you implicitly, Ellen."

"Then you must know me better than I know myself." Ellen's laugh was tense, and Courtney had the overwhelming desire to kiss her until she went limp in her arms.

"Do you want to talk about last night?" Courtney asked tentatively.

"Not really."

"How about what happened between you and Sam then?"

Ellen's features softened, and she told Courtney about her discussion with Sam. She sounded relieved, happy to have the disagreement behind them or at least on the table. Clearly their fight had weighed heavily on her. At that moment, Courtney realized what mattered was the happiness in someone's voice, the light in their eyes, and not the big office in the corner and the big paycheck and all the accolades. The little things had always mattered, but Courtney had learned to shut them out and shut them off. She loved the subtle changes of expressions in Ellen's face, in her eyes, and in the movement of her hands as she talked. With each word Ellen looked as though she were shedding a heavy burden, and it mattered to Courtney.

Ellen had stopped talking to study Courtney. "You okay?"

"Yeah. I was thinking, though, how sometimes it's too late to fix things that go wrong. I'm glad you and Sam are patching things up. That it's not too late for you guys."

"Me too. I thought I'd blown it there, getting so pissed off at her for dating someone who's married. You were right on the phone earlier today, about me having to stop treating her like she was Susan. I needed to really listen to her, and I'm so glad I did."

"It must not have been easy for you."

"It wasn't. But it's not easy going through your days thinking the worst about people, either. Frankly, I'm sick of that."

Courtney's hand bridged the distance between them and snuck into Ellen's. Their fingers immediately intertwined. "I'm proud of you for coming to that conclusion."

"Well, it's not about me, I've realized. I really do want Sam to be happy."

"I'm a bit jealous, you know."

Ellen's eyebrows nearly jumped off her forehead. "Of Sam?"

Crap. Had she really said she was jealous? She wanted to backtrack but thought better of it. Ellen would call her on it anyway. "Of having a best friend like that," she quickly amended. It was true, she envied the close bond they had. She also envied Sam for getting to spend so much time with Ellen, for being so emotionally close to her.

"You don't have a best friend, Courtney?"

"No, not really." She had a few friends, but not a best friend in a long, long time, and that had mostly been okay with her. She'd not had the time or interest in being that intimate with someone, of investing so much of herself in someone else, not when she had her career to keep her occupied. There was always another game to develop, another boss to impress, another promotion to gain. Courtney liked being the best at everything she did and had always been quite willing to pay that price.

"What about your past girlfriends?"

That was a laugh. Even Celine, who she'd been with longer than anyone, she'd never really let in. They had never shared everything the way Sam and Ellen did, nor had they even shared as much as she and Ellen had already. She should have shared more and put herself out there more, Courtney realized. Especially when Celine wanted to talk about having a baby. "I was a selfish jerk most of the time, Ellen."

Ellen looked mildly surprised. "You don't seem that way to me at all."

Courtney answered her look with a wry smile. "Not even

that night you first met me at the bar?"

"Oh. That. Okay, you have a point there."

Courtney rolled her eyes jokingly. "I've had a lot of practice at being a selfish jerk, trust me."

"So what's changed?"

"Everything." The plane crash started it, but now she had the time on her hands to see and feel what she had been missing. The clutter in her mind was gone, replaced with a quiet urgency to figure out what it all meant, to set herself on a different path. Meeting Ellen had been pivotal too. Not so much in setting her on a new path, but in finding a compass with which to guide her journey. "But I'd really rather not talk about that stuff right now."

"You wouldn't, eh?" Ellen's voice practically purred, and the habitual little *eh* these Canadians often tossed in at the end of their statements was endearing to Courtney now. "Is there something else you would like to talk about?"

"Yes. This." In one sweeping movement, Courtney scooted closer and gently brought Ellen's face to hers. Without even thinking about what she was doing, she closed her eyes and kissed Ellen tenderly, slowly, their lips barely touching. Ellen muffled a startled reply, but her lips willingly joined Courtney's, answering her gentleness in kind. They kissed softly for a long time, or what felt like a long time to Courtney, neither giving any signals that they wanted to stop or, alternately, go further. It was sweet and lovely.

It was Courtney who pulled away first, driven by a sharp need to look into Ellen's eyes. What she saw there was desire, supplication, surrender, but also a quiet determination. Ellen was not afraid of what might happen, nor was there a hint of apology or regret in her eyes. She was not about to bolt like she did last night. It was exactly what Courtney needed to see, that Ellen wanted this as much as she did.

Ellen resumed the kissing, pressing more firmly against Courtney's mouth this time. Her tongue surprised Courtney, the tip of it beginning a slow tracing of her lips. It was the most erotic thing Courtney thought she'd ever known and was confirmed by the quickly growing patch of wetness between her legs. She could do this all day with this woman, without a doubt, but her hormones were having more advanced ideas. When the tip of Ellen's tongue finally parted her lips and darted inside, Courtney moaned softly. *Damn hormones!* They were getting very demanding now, trying to take over, trying to show her who was boss.

Their tongues teased and played, each woman taking turns being the aggressor. Courtney loved the feeling of Ellen filling her mouth, loved feeling Ellen's desire dancing in her, loved the combination of raspberry and peppermint her mouth tasted of. Courtney had been embracing Ellen. Now she pushed her body against the smaller woman, who shifted beneath her until Courtney lay fully on top of her on the sofa. Courtney's mouth drifted to Ellen's neck, the flesh soft but firm, the subtle smell of her perfumed scent there enchanting Courtney. Gently, she sucked and nibbled the delectably soft part of Ellen's throat, above her collarbone. She felt Ellen shiver pleasurably beneath her.

"Is this okay?" Courtney whispered, stopping to take Ellen's ear lobe gently between her teeth.

"Oh, yes." Ellen's words faded into a soft moan.

Courtney made herself slow down, wanting to remember every facet of this experience—how soft Ellen's skin felt beneath her fingertips and lips, how she tasted, smelled. She wanted to remember each intense sensation rippling through her own body. She was turned on—achingly so—but in awe too. *This* was how loving another woman was meant to be! Ellen was meant to be savored, not devoured. Adored slowly and languorously over hours.

Courtney smiled between the kisses she doled out. She slid her right hand along Ellen's hip, grazing her fingers along her side and over the light, smooth cotton of her blouse. She drew small circles, followed an invisible line, then firmly spread her fingers across Ellen's tummy. She thrilled in the little jolt Ellen gave from her touch.

Ellen drew Courtney's face to hers again and kissed her thoroughly. Their lips melded softly and perfectly together as if they'd been doing this for years. It astounded Courtney how easy and right it felt. Desire and patience had struck the right balance for her. She wanted to keep kissing Ellen, wanted to keep feeling her twitching stomach beneath her hand, and the length of her body under hers, for...oh, about the rest of her life.

"What are you giggling at?" Ellen whispered against Courtney's mouth.

"I was giggling?"

"Yes, a little."

Courtney laughed more fully now, surprised by the happiness burgeoning inside her. Not just happiness, but foot-stomping, gut-splitting bliss. It was completely foreign to her yet so wonderful and so familiar, like somewhere deep inside she'd known it before. Another life maybe? *God, who ever would have thought I'd feel* blissful*!* "Sorry, I'm just...happy."

"Me too." A look of concern flashed across Ellen's face.

"What's wrong?"

Ellen bit her bottom lip for a moment, nodded once.

"You haven't been with anyone since your ex, have you?"

"Guess it shows, eh?"

Ellen was trying to lighten the moment, but Courtney was having none of it. "I don't want you to be uncomfortable in any way. If it's too much—"

"It's not too much. It's lovely. It's just...you know, so many emotions going on all at once."

Courtney stroked Ellen's cheek. "Tell me what you're thinking."

A small tear gathered in Ellen's eye, and Courtney could see her trying to fight it back. "I haven't done this with anyone since...you know. And I just... Crap, I'm sorry."

"Don't be sorry, Ellen. Tell me."

"It feels wonderful with you like this, but it feels a little weird too. I don't want to be doing this just to get back at her or to use you or anything like that. I am not doing this to get past Susan."

Courtney brushed away a lock of hair from Ellen's forehead. "I know it's not about that, and you need to believe it too, okay?"

Ellen's response was to kiss her, and something shifted inside Courtney. She had no idea where all this was going, and maybe that was the point. Maybe she was only supposed to enjoy the moment, to give and take fully, to shut her mind off and just feel. After all, wasn't that all life was? Moments crashing upon moments?

The kissing felt wonderful inside, her belly fiery and ticklish. Her hand crept down to Ellen's tummy again, then slid further up until it boldly found her nipple. It was rigid already, and the hardness of it made Courtney hard too. Hard and wet. She thumbed Ellen's hard tip lightly, and it grew even more rigid, straining at its cotton confines. Ellen moaned, pulling her mouth away from Courtney's and turning her head to the side. Her eyes were squeezed shut, her mouth tight with ecstasy. Courtney continued to stroke Ellen's erect nipple, then the other, eliciting more soft moans from her. What she really wanted to do was rip those buttons off and suck on her nipples, run her tongue around the perimeter of them, then take each one into her mouth again. Just the thought of what she wanted to do made her gush into her underwear, and she squeezed her thighs shut. Her clit was pulsing and throbbing madly, and Courtney was sure she would explode if Ellen were to reach down and even just graze her right now. So much for having to fake an orgasm, as she had done with her one-night pickups in Vancouver. Courtney would never have to fake an orgasm with this woman.

"Courtney," Ellen managed between gasps. "Please...I need you to..."

"You need me to what?" She needed Ellen to say the words.

"Touch me. I need you to touch me, my skin."

Courtney didn't need a second invitation. Less gentle than she'd been up until now, she pulled Ellen's shirt up, pushed her bra out of the way and latched her mouth to Ellen's nipple. *God, how incredible*! Soft but hard, warm in her mouth and against her tongue. She sucked and stroked, sucked and stroked, fast and slow, hard and soft. It was driving Ellen wild. She squirmed beneath her, her chest rising and falling like that of a runner in a full sprint. Courtney moved to her other nipple, tonguing around it before sucking it fully. She was slowly spreading Ellen's legs with her thigh, wanting so badly to feel Ellen's hot center against her own.

"Oh, God, Courtney. You don't...know...what...you're... doing to me."

Courtney chuckled. "I think I do, actually."

Ellen's hips rose up to meet hers, begging for friction. Courtney was only too happy to oblige. She ground into Ellen, allowing the pleasure to take root in her legs and wind its way up, like ribbons softly caressing her inner thighs, licking her center. If she wasn't careful she was going to come right now, through her shorts up against Ellen like this. Still she ground rhythmically into Ellen, who met her thrusts in perfect time. Ellen was pushing her breast hard into Courtney's mouth too, her intentions more than clear. *Oh, yes! This is so perfect, so fucking good!* She wanted this so badly, and she wanted much more too. Courtney's breathing was escalating in time with Ellen's. She could not take this much longer. Neither could Ellen, she suspected. They were both nearing the edge, already at the point of no return.

Courtney reached down between their writhing bodies until she found the button and zipper of Ellen's pants. "I need to be in there," she whispered urgently into Ellen's ear.

"Yes."

Such a simple, glorious word. It sent an electrifying pulse through Courtney. Deftly, she undid the button, pulled the zipper down and thrust her hand inside to cup Ellen's mound, so warm and moist through her cotton panties.

"Oh!" Ellen groaned, and Courtney thought deliciously, honey, I haven't even gotten started yet.

Up on one elbow, Courtney began to rub her palm lightly over Ellen's center. She watched her eyelids flicker wildly, watched her mouth gasp for much-needed air. Her chest, her beautiful smooth, creamy chest, rose and fell briskly with each breath. Courtney's fingers danced lightly over the soft delineations of Ellen's secret

157

flesh, sparking her imagination with how she would look, feel and taste beneath the cotton. As Courtney's fingers traced and tickled and caressed, Ellen groaned louder and began to reach for Courtney's wrist.

"Yes?" Courtney burred, knowing full well she was driving Ellen crazy.

"Oh, Courtney, I need you to touch me! Please!"

Courtney chuckled devilishly. "Your wish is my command, my dear."

Ellen roughly clasped Courtney's wrist, shoved her hand inside her underwear and pushed it hard against herself. It was Courtney's turn to have her breath sucked away. Ellen was hotter, harder and wetter than she could ever have imagined. It was heavenly. It was melted chocolate and sweet champagne all at once, right there at the end of her fingertips. She closed her eyes and let her fingers explore Ellen's soft, slick folds. Colored lights danced behind her eyelids in time to pulses deep in her belly that were growing more and more insistent with each passing minute. She was so turned on, so attuned to Ellen's body. Ellen was quietly rocking against her hand, moaning softly, and Courtney slipped a finger inside.

"Oh, yes!"

Yes, indeed! Courtney was met with a warm, enveloping wetness that sent her to yet another excruciatingly sweet level of arousal. She wanted Ellen's finger inside her too, Ellen's hand on her, bringing her to urgent, necessary and immediate climax. She wanted to explode, gush right into Ellen's hand, as Ellen was about to do to her. It was all she could do to wait and enjoy Ellen's impending climax, her little thrusts taking Courtney deeper and deeper inside her. *Oh, my god.* It was the sweetest, purest, most wonderful torture ever, and Courtney loved every second of it.

Her finger pumping inside, Courtney began to work Ellen's clit with her thumb, slowly at first, before her circles grew tighter and harder. Ellen practically screamed her name now.

"You are so ready, Ellen! You are so turned on for me, aren't you?"

"Oh, God, yes! Yes, yes!"

Courtney pressed harder and faster, thrust deeper too, until she felt the rumblings begin in Ellen's legs and work their way up like a tidal wave storming in. Ellen exploded in one huge, tight spasm, her breath leaving her in a rush at the same time. Every muscle seemed to tighten and jerk as the one large spasm gave way to a thousand little tremblers. Courtney withdrew her hand and held Ellen's quavering body tightly to her own. She kissed Ellen's neck, her chin, her cheek, until her breathing returned to normal and her trembling abated.

"Everything okay?" Courtney asked quietly, a little worried about the answer.

The slightly bashful way Ellen looked at her sent a tingle through Courtney. "More than okay. Wonderful."

Courtney smiled her relief. "I'm so glad."

Ellen squirmed out from under her, surprising Courtney by climbing on top of her and pinning her wrists to the couch. There was a mischievous glint in her dark eyes that shot new flames of desire through Courtney's core. It seemed there were many layers to Ellen, and Courtney looked forward to exploring every one of them.

"I want to show you how wonderful I feel," Ellen whispered against her ear.

Courtney swallowed. She didn't know how long she could keep behaving. She wanted—was practically ready to beg—for Ellen to just fucking *take* her. "Oh, yes, I want you to." Her voice had turned all ragged and breathy. She hardly recognized herself. She was a quivering lump of helplessness that wanted and needed this woman to make her come. Courtney couldn't remember ever needing it this urgently and this deeply before.

Ellen seemed to sense her urgency as well. Her hand was suddenly on the crotch of Courtney's shorts, moving up and down, and the room began to spin for Courtney. She couldn't think anymore—couldn't think about whether it was too fast or too slow, too hard or too soft, whether it was really going to happen or some ungodly act was going to suddenly intervene before she could come. Like a goddamned fire alarm or something. No. There was only Ellen's hand on her crotch, now Ellen's hand diving underneath her shorts, beneath even her underwear. Courtney stopped breathing as Ellen's fingers found her. It was exquisite torture, the best kind, as those fingers danced across her flesh, tickled her clit, circled her opening. *Oh, God!* Courtney moaned her pleasure, which started down in her toes. Then the rippling, core-shaking waves began tearing their way up her body, crashing against her shores. When Ellen began concentrating all her efforts on her clit with short, intense strokes, Courtney finally exploded. She cried out, went still, then shook ferociously. Ellen's hand stayed with her until Courtney quieted. Silently, they held each other for a long time. Courtney was pretty sure she'd drifted off to sleep, the two of them pressed tightly together.

Ellen stirred some time later. Courtney awoke to her trying to extricate herself from the sofa.

"You okay?" Courtney asked sleepily.

"Yes, but I think I should go."

Courtney sat up quickly. She was awake now and a little alarmed. "You don't have to, you know."

Ellen smiled. Try as she did, Courtney could see no signs of regret, thankfully. "I don't want Sam to worry."

"Is that the only reason?"

Ellen sat down beside Courtney and kissed her lightly on the cheek. "I'm fine, honest. It would feel a little...strange if I spent the night with you when I'm not even sure...you know."

"If we're dating, or what?"

Ellen nodded. "Exactly. That and the fact that I haven't spent a night with a woman since Susan. I haven't done anything with another woman since Susan."

"And you're a little freaked out?"

Ellen thought for a long moment, then smiled nervously. "Maybe I am a little. Does that bother you?"

"Honestly, it would bother me if you weren't freaked out a little."

Ellen suddenly kissed her long and hard on the mouth.

"Wow! What was that for?"

"For being you."

No one had ever said that to her before. One simple sentence, and yet it made her feel like the whole world was in her hands.

Ellen rose and began gathering her things.

"You're going to call me, right?" In spite of Ellen's words a moment ago, panic rose in her.

"I most certainly am." Ellen winked.

As they kissed goodbye at the door, it occurred to Courtney that her shorts were still undone.

CHAPTER FOURTEEN

Gambling tip: Your bankroll should be one hundred times your smallest bet.

The noise of clattering dishes and utensils crept slowly into Ellen's consciousness. Sam was puttering in the kitchen, she realized, and while it would be rude to stay in bed while she was cooking breakfast, Ellen yearned to lie around like a love-struck teenager, replaying every minute of last night in her mind. *Shit.* She was pretty sure those delicious couple of hours at Courtney's last night would be evident in the color of her cheeks and in the lightness of her voice this morning. She was invigorated, satiated, thrilled. Courtney's kisses and touch had chiseled years off her. Chipped away the sorrow and bitterness weighing her down these last few months too. Sam would take one look at her and know *exactly* what she'd been up to last night.

Ellen hadn't intended on going to Courtney's to make love to her, but neither had the prospect frightened her once she realized that was exactly what would transpire. She had been so turned on, wanted to make love with Courtney so badly, needed Courtney's mouth and hands on her with a greedy hunger that shocked her. She hardly recognized herself. But dammit, she was not about to feel guilty. Courtney was single and so was she. Well, perhaps not in the eyes of the law quite yet, but in her heart and soul, Susan was out of her life forever and their relationship was now in her past. She would never again allow herself to become the person she had with Susan, would never let herself become so unhappy again. It was more than time to move on, and while it was true she might never see Courtney again after the next two weeks, so what? She could enjoy this for what it was—a good time with a woman she really clicked with and was incredibly attracted to. It was all part of her transformation, a moment in her life where, for once, she was reaching for a sliver of happiness.

Sam was knocking softly on her door. "Breakfast is ready if you're in the mood. Yes, you heard right. I'm actually cooking, though it's only eggs."

"Okay, I'll be right there."

Ellen crawled out of bed and threw her robe on over her pajamas. Her body felt as if she'd run a marathon. She was sore but in a wonderful way. Every movement now reminded her of last night's toe-curling, plundering pleasure.

"Well, look at you!" Sam beamed at her in the kitchen.

"What? Something wrong?"

Sam laughed and waggled her eyebrows suggestively. "Only that glow you have about you!"

Ellen felt her face warming. *Crap.*

"C'mon, El."

"C'mon, what?" Ellen played dumb.

"Spill it!"

Ellen pulled a mug down from the cupboard and filled it with coffee from the carafe, stalling for time. She sighed deeply. She knew the jig was up. After all, Sam had spilled her guts to her yesterday. And while there was a component to her relationship with Courtney that felt like some sort of delicious, secret affair,

163

there was no reason to keep it from Sam.

"What exactly am I supposed to spill?" She at least didn't have to make this easy for Sam.

Sam plated up their eggs and toast and set them on the table. "Oh, come on. What's up with you and Courtney? You owe me, you know. And I'm pretty damned sure you were with her last night."

Ellen sat down in front of her breakfast and inhaled deeply. It smelled delicious and she'd certainly worked up an appetite last night. "Thank you, this is wonderful, Sam!"

"I figured you could use some nourishment this morning."

"Meaning?"

"You know what I mean." Sam pointed her fork menacingly at Ellen, but there was a grin behind her gesture.

"All right, all right." Ellen had no real reason to feel embarrassed or coy about Courtney. She'd been keeping her— *what? relationship?*—with Courtney from Sam, and she wasn't sure why. Her time with Courtney was spectacular physically and emotionally. Courtney made her feel like she was special, desirable, fun to be around. She made her feel like she could truly make a fresh start with her life if she wanted to. Like she could reinvent herself and be the person she really wanted to if she would allow herself. A secret smile blossomed in her mind, if not on her face. "It's true. I've been seeing Courtney the last few days."

"Well, duh," Sam said between bites. "Is it serious or are you just fucking each other's brains out?"

Ellen nearly spit out her coffee. "Sam!"

"Oh, stop playing virgin poster girl." Sam winked indulgently. "It's written all over your face."

Ellen was tempted to feel her cheeks to see if she was blushing, but she resisted. She could stall no further. "Fine. We had sex last night." That was what Sam really wanted to hear, after all.

Sam's eyebrows rose comically. "Wow, you gave it up pretty darned quick."

"Pardon?" Ellen gaped at her friend.

164

"Shit!" Sam's eyes widened, a momentary look of guilt on her face. "I meant you gave it up to *me* pretty quick what you two have been up to. I didn't mean to, you know, suggest anything else."

Ellen broke into laughter. "You least of all, my friend."

Sam cowered behind her coffee cup. "I know, I know. But we're talking about you, Ellen Turcotte. So, you really like her?"

This time, Ellen couldn't keep the smile off her face or out of her voice. "Yes, I really like her."

"Well, I liked her right away when we met at the casino. But if you don't mind my saying so, she seems a little more...I'm trying to be delicate here...adventurous by nature than you."

Ellen had a flash of their day ziplining. She was proud of herself for taking such a chance and thoroughly enjoying it. She'd missed a lot in her life by standing on the sidelines, playing it safe, sticking with what she knew. "She is, but as you've reminded me several thousand times before, almost everyone is more adventurous than me!"

"Ouch. Okay, I deserved that little barb. Look, seriously, I think it's awesome that you're with someone who is a little bit on the daring side, you know? You need a little bit of spark in your life right now, and I think Courtney could be very, very good for you."

They could be good for each other, Ellen thought, because they seemed to understand one another and what each had been through recently. She thought back to her conversation with Courtney about missing the plane that crashed, about how much it had troubled Courtney and made her re-examine her life. They were both at a crossroads, unable to go backward, but not quite sure of the path forward. "We have a lot more in common than you might think. She's smart, funny, thoughtful, sensitive. God, she is so *not* the person I thought she was that night in the bar. I thought she was a reckless drunk. Another Susan."

Sam chuckled knowingly. "I'm sure she's not, or you wouldn't be seeing her."

"You're right about that. I am certainly not about to go through all that again."

"No, you're much too smart for that and too good to yourself to let that happen again."

"Sam?" Ellen treaded slowly, wary of the answer but wanting her best friend's opinion. "Do you think I'm moving too fast?"

"With Courtney? Hell, I thought you were moving too *slow*, remember?"

"I'm serious."

Sam's smile was reassuring and her eyes were kind, giving Ellen exactly the reassurance she needed, particularly since she'd been so hard on Sam over Rebecca. "Ellen, I'm thrilled you're having fun, that you found someone who makes you feel alive and desirable. It's exactly what I've wanted for you. You desperately needed this."

"But I'm not legally divorced quite yet from Susan."

"Divorce, shmorce. Susan is history. I know you better than anyone, and I know that after what she did to you, that was it for her. She was out of your life forever. Whether you realize it or not, you've been moving on from Susan for months. Courtney just drives home the fact that this is a whole new life for you now. I say enjoy the moment."

Sam was right of course. The divorce papers were just a formality. Still, she wasn't yet used to the new Ellen, the one who would embark so quickly on a sexual relationship with someone. She finished her eggs and toast, enjoying the companionable moments of silence. Sam got up to refill their coffee mugs, and it struck Ellen how infrequently she and Susan had had moments like this, chatting over a leisurely breakfast or quietly enjoying the newspaper together over coffee. It wasn't just their mismatched work shifts, because even on days off, they rarely spent quiet time together, simply enjoying one another's presence. Ellen had figured it was the way things unfolded after so many years together, that growing apart was normal. They'd been two individuals moving in the same sphere for a long time.

"Sam?"

"Yes?"

Ellen was close to tears suddenly, and it surprised her. She shook her head lightly, trying to shake the tears off like shaking rain from a jacket.

"What's wrong, honey?"

"I think I've finally realized something. My God, I was totally in denial."

"Okay, go slow and tell me what you're thinking."

Ellen remembered the moment she'd walked in on Susan in bed with another woman, how the sight had at first shocked and numbed her, then had caused such searing pain it was like dying a sharp and painful death. And part of her *had* died that day—the part of her that believed in the woman she loved, the part of her that took monogamy and commitment for granted, the part of her that figured the ground beneath her was solid and predictable. "God, I was so blinded by my own anger and rage and jealousy. I totally convinced myself that Susan's infidelity killed our marriage. How could I have been so stupid?"

"What? There was nothing stupid about it. She fucked around on you. I'd say that's a marriage killer."

Ellen shook her head vehemently. "Of course it is, but Jesus. Our relationship was over a long time before that. I never realized it before, or maybe I hadn't wanted to admit it to myself. Susan's affair was the exclamation point, the thing that finally pushed us across that line for good."

"I'm not sure I follow. I always assumed you guys were doing okay before that happened. You never said anything was wrong."

"I never said anything was great either, did I?"

Sam shook her head.

"You get into the rhythm of a long-term relationship, you know? There's no real ups or downs anymore, you go about your daily life. Kinda like sleepwalking through it, and before you know it, years go by. Hell, you don't even know you're not happy anymore. Life happens and you forget you're supposed to be happy."

"God knows I don't know a lot about long-term relationships, Ellen, but it seems to me that it should be about a lot more than

167

sleepwalking through life. And you shouldn't have to sit and ponder whether you're happy or not."

"I know. You're right. But I thought that was the way it was, that it was normal to have so little joy in each other and in our relationship anymore, that it was just the natural progression. God, was I wrong."

This epiphany that their marriage had been on the rocks for years surprised Ellen a little. Or maybe what surprised her was that it had taken her this long to realize it. Oh, they'd tried to patch up their leaky boat at times, or ignored it altogether, until Susan beached it for good with her betrayal. Truth was, they'd been caught on a sandbar for years. Even the alcohol was only a symptom of how far apart they'd grown over the years and it was only one of the wedges between them. Fresh tears gathered in Ellen's eyes. The tears were for failing to recognize much earlier what her marriage had become. They could have avoided so much hurt if they had realized the trouble they were in, talked about it, come to some sort of resolution a lot sooner.

"Oh, Ellen, I'm so sorry."

Ellen slumped. She'd spent the last several months grieving for a woman she hadn't loved in a long time. She and Susan had filled a kind of emptiness in one another, but they hadn't fulfilled each other in the true sense of the word. It was time to admit that they'd both failed and to accept that it was over. "You know, until now I couldn't let go of Susan's betrayal. Of what she'd done to me. But I think I'm finally seeing that all she really did was put us out of our misery."

"That doesn't make it any easier I suppose."

"No, but at least I understand now."

"Do you think her affair was her way of sabotaging your marriage?"

"Maybe. Or maybe it was a natural progression of how far we'd grown apart."

Sam finished the dregs of her coffee and set her cup down. "Do you think being with Courtney is making you realize these things?"

"Maybe. Or maybe time and distance are giving me a clearer perspective. I don't know, but dammit, it feels like I've suddenly lost twenty pounds from around my neck."

Sam beamed at her. "Does that mean you'll go dancing with me tonight?"

"Oh, no! I'm not that freewheeling yet. Give me at least a day or two to get used to the new Ellen."

"Oh, all right! But only a day or two. And I'm definitely going to make sure we go dancing again before you leave here."

Sam would hold her to that, she had no doubt. Ellen's thoughts strayed to Courtney. She couldn't wait to talk to her about the realizations she'd come to this morning. She wanted to share this important moment with her, this new threshold she'd crossed.

"Ellen, do you have a date with Courtney tonight?"

"No. Why?"

"You mean you don't even know when you're seeing her again?"

"No. We hadn't talked about it yet."

"You need to get off your butt and call her."

Ellen grinned at her friend. "Any particular reason why you're throwing me at her?"

"Yes. Because for the first time in a long time you seem happy, and I want you to keep the momentum going!"

"How about I see if she wants to join us somewhere for dinner?"

Sam stood and began clearing the table. "Nonsense. Go have dinner with her yourself. The two of you. There's plenty of time for a party later."

The self-help books had been a good start, but they were not enough. Jeff had suggested that a therapist could help her heal much faster—and then recommended one. Courtney liked her immediately. Liz, as she encouraged Courtney to call her, was old enough to be her mother but seemed hardly the maternal type. She had blue eyes that could carve you up like a jagged wedge of ice and an ass-kicking attitude that Courtney respected. Liz was kind but impatient to get at the heart of the matter, which meant they could cut through a lot of bullshit. Courtney didn't want her hand to be held; she wanted to move on, to have a purpose in life. She wanted Liz to help her leave for good this helpless place she was stuck in.

They'd already covered why Courtney was there, and Courtney was long past feeling weak or weird about seeing a therapist. She wanted help. Now. Liz was prodding her about the changes she had undergone since the crash. In fact, Courtney decided, the plane crash had been equivalent to having ten different objects thrown at her at once—satisfaction with her job, questions about life and death, questions about why she had been spared, the feeling that nothing seemed real or permanent anymore—and all of it coming on the heels of her breakup with Celine. It was like juggling knives. It was too much too fast, not to mention confusing. Which was why she'd had the overwhelming need to drop out suddenly, she told Liz. That seemed like her only choice at the time, because she felt she'd go crazy simply trying to resume her life as it had been. Nothing made sense anymore. Nothing fit. There had been no choice but to smash it all into a million pieces and start over.

"You do know that when something like that plane crash happens to you, Courtney, it's supposed to change your life. You can't cheat death the way you did and expect everything to go back to the way it was. What you have been going through is perfectly normal."

"But I didn't expect things to change so drastically. It's like *every* part of my life changed all at once, you know?"

"Like a big piece of glass that suddenly shattered?"

"Yes, exactly."

Liz explained post traumatic stress disorder, much of which Courtney had already read about. She quizzed Courtney on her eating, sleeping and drinking habits, her dreams and nightmares and her ability to concentrate. She was suffering from classic PTSD symptoms, Liz said, but the prognosis for recovery was very good, particularly because she was getting help before the symptoms became disabling.

"Once you accept that a tragedy like this changes you, only then can you begin to accept those changes and to fully adapt to them. You won't be the same person you were, but you will learn to celebrate that, to be thankful for that."

"It's just...I've never really not had control of my life and not controlled the changes before, you know?"

"But that is one of the big mistakes we make as human beings. We control most things, which is how we got to be at the top of the food chain, but we do not control everything all of the time. Man-made things fail sometimes. And the earth too—hurricanes, earthquakes. Nothing stays the same forever. Things break down, and when that happens, the order of everything changes."

Courtney thought about that. Much of her life had stayed the same for a long time. She'd been at her job a long time, had lived in the same condo for a long time, had a couple of casual friends who went back decades. Celine had only been around for three years, and Courtney had driven her away, bit by bit. Celine's leaving hadn't truly come as a surprise. In fact, Courtney had been alone much of her life, particularly since her mother's death ten years ago. "Okay, so I can't control everything in my life. But I don't want to be at the whim of it either, cast around like a leaf in a windstorm or something. That's no way to live."

"No, of course it isn't. You control what you can, and the things beyond your control, you learn to control how you react to them. You make choices, Courtney, and that's what you take control of."

Courtney had made some pretty lousy choices the last few weeks. Then again, she'd made some good ones too. She thought of Ellen. Beautiful, intelligent, kind Ellen, who could turn her on with a look or a touch and who made her want to not only find joy in her life again, but to live every day with joy and laughter and feeling. Ellen was worth whatever Courtney had to do to make sense of her life right now. Ellen wasn't a flotation ring bobbing within reach of a drowning person; she was a reason for wanting to grab that ring and pull herself from the turbulent waters.

"I do want to take control of my choices," Courtney said forcefully. "I guess I'm not sure I know where to begin."

"Then start small. Start with how you're going to spend your day. Hell, start with what you're going to eat for breakfast. And then when you think about how you're going to spend your day, try to plan to do one thing that's productive and positive."

"What, like doing my laundry or something?"

Liz laughed reluctantly. "Yes, it can be as simple as that. Or it might be connecting with an old friend, or reading a book, or writing in the journal I'm going to give you to work on each day. I want you to start doing routine things, preferably at the same time every day, and you're going to record it all in your journal, as well as whatever thoughts pop into your head."

"Crap. You mean there's work involved in this?"

Liz's blue eyes twinkled. "Isn't there work involved in anything worth achieving?"

Courtney knew that to be true, but this was unlike any kind of work she'd ever had to do before. She was game for it, though, because she wanted her life back. If she was going to be a changed person, a new and improved Courtney, she wanted to get on with it.

She left the therapist's forty minutes later with a journal and workbook in her sack. She would ride her motorcycle to Stanley Park, find a spot on the grass and get to work.

As she was about to start her bike, her cell phone rang. It was Ellen's number. She was ridiculously relieved and giddy at the sight of it. She hadn't wanted to admit it, but she had been afraid Ellen wouldn't call again. She was worried that last night had spooked her, that things had happened too quickly between them.

"Hey, good-looking," Courtney answered.

"Wow. Were you expecting someone else on the other end?"

Courtney shook her head but she was grinning. Just hearing Ellen's voice made her heart do a little dance. "No, silly, you were the good-looking one I was expecting."

Ellen chuckled sheepishly. "I guess I'm not used to compliments."

"Well, I'm giving you about five minutes to start getting used to them."

"Boy, you move fast!"

Courtney swallowed, nervous suddenly, but she had to get the question out there. "Speaking of fast, are you okay today?"

Ellen's slight hesitation was a slow death for Courtney. "I am more than okay. I feel great! How about you?"

Thank you, God! Ellen was doing just fine. "I feel much better knowing you feel great." Courtney tried to keep her voice level. "I was a little scared."

"Sorry, I didn't mean to scare you. Were you worried because I didn't stay all night?"

And because you didn't call me first thing. "Yes. I was worried that in the light of day, maybe you had some regrets."

"To be honest, last night I wasn't entirely sure how I'd feel this morning. Shit, Courtney, I feel like such a virgin. I don't even know how this dating stuff is supposed to work."

"It's okay, honey."

"Honey?" Ellen's voice, soft and warm, embraced the new pet name.

"Yeah, is that okay?"

There was a definite smile in Ellen's voice as she practically purred, "Yeah. I like it."

"Good. Another thing to get used to. What I was going to say is I'm no expert on dating, either. So can we forget what it is we're supposed to do or not supposed to do, and talk about our feelings and do what feels right?" *Oh, my God, is this really me speaking?* Courtney barely recognized herself anymore sometimes. *Jesus, one session with a therapist and already I sound like a self-help guru.* Jeff would laugh if he could hear her now.

"How about we talk over dinner tonight?"

"That sounds fabulous. Do you feel like Chinese?"

"Sure. There's got to be a ton of great Chinese restaurants in this city."

"There are, and they all do takeout."

"What?"

Courtney laughed playfully. "Why don't I order out and you can pick it up on the way over. Or am I being too bold?"

Courtney could hear Ellen suck in an excited breath at the other end. "What time do you want me?"

Courtney held back the answer she really wanted to give, which was "now." "How about any time after five?"

"I'll be there. Can I bring wine?"

"That sounds perfect."

Perfect would be wine and food in bed and starting much sooner than five o'clock, but Courtney vowed to try and behave. Just because Ellen hadn't bolted from her yet didn't mean she wouldn't if Courtney pushed too hard. It was the first time Ellen had been with anyone since Susan, and she might still have moments of doubt or fear. Courtney would be patient. *They* would be patient and work through this.

CHAPTER FIFTEEN

*Definition of "surrender": In blackjack, to give up half your bet
for the privilege of not playing out a hand.*

The two paper bags in her hands were still warm, the smell of
fried and battered chicken balls, rice and fried wontons wafting
up and igniting Ellen's hunger. She juggled a bottle of white wine
too. If Courtney didn't answer the door soon, there was going to
be one hell of a mess on the hall floor.

Courtney flung open the door. Ellen's heart leapt, and she
knew she could go on juggling bags of food and wine for hours
if she had to, if it meant being in Courtney's presence like this.
God, she was beautiful. Her smile and the look in her eyes, Ellen
knew, were reserved for her only, enveloping her in a very special
intimacy. It was like pulling the shutters up on a bucolic scene
meant just for the two of them.

Courtney gallantly rescued dinner from Ellen's hands. Ellen
followed her into the kitchenette.

"You are a sight for sore eyes," Courtney growled, turning and giving Ellen a heart-stopping kiss.

"Wow. Remind me to bring you food more often."

Courtney pulled her into a tighter embrace. "I assure you it has nothing to do with the food and everything to do with this." She kissed her harder and longer, her tongue playfully parting Ellen's lips and darting inside.

Ellen's legs felt wobbly, even though Courtney's arms were strong around her. She closed her eyes tightly and let her thoughts and then her body drift on a pleasurable wave. She gave everything she had to the kiss—all the years of pent-up desire she'd never expressed, all the feelings of love and lust and passion that Courtney had helped her discover. Ellen supposed she'd always been a passionate woman deep inside; she'd tamped it down all these years, allowed it to be slowly snuffed out bit by bit, a piece at a time. But she was free now, free to put it all out there, free to rain her passion down on this woman who seemed so attuned to her body and mind. It couldn't be wrong to let herself feel and give so much to Courtney in this moment. Even if Courtney were to hurt her eventually, it wouldn't be wrong for Ellen to put her passion on the line like this. This was who she was, a woman who loved deeply and wanted to be loved just as deeply.

"You make me so wet," Courtney whispered thickly in her ear as her hands traveled up and down Ellen's sides.

Courtney's words and actions made Ellen wet too. It was like she was sixteen again, so thoroughly turned on and so quickly, too, from a kiss and a few words. *My God, I'm absolutely gushing for this woman.* And that was okay too. Ellen was so glad she didn't have to pretend she wasn't extremely turned on, glad they didn't have to go through some sort of dating ritual first. They were two adults who cared for one another and were attracted to one another. It was more than okay to respond.

"Ohhh, Courtney." Ellen could get nothing else out, her desire hot in her throat now, nearly choking her. She wanted Courtney so badly. *Goddamn!* She looked so good, smelling of lavender body wash, her hair still damp from a shower, curling wetly at her neck.

Courtney backed Ellen against a wall, cupping her ass and pulling her into her, tasting her neck and throat. Ellen exposed more of herself to Courtney's hungry mouth. Her flesh prickled pleasurably at her electric touch, which was alternately tender and boldly aggressive. Courtney was a skilled lover who knew exactly what she wanted and knew what Ellen wanted too. Which was to be plundered. She wanted to demand that Courtney take her—hard and fast. To scream, "Fuck me, Courtney! Now!" She was too shy to say the words, but Courtney did not need the verbal encouragement. After unzipping Ellen's shorts in agonizingly slow fashion, she slid Ellen's shorts and underwear down her hips in one swift stroke until they gathered at her ankles like restraints. Ellen couldn't go anywhere right now if she wanted to, and boy, she did not want to!

Courtney's fingers found her. "Oh, baby, you're so wet."

"Oh," Ellen moaned from deep in her throat. Courtney's fingers dancing over her was the most exquisite, most pleasurable pain she'd ever known. "Oh, God, I want you."

She felt Courtney smile against her neck before she plunged a finger inside Ellen. *Oh, my God!* Ellen melted all over again. Her legs threatened to give out on her, but Courtney was strong against her and held her up.

"I've got you, baby." Rhythmically, Courtney's finger pumped inside her, slippery and warm with Ellen's wetness.

Ellen's eyes rolled back in her head, as the pleasure dance continued. It was as though time had stopped completely while she perched on this precipice, dueling between control and complete abandonment, both beckoning and rejecting orgasm. She wanted this sweet torture to go on and on, didn't want to come too fast.

She felt Courtney drop to her knees in front of her. *Oh, God, she's going to...* Yes, she was. With lightning quickness, Courtney's warm mouth was on her, a sweet and tender counter to her thrusting finger. She was kissing Ellen's clit, then sucking it gently between her lips, while her finger beat a frenetic rhythm inside her. Ellen wanted Courtney to go on forever like this, tasting her, teasing her, propelling Ellen's desire to surprisingly new levels, turning her body to liquid with her very skilled tongue and fingers.

Ellen gasped for air as the first tremors of orgasm began stirring in her legs. The quaking began, slow and steady, then faster and deeper as it roared forcefully up, pushing everything else aside in its need to ignite and explode. It was far too strong to push below the surface now. She gave way to it, allowing the wracking and shuddering to wash over her in a powerful, thundering wave that claimed every inch of her body and soul. She was powerless against it, just as she was powerless against her desire for Courtney.

She cried out, grasped Courtney's head between her hands and pushed her face hard into her one last time. Courtney eagerly obliged, her tongue flicking firmly and briskly against Ellen, her finger perfectly answering the pulses of Ellen's orgasm. Together they rode it all the way, through every surge and plateau, every last tremble in Ellen's body. Courtney kept one strong arm around Ellen's hips the whole time, and as Ellen bucked for the last time against her mouth, she felt Courtney smile against her wet, quivering flesh.

"Oh, my God," Ellen mumbled, breathless still. She'd never been so comprehensively made love to in her entire life. It was not only the physical pleasure she'd experienced that still tingled throughout her body. The Goddess had smiled on her very soul. Making love with Courtney was a thousand beautiful sunsets, a million tiny stars blinking down at her from a blanket of darkness.

Courtney stood and wrapped Ellen in a tender embrace. For a long time they didn't move. Ellen wished soft music were playing so they could sway together in time to it. Maybe a little Frank Sinatra or Ella Fitzgerald. Something romantic. Something that mirrored the way Ellen felt about Courtney at this moment.

Fingers caressed Ellen's cheeks and forehead, then Courtney

tilted her chin up to look into her eyes. There was a flash of deep satisfaction in those green eyes, and Ellen giggled.

"All right, Courtney Langford, that was absolutely the best orgasm I've ever had in my life."

"Yes!" Courtney punctuated the air with a fist pump, then kissed Ellen deeply. "You, my dear, were wonderful, and if I could do that all day long to you, I would."

Ellen nearly swooned, excited by the very thought of spending an entire day like this, being brought to orgasm over and over again by this wonderful lover. *Lover, yes, My lover.* Courtney was indeed her lover now, and the word was both strange and magical in her mind, like something exotic she was tasting for the first time. "If you did that to me all day, I don't think I'd ever be able to walk again."

Courtney laughed smugly. "You wouldn't need to. You could stay in bed and I could bring you anything you needed." She kissed Ellen again, playfully tugging on her bottom lip with her teeth. "I'd love to see you in no condition to walk."

Ellen chuckled against Courtney's lips. "Keep it up and you may get your wish."

"Is that a challenge?"

"Is there any doubt?" Ellen waggled her eyebrows.

"Game on, little girl! But first I want you to get your strength up. Maybe we should actually eat some of this food you brought."

"That's a great idea. And a little wine to quench our thirst." Ellen reached down for her shorts and underwear.

A hand halted her progress. "You don't need to put these back on, you know. They're just going to be coming off again after dinner."

Ellen playfully smacked Courtney's hand away. "I am not going to sit naked eating dinner while you get to sit there fully clothed."

Courtney dashed off and returned momentarily with two white terrycloth robes. "How about we both slip into these, is that a deal?"

"That, my dear, is a deal I can most definitely make."

"Good, then kiss me to seal it."

Ellen fell into another heart-stopping kiss that could so easily have led to more. Already she was tingling in anticipation of Courtney's touch. And that tongue! *Oh, my God, I need that tongue on me again.* Fleetingly, Ellen wondered if she could hole up here with Courtney for days, having sex hour after hour until they fell asleep, exhausted, only to wake up in each other's arms and have one another again. She was becoming a sex maniac. Or maybe a sex addict! First gambling, now this! Where was all this depravity going to end? She wanted to giggle. *Oh, my God, I can't keep my hands off this woman!*

Courtney was eyeing her suspiciously. "What?"

"Nothing," Ellen lied, secretly smiling inside. There were far worse things than being addicted to the orgasms Courtney was so expertly giving her.

The food was barely warm, the wine hardly chilled, but neither woman cared. They were famished and eager to replenish themselves for another round of making love.

After they filled their stomachs, Courtney suggested they move into the bedroom with their glasses of wine. Sitting up against the headboard, their robes still clasped around them, Courtney grinned at Ellen.

"What?"

"I always knew you were capable of such passion, you know. The way you came today, my God! It's like every single part of your body and your heart exploded. And all for me!"

Ellen felt a blush working its way up her face. "I think I even surprised myself a little, to be honest."

"That's because you're not used to great sex, obviously."

"Oh, and I suppose you are? Okay, wait, don't answer that!"

Courtney leaned over and kissed the tip of Ellen's nose. "I have never, ever wanted to pleasure a woman the way I want to pleasure you, Ellen, my dear."

Ellen gazed into Courtney's eyes, needing to read if she was teasing her. She wasn't. Ellen was warm and tingly all over. "Why me?" she whispered.

"Because you are a wonderful, special, beautiful woman who makes my heart sing."

Ellen's mouth fell open. No one had ever said anything like that to her, ever. A joyful shiver raced through her. That she could make another woman's heart sing was a gift to her. She kissed Courtney in a simple, tender way that spoke of her joy at being exactly where she wanted to be. Nothing before or to come mattered, only this moment. Ellen was so *here*, enjoying every second of it.

Ellen parted Courtney's robe, then her own, wanting skin on skin. She moved on top of Courtney, moved her breasts against Courtney's, feeling their nipples hardening simultaneously. Courtney moaned, and Ellen dropped her mouth to Courtney's throat, trailing kisses down to the center of her chest. Her breasts were compact, firm, functional like the rest of Courtney's athletic body. Ellen moved her mouth over one nipple, suckling it gently, before moving to the other. Courtney's body began to stiffen beneath her.

"Oh, Ellen." Courtney was already breathing heavily. "I don't know if I can go slow this time."

Slow torture might have been fun, but Ellen wasn't that cruel. "Whatever you want," she whispered seductively. "And I mean that."

Courtney's eyebrow quirked. "Anything I want?"

Ellen had only a moment's pause. She winked. She was ready to give anything to Courtney. "Anything."

Courtney's eyes fluttered shut. Her voice was thick with desire and anticipation when she said, "I want to feel your mouth on me."

The words unleashed a steady throb of desire in Ellen and wetness that now spilled out onto her thigh. She'd hoped Courtney would say that, because she wanted to do to Courtney exactly the things Courtney had done to her. "I would like nothing better."

Slowly, she slid the length of Courtney's body, stopping to plant tiny kisses on her stomach, which was both soft and hard at the same time and quivered ever so slightly beneath the touch of her lips. Pausing now over Courtney's hot center, Ellen breathed her in, imprinting her unique scent in her mind. She dipped her head, her tongue tentatively homing in on its velvety target. Soft, wet, lusciously full, like freshly picked fruit. Ellen stroked boldly, exploring every slick contour, flicking her tongue against the hard bud of Courtney's clit. Courtney squirming beneath her, began quietly invoking her name over and over—the prayer of a needy lover.

When Courtney came, she erupted quickly and furiously, so much so that Ellen could barely keep up with her wild bucking and writhing. It was like riding one of those mechanical bulls at a bar. Ellen wanted to laugh at the image, but she held on and rode the last shivers of joy with Courtney. She slid up and nestled into the crook of Courtney's shoulder. They both lay silent, smiling, both basking in their post-lovemaking glow.

If Ellen never had to leave this room, if the next hour never rolled over on the digital clock beside the bed, if tomorrow never dawned, it would be all right with her.

To Courtney, sleep was a type of cleansing ritual. Or at least she hoped it could be. Every night she fantasized about waking in the morning feeling refreshed and renewed, like a commercial for laundry soap or fabric softener, where the person wakes up in a cascade of sunshine and soft, freshly fragrant sheets, and is bursting with hope and vigor. That was what she wanted for herself, a morning of waking and finding that she had shed the part of her mind that kept bringing back the plane crash, kept besieging her with survivor's guilt. But each morning was the same. She was still the same old Courtney. Changes or metamorphoses were painstakingly slow and frustratingly gradual.

When she woke up next to Ellen, Courtney had none of those unrealistic expectations that life would be different today, that all her problems would be gone. Nor was she anticipating—the way an alcoholic struggling with sobriety might, she imagined—that the day would be a bad one, the day she fell off the wagon. Surprisingly—and it was thanks to Ellen's presence, she was sure—she felt very rooted in the moment. Somehow, she knew, her day was going to be fine, because nothing else mattered but this one single moment.

After watching Ellen sleep for what felt like an eternity, Courtney woke her with soft kisses. They made love again for the fourth time in the last fourteen hours, then lounged until their hunger got the best of them. During breakfast at the hotel restaurant downstairs, Courtney watched Ellen devour her French toast and fresh strawberries. She smiled, noting with pleasure the rise of excitement in her stomach. She had spent the night devouring Ellen in every possible way, with all her senses, and Ellen had done the same to her. *Shouldn't it show somehow? Shouldn't we be blushing or glowing or falling down exhausted or still shivering with orgasmic pleasure? Shouldn't we be looking ridiculously self-satisfied?* But no. They were sitting doing something as mundane as talking about the week ahead and eating a late breakfast with a dozen other patrons, alone or in pairs, who might well have been up to the same activities they had been for all Courtney knew.

"Do you want to do something today?" Courtney finally asked the question she'd wanted to ask all morning.

"Actually, I should probably spend some time with Sam. She's off today." Ellen added a smile almost as an afterthought, like throwing a cherry on top of an ice cream sundae to dress it up.

"Okay. How about tonight? We could go to a movie or something." Courtney tried not to sound anxious, even though she was knotted up inside.

Ellen swallowed the last bite of her French toast. "I should check with Sam first, see if she has anything planned."

Okay, this isn't going well. She was getting the old brush-off, the Dear Jill letter in verbal form. They'd fucked their brains out, enjoyed every minute of it. Now Ellen obviously had cold feet and was ditching her. *Didn't she find last night and this morning as special as I did? What the hell happened?*

Courtney sulked behind her coffee cup until she could no longer contain her hurt and curiosity. "Ellen, did I do something wrong? Or something to upset you?"

"What?" Genuine surprise flashed across Ellen's face.

"You don't want to make plans with me today or tonight. Is it, you know, that you don't want to see me again?"

"Of course I want to see you again. It's nothing like what you're thinking. I thought tomorrow we could spend the day together." She was trying to sound casual, but there was something in her tone that Courtney couldn't quite put her finger on, something evasive.

"Are you sure you're okay with everything that's happened? I mean, with you and me?" It was a bit like Twenty Questions, getting at the root of what was bothering Ellen, and Courtney was sure something was. She would need to be patient enough to probe gently and not come down like a ton of bricks, as she usually did with her employees when they couldn't solve a technological glitch in a new game under development. Instinctively, she knew such tactics wouldn't go over well with Ellen.

"Yes, Courtney. I'm a big girl and…" Ellen leaned closer to whisper. "Sleeping with you did not scare me or make me want to run away. That is not what I'm doing, I promise."

"You're sure?"

"Yes, I'm sure. I think I need a little space today. You're the first one since—"

"Susan, I know."

"And it's all new to me, and I don't know what—"

"It's okay, Ellen. Take a deep breath. We don't have to do anything or follow some script, okay? We can take it as slow as you want." Courtney's words were meant as much for herself as for Ellen.

Relief swept across Ellen's face, immediately softening her features. Courtney knew she'd hit the bull's-eye. Ellen needed to step back for a moment, and Courtney vowed to be okay with that. She would have to be. Hell, it would probably be good for her to spend the day alone too. She had problems of her own to solve, with or without the diversion of Ellen's presence.

They said goodbye with a quick kiss, promising to talk later. As Courtney watched Ellen walk down the street, she was flooded with a calm sensation, a quiet knowledge far deeper than her gray matter, that told her this was the woman she was going to spend her days growing old with. It was like diving into a tropical pool and being bathed in that warm, welcoming, cushioning, life-giving water. She smiled to herself and wished she could feel this way about every part of her life. *Just don't fuck it up with her, Courtney.*

Courtney spent the rest of the day in her room. She divided her afternoon into blocks, an hour at a time. Liz would approve of that. An hour of tending to chores like sending laundry out and doing her banking, an hour of journal work, an hour of reading, an hour of napping. And she didn't even think about Ellen. Didn't think about much of anything, and let her journal work and her novel provide her escape. It was a relief not to be pissing the day away in a bar, getting drunk, watching strangers pick up other strangers, or worse, trying to pick up strangers herself.

Courtney looked around her room. It was nice enough, with a small kitchenette, separate living room and a bedroom. It was like an apartment with all the frills of a hotel—and a great view of the marina. But she couldn't live like this forever, hiding out from all her adult responsibilities. She had gone from one extreme to the other, from working like a dog, putting her career first, to all of this...this nothingness. She told herself she was doing what she needed to do to take care of herself. She was recharging her batteries and figuring out what she wanted to do with the rest of her life, like some college dropout hiking through Europe. This was her proverbial year-off-from-school to navel gaze. It was all badly needed, this righting of herself, but it was also a big fat excuse to play hide-and-go-seek.

Courtney stretched out on the sofa, staring at her socked feet. She could not and would not go on like this forever. Something had to give. But she did not have to solve every last problem today or even in the next twenty-four hours. She had time. If nothing else, the doomed plane she had missed taught her that, for her at least, there was time to start over again, to figure it all out. A giant do-over—that was what she'd been given. She might never get another one. She would not waste it.

CHAPTER SIXTEEN

Definition of "push": A tie between a dealer and a player. A push in blackjack occurs when both the player and the dealer have unbusted hands with the same total points.

Ellen clutched Courtney tightly as they zipped along the highway on her motorcycle, the mountains looming on their left as they headed north. She hadn't spent much time on a motorcycle before, but she was beginning to relax more into it. Courtney had been totally right about riding. It was a great way to see the mountains and their snowy caps, the little streams that ran below them, and the lakes that opened up like jewels, presenting themselves suddenly as the bike rounded a bend. The pine smells and the clean, cool crispness of the mountain air made Ellen smile as she breathed it in.

They had picked up takeout—sandwiches and cut veggies—in Squamish, and Courtney drove them a few more miles north until they came across a small, uninhabited park off the road.

"Is this okay?" Courtney asked after silencing the engine.

"Darling, it's perfect!"

And it was. Rolling green hills, the mountains to look at, and best of all, total privacy.

Courtney turned around and grinned at her. "'Darling'? Now *that's* perfect!"

Crap, did I really say that? Ellen hadn't called anyone an endearing term like that in years, yet she'd blurted it out without thinking. She knew she was blushing furiously and was glad for the full-faced helmet she still had on.

They found a flat spot to lay a blanket down and sat munching on their turkey sandwiches, their shoulders touching companionably. Seated behind a knoll, they were totally private from the road. Even the sounds of traffic were mercifully distant and muffled.

Courtney snuck a kiss between bites. "You seem quiet today. Is everything okay?"

Ellen was touched, and a little scared, by the way Courtney looked at her, so unguarded and full of caring and concern and so nakedly fond of her. Courtney was sweet on her, as her mother would phrase it. It was obvious in the ways she touched Ellen and spoke to her and the way she looked at her. This was far deeper than a sexual attraction or companionship; much more than casual dating. They were quickly approaching something far more complicated, and Ellen wasn't sure what she was ready for. She didn't want to feel pressure, nor did she want to ignore her growing feelings. It was a delicate balance she had yet to figure out.

"Everything's fine," Ellen assured, trying to sound lighthearted. It occurred to her then that maybe she looked at Courtney exactly the same way Courtney looked at her—like a woman on the cusp of falling in love.

"You know, you're good at saying everything is okay, but I don't always believe you."

Ellen swallowed. She and Susan had moved at odds with one another most of the time, ships passing in the night, and so she'd gotten away with retreating into herself or pretending that everything was fine. It'd always been easier that way. Courtney was gazing at her in a quietly challenging way, however, making it clear that she was not going to let Ellen off the hook. Being with her was entirely different from any other kind of love relationship Ellen had ever been in.

"Does it feel strange to you sometimes? Being with me?" Courtney asked gently.

"You mean being with someone other than my ex?"

"Yes."

Truth was, it felt incredibly strange at times. Yet at other times, being with Courtney felt amazingly familiar and right, like a drill bit fitting perfectly with a screw head, clicking solidly into place. It was a coming home of sorts.

"Being with you…" Ellen tried to choose her words carefully. "It's a little like losing my bearings, and yet it's also strangely like finding my bearings too. I don't know how else to describe it."

Courtney nodded, gazed off toward the mountains. "I know that feeling of losing your bearings. Believe me. And I feel like maybe I'm starting to find mine too."

"I'm so glad you're feeling some direction again." Ellen couldn't imagine what it had been like for Courtney these last couple of months. Well, she sort of could, having gone through the trauma of ending a long-term relationship and experiencing that feeling of being lost and trying to figure out how to start over again. But Courtney had come close to losing her life, and *that* Ellen could not totally relate to.

"Do you miss her?" Courtney asked bluntly.

Ellen was so caught up in her thoughts, she wasn't sure who Courtney was talking about. "Who?"

"Susan!"

"Oh, her." Ellen laughed hollowly. "I did at first. Then I missed having another person around like I was used to. I don't miss her anymore. I miss the idea of her sometimes, but not the person she is."

"Do you think there's any chance, you know, you might…"

The worry evident on Courtney's face surprised Ellen. "Oh,

God, no. I'm not going to get back with her, if that's what you mean."

"Okay, good." Courtney swirled the remaining cola in her can for a moment, deep in thought. "But you're not ready to move on exactly?"

Ah, so here it is. The conversation they'd been inching toward since they'd slept together. The old where-is-this-all-going discussion. Ellen wished she had the answers, but she didn't. She wished she could give Courtney blanket assurances, but she couldn't do that either. "All I can say is that I think I am much closer to moving on, whatever that may be, than I was a month ago. It's a process, and one that I'm taking slowly but surely."

Courtney looked at her earnestly, a tiny flash of fear in her eyes that made Ellen's heart break a little. "Ellen, do you think moving on includes being with me?"

Ellen's heart skipped a beat. The question was simple, but what was Courtney really getting at? Did she want them to go to the next level together? And if so, what did she think that was?

The thought of Courtney wanting something more permanent between them gave her pause, because she was not ready to give more. It was equally disconcerting to think Courtney might be thinking the opposite, that what they had was merely a fling that they should leave behind. Ellen didn't want that either.

"I'm more than okay with where we're at right now. I'm happy with you. Happier than I can remember being in a very long time. It feels right with you."

"I detect a *but* in there."

Ellen shrugged lightly. "I don't know what to say. I leave here in a week and you, well, you'll either stay here or move somewhere else. I don't know what it all means." Tears began to well up, and Ellen had to fight to keep them down. "If it's all right with you, I'd rather not think about any of that stuff and just enjoy the day as it comes. Okay?"

"I'm all for that." Courtney leaned over suddenly and kissed Ellen. Not a quick kiss, but a long, deliberate, intense one that made Ellen forget where or who she was.

"W-wow," Ellen stammered as she collected herself. "I, ah, suppose you think a kiss like that can fix anything, eh?"

"Why shouldn't it?" Courtney's smile brimmed with bravado, but her eyes were deadly serious. "Maybe a little more kissing and a little less thinking is exactly what we need."

Ellen didn't need any more convincing. She lay back on the blanket with Courtney and they made out like a couple of amorous teenagers. She felt like a horny kid around Courtney, hardly able to keep her hands off her. If kissing and making love could solve all their issues, they'd have it made and the world would be theirs.

"Susan was a fool to treat you the way she did, and she was a bigger fool to let you go," Courtney interjected, bringing Ellen's lusty thoughts to a crashing end.

"Maybe it was the best thing she could have done for me."

"True. I'm very happy she did. Are you?"

"I wasn't at first. Hell, until very recently I was still so hurt and pissed off at her for doing what she did to me, to us." Ellen, flat on her back, closed her eyes and let the sun warm her face. She longed for the day when Susan wouldn't pop up in her thoughts anymore or when the subject of Susan wouldn't dominate conversations. But talking about her and thinking about her and their relationship was all part of working through the breakup. She couldn't slot things in their rightful place until she reconciled the hurt and the betrayal and admitted the truth of what their relationship had become over the years. She wasn't necessarily ready to move on to Courtney or someone else, but she was ready to put the past behind her. "As miserable as things had become between Susan and me, it wasn't always like that, you know."

Courtney propped herself up on her elbow and gazed at Ellen, her other hand absently stroking Ellen's bare arm. It had a calming, loving effect on her. "Go on."

"I just don't want you to think I'm a complete idiot, that I put up with a shitty relationship for years and years. I'm not that kind of person. I would have come to my senses eventually, even if I hadn't caught her screwing around."

"I know that. I know you're a smart woman."

Ellen thought back to the early days of her relationship with Susan, both of them in their late twenties, full of plans for the future, buying the condo together, the winter vacations in Cuba and Aruba, the summer camping vacations on the East Coast, Susan proposing to her on the deck of a boat in Key West, during a women's sunset cruise, and how all the women had clapped and cheered and encouraged them. Ellen thought it was their sunset they were riding off into, except soon after that the drinking increased. Susan's moodiness worsened and her unexplained absences grew longer. They stopped taking vacations, stopped talking. Stopped doing much of anything together and merely existed.

Before Ellen could stop herself, tears began sliding down her cheeks. She was embarrassed, but Courtney tenderly wiped them away with her fingers.

"It's okay, baby," Courtney soothed, kissing her wet cheeks. "It's okay to be sad about it. It was a big part of your life, and now it's over."

"Yes," Ellen murmured, letting herself be held by Courtney. Yes, Susan had been a big part of her life, and yes, it was over now. She could begin again—she was still young, could still move past the bitterness and disappointment she felt over those lost years. She would hope again and love again, and it was Courtney who was giving her that wonderful gift, helping her believe it was possible, though it was far too soon to delve deeper than that, to know whether Courtney was her pot of gold at the end of the rainbow or merely a pleasurable stop along the way.

Ellen rolled on top of Courtney and began playfully kissing her neck, nipping and tickling.

"Oh, you want to play that game, do you?"

Ellen shook her head and laughed. "No, but I'd like to find a hotel room right about now so I can ravage you."

Courtney's eyes darkened with desire. "Now you're talking.

Whistler's only a few more miles up the road. I would love to spend the night there with you."

"But I didn't bring a change of clothes or anything."

"So what. Let's wing it, Ellen. We can buy some lame tourist T-shirts and underwear when we get there."

Ellen threw her head back and laughed, her troubles falling away as easily as leaves from a tree in autumn. "Let's do it, darling."

Courtney's cocky grin was sexy as hell. "I like the way you think!"

The ski village was quiet, with only the occasional tourist wandering through it. Perfect for a spontaneous, romantic getaway. Ellen and Courtney had their choice of rooms, and they chose one with a stunning view of Blackcomb Mountain. Eyeing the distant, tiny specks that were the chairlifts, Courtney reminded herself for probably the sixty-fifth time to come back some winter and tackle those slopes with her skis. She'd been to Aspen a few times and had loved it.

"Sam's okay with you being a loose woman with me here?" she asked slyly.

Ellen had phoned Sam to tell her where she was. She made a motion of throwing her cell phone at Courtney but held back. "Oh, so *I'm* being the loose woman, am I? That's a good one!"

"If the shoe fits, baby."

"Oh, you're going to get it for that!" Ellen did a running tackle, surprising Courtney with her strength as they landed in a heap on the bed.

"You're pretty strong for a—"

Ellen narrowed her eyes. "For a what, wimp?"

"College professor was what I was going to say."

Ellen began tickling Courtney. She put up with it good-naturedly, even though she could have easily turned the tables and pinned Ellen beneath her. "Okay, okay, you are a fierce warrior, Ellen Turcotte. I give up."

Ellen smirked, her brow raised skeptically. "You're just humoring me and I know it."

"You know how you could humor me?"

"I have some ideas, but I'm dying for you to tell me."

"Wanna go for a dip in the hot tub and the pool? They're on the rooftop terrace and they promise a great sunset view of the mountains. And with any luck, we'll have it all to ourselves."

A lazy grin broke across Ellen's face. "That sounds fantastic. There's only one problem, darling. We don't have swimsuits and I am definitely not brave enough to skinny-dip in public, fierce warrior though I am!"

Courtney laughed. "Okay, okay. How about we wear these new T-shirts and boxers we bought downstairs."

"Do we dare risk going out in public with boxers that have grizzly bears on them?"

Courtney made a face, remembering the shop's limited selections. "It was either those or the pink-flowered underwear."

"You're right. I will proudly wear my grizzly bear boxers and Whistler T-shirt to the pool with you."

They lucked out. They had the place to themselves, at least for the time being. They started out in the massive hot tub, settling into near-scalding water that was a nice contrast to the chill in the evening air, and held hands beneath the burbling water. Courtney laid her head back, closed her eyes. She could hardly believe she was sitting here with a gorgeous Canadian woman who seemed utterly compatible with her in so many ways. And where Ellen wasn't compatible, she was complementary. Her sense of humor, her nimble mind could more than keep up with Courtney's, and in bed... *Wow!* Courtney had never been with another woman who could rock her world in bed the way Ellen could. It wasn't just skill, either, though Ellen was certainly adept in the ways of lovemaking. It was really about the emotional level they had reached. Never before had she been able to let down her defenses like this or expose this kind of vulnerability. Courtney had fully intended to do some serious soul-searching on her own, but it was so much better doing it with someone at her side and in her arms. It made her much stronger and more hopeful, knowing Ellen cared about her and was there for her, sharing this with her.

There was more Courtney wanted to share with Ellen, and more she needed to figure out first. She sensed the same was true of Ellen. Neither wanted to share absolutely everything about how they felt about one another. They both had their reasons for holding back, the biggest one being the transitory nature of their circumstances, Courtney presumed. *What the hell were the odds of meeting a woman and falling in love with her in a place where neither of us live? Christ!*

"You look deep in thought," Ellen observed.

Courtney smiled, gazing into eyes that were dark as oil but with amber highlights. The undisguised delight and affection she saw there made her tingle all over. "I don't want to think anymore."

"Neither do I." Ellen gave Courtney a long, slow, tender kiss that surged all the way down to Courtney's toes.

They fooled around in the hot tub, caressing each other's breasts through their wet T-shirts, slipping a hand down to one another's crotch, promising, with a playful look, much more later. They giggled like naughty children when a woman and a pre-pubescent boy appeared, towels in tow and totally oblivious to their lusty activity in the hot tub.

"It's getting a little hot in here," Ellen whispered with a giggle. "Shall we cool down in the pool for a few minutes?"

"Yes, and then we need to go make some heat again in our room."

The pool was cold after the hot tub. They frolicked briefly, behaving themselves for their audience. Moments later they were in their room, their clothes gone, and they were making love, sweet and tender. The heat they generated was a slow, steady sort and not the pan-fried searing of their previous sessions.

Lying with Ellen afterward, Courtney felt a dry constriction form in her throat. Of its own accord, her mouth began to tremble. Suddenly tears filled her eyes, causing the ceiling above her to blur. It seemed for a moment like a false alarm, the result perhaps of extraneous emotions from their lovemaking. But then, all at once, Courtney was overcome. Her body quaked, her breath left her and sobs exploded with force.

"Oh, sweetie." Ellen, who had been nestled in the crook of her arm, clutched her tightly. "What's wrong?"

Courtney couldn't speak. Even if she could have, she didn't know what to say. She was crying about everything and nothing—Ellen and the love she was feeling for her, gratitude for finding Ellen, grief at the prospect of their parting, regret for not having loved Celine or any other the way that she now realized she was capable of. She cried over her own helplessness too. She'd helplessly avoided that doomed flight, she'd been helpless to save her colleague and friend, Danny, and she was helpless at helping herself, though she had taken great strides toward that end lately.

"Don't cry, baby," Ellen soothed, planting soft kisses on Courtney's cheek and forehead, tenderly caressing her hair away from her face. "It's going to be all right."

Courtney cried until she was spent, like a candle burning through its wax. Afterward, she was weak but comforted, thanks to Ellen's patience and loving, gentle attention. There was still more churning inside her, however. She was worried about Ellen leaving in a week, and what would happen to them after that. She couldn't talk about that now, though, because it hurt too much. She did want to talk about Danny. She hadn't shared that part of her story with Ellen yet, nor with Jeff or her shrink, and she wasn't sure why. Probably because thinking about Danny made her feel like such a shit.

"I wish," Ellen whispered soothingly, "that I could snap my fingers and make it all better for you."

Courtney summoned a weak smile. "I wish you could too. But you being here helps. More than you could ever know."

Ellen looked up into Courtney's eyes. "I have big shoulders, Courtney. I want to help you in whatever way I can."

If it were only that simple, Courtney thought. She took a

deep breath and let it out slowly. "There's someone I want to tell you about."

There was a flash of panic in Ellen's eyes, but she said nothing.

"Don't worry, I'm not married or with anyone, if that's what you're thinking."

Ellen laughed uncertainly. "Sorry, you scared me for a minute there."

Courtney grew pensive. "Danny's his name. He was my best game developer. He'd only been with the company for a couple of years, but he shone from day one." Courtney's voice cracked. It took effort to get it back under control. "He established himself quickly as my best and brightest. The kind of employee who makes everyone around them look better, you know?"

Ellen nodded.

"We had this really good rapport. Sort of like he knew what I wanted before I asked for it. Hell, before I even knew I needed it. He was one of those real genuine people. Trusting, honest, funny. He was almost like a kid brother to me." Courtney smiled. "He would follow me around like a puppy most of the time, wanting to hang out after work or go for lunch and talk nonstop about work. I shut him down most of the time. I mean, he knew I was gay and everything, but I just, I don't know. Sometimes when you work ten hours a day with someone five days a week, the last thing you want to do is hang out on your time off, you know?"

"Of course. You needed your space. There's nothing wrong with that."

"No, but I treated him like shit a lot of the time. I didn't give him enough credit sometimes. He kept bugging me and bugging me to let him go with me on a road trip. I felt guilty because I always blew him off, so this time I let him."

Ellen stiffened beside her, as though she'd already guessed the outcome.

Courtney stared at the ceiling. It was a few minutes before she could speak again. "He made the flight and I didn't."

Ellen gasped. "Oh, God, Courtney. I'm so sorry."

There were no tears for Courtney, only quiet anger. "I never should have let him. It's not like I even needed him there. He'd done a lot of work on that damned game, though, so I thought it would be interesting for him to come along and hear about the ad campaign for it. Kind of like a reward for him."

"It's not your fault."

"He shouldn't have been there. I should never have let him come along, Ellen. And at the very least, I should have been on that damned plane with him."

Ellen touched her face, stroked it lightly. "Oh, Courtney, it's not your fault. What happened was totally unpredictable, totally beyond your control. There was nothing you could have done, except be on that plane yourself. Thank God you weren't."

"Maybe that's what should have happened."

Ellen jerked up onto her elbow, staring hard and angrily at Courtney. "Courtney Langford, don't you ever say that! You survived. You're here. So what are you going to do about it? Huh?"

Courtney shrugged and remained stubbornly silent.

"If you want to be the final victim of that plane crash, slowly killing yourself with guilt or erratic behavior, fine. Because that's what's going to happen if you don't find a way to get past this. Life is going to pass you by, dammit. Is that what you want, to be left behind like roadkill or something?"

"So what if I do?"

Ellen's eyes were dark as coal and her mouth a hard line.

She's adorable when she's pissed off, Courtney thought. She wanted to smile but didn't dare.

"I don't want you to waste your life. You've got too many things going for you for that. You're too smart and too good to let that happen. And I want you around, okay? I want you in my life! I care about you, don't you see that?"

"You do?"

"Yes, you dumbass! Don't you know how much better you've made my life by coming into it?"

Courtney grinned, her mood shifting. Were all those poetry

books and romance novels right? Was the secret to life the love of a good woman? Could it possibly be that simple? "You've made my life so much better too, Ellen. Thank you for coming into it."

Ellen's smile was radiant as she leaned down and kissed Courtney. It would have been the perfect time for Courtney to tell her she loved her, but she didn't. She closed her eyes and accepted the kiss, then pulled Ellen into her arms.

Ellen fell asleep before Courtney did. Staring up at the blackness that was the ceiling, she thought of Danny again. She hadn't allowed herself to think of the final moments of the crash before this, but she did now. Did he have seconds, minutes to comprehend what was happening? What went through his mind? What would have gone through her own mind had she been on that plane? Would she have thought of regrets, of what she still wanted to accomplish?

Courtney felt tears threatening again, but she swallowed them, not wanting to wake Ellen. Sometimes bad things happened to good people. It was all a big random spin of the wheel. Maybe the fact that she had been spared didn't mean a damn thing about what she deserved or didn't deserve. It wasn't about fairness; it couldn't possibly be. Maybe all it really meant was that she had more time. More time to live her life and more time to enjoy being alive, more time to make mistakes, more time to triumph, more time to love, more time to appreciate what she had.

Courtney stroked Ellen's hair. She was so grateful for her. Ellen made her appreciate how wonderful it was to be alive. How much there was to live for. Ellen would miss her if anything happened to her now. For that, Courtney was grateful.

It was a while before Courtney fell asleep, and as she did, she let her mind drift. She imagined she was rolling along on tiny waves in the sea, bobbing, going nowhere, but perfectly content.

CHAPTER SEVENTEEN

Definition of "showdown": In poker, after the last betting round, the players who remain in the pot must show their hands in the showdown to determine the winner.

Courtney turned down Sam's offer of another beer; it was far too tempting. Instead she grabbed a Coke from the plastic cooler and leaned against a tree in Sam's backyard, holding the cool can to her forehead and allowing the beads of sweat from the can to mingle with her own. She didn't see Jeff come up behind her.

"Having a tough time, eh?"

She blinked at him, worried she might start crying any minute. The prospect of Ellen leaving in a few hours had sucked the breath out of her. Her chest hurt. "That obvious?"

His smile did nothing to reassure her. "Not really, but you're not exactly the life of the party. I know you well enough to know when you're upset."

"Sorry."

"Don't be. If it were me, I don't even know if I would have come tonight."

Skipping Sam's farewell barbecue for Ellen wasn't an option, at least not for Courtney. It would have been disrespectful to Sam and Ellen. No matter what the terms were or how hard it might be, she needed to spend this last evening with Ellen. "You would have come if it were you," she said plainly.

"All right, all right." Jeff acquiesced with a sigh. "But dammit, I hate to see you hurting like this."

"I'd be hurting whether I was here or not." That was certainly the truth. Ellen was leaving tomorrow, and worse, she'd refused so far to talk to Courtney about where they stood, about what would happen to them now. Whether there still was a *them*. They'd been practically inseparable the last few days, enjoying one another's company, delighting in one another's bodies, and yet Ellen kept a small part of herself separate and distant, as though to soften the blow of their separation. No matter how hard she tried, Courtney hadn't been able to tap into that secret, most private part of Ellen. It was frustrating as hell because she didn't want to be protected or spared. She wanted to share everything with Ellen, even the pain.

They stood watching Ellen play Hula-Hoop with Ashley, the young daughter of Sam's girlfriend, Rebecca. Ellen was quite good at it, and her actions reminded Courtney of their lovemaking, of Ellen's hips rising up to meet hers. Ellen was lovely, throwing her head back and laughing as Ashley encouraged her to keep going. She looked relaxed, happy. Courtney tensed, seeing her like this, because it was proof that Ellen was fine without her, that she didn't need Courtney in order to be happy.

"I don't think she's going to want to see me again," she said matter-of-factly.

"Are you kidding me? Of course she's going to want to be with you! How could she not? I see how you two are together. You love each other."

Courtney appreciated Jeff's blind support, but it wasn't helping. Ellen was ready to move on with her life, ready to leave

Susan and that part of her life behind. Courtney was glad about that. She wanted Ellen to be happy. *But dammit, I want her to be happy with me! I want us to be happy together. I want her to move on with me.*

Reading her mood, Jeff put an arm around her shoulders. "If it's meant to be—"

"Bullshit," Courtney grumbled. "That's a load of crap and you know it. Since when is love like a roulette wheel, meant to land on your number or not?"

"Oh, Christ, I don't know. I'm not exactly an expert on love, okay? But seeing you two together, seeing how you light up when she's around, how different you are with her—"

"Different?"

"Yeah, you know, more at peace or something."

Yes, that was it. She was more at peace around Ellen. She was happy around Ellen. Happier than she'd ever been in her life.

"You're in love with her," Jeff said. "You're not going to let her fly off tomorrow without telling her that, are you?"

Ellen was trying to get Ashley to spin the hoop around her hips. She was trying so hard to show the girl how to do it, but one had to have hips to do it well, and children do not. Still, Courtney admired Ellen's perseverance, and Ashley was clearly enjoying the attention. Courtney smiled at Jeff, remembering the first time she'd met him at the casino. "So you think I should up my bet, huh?"

Jeff gave her shoulder a squeeze. "Exactly. You've been playing far too conservatively. It's time to take a bit of a risk, don't you think?"

Courtney wasn't averse to putting all her cards on the table. It was damned scary, but it would be worse if she didn't. If she walked away now, without knowing how Ellen truly felt about her and without Ellen knowing Courtney's feelings, it would haunt her for the rest of her life. It was like folding a winning hand.

"You're right," Courtney said coolly. "It's time to up the ante."

Sam grabbed Ellen's hand and led her through the back door and into the kitchen, where they could be alone.

Ellen kissed her friend on the cheek. "Thank you so much for having this little party for me. You didn't have to, you know."

Sam grinned and held up her beer bottle, tipping it in salute. "I wanted to give you a nice sendoff. I figured it might get you back here a hell of a lot sooner than three years. I really want to see you more often."

"You can count on that."

"I had an ulterior motive in throwing the party, of course."

"I would be shocked if you didn't, my friend!"

Sam laughed, her mood cheerful. Around Rebecca, she seemed truly happy, almost drunk on life. It was a side of Sam that Ellen rarely witnessed, and it was wonderful to see. "I wanted you to meet my girl before you left."

Ellen hadn't had a chance yet to talk to Rebecca for more than a few minutes, but she seemed like a nice woman—open, friendly and charming in a down-to-earth way. She and Sam were obviously smitten with one another, and Ashley was a treasure. She could totally see the three of them as a family. "I think Rebecca's wonderful, Sam."

"You do?" Sam asked eagerly. "I know she's young, and she has baggage and all—"

"Stop." Ellen held up her hand. "You love her and she clearly adores you. In fact, the way you are around her, I've never seen you like that before. And as for baggage, jeez, who doesn't have baggage? We all do, and someone once told me it's about how you carry it."

Sam was blushing, but Ellen could see that her words had reassured her friend. Sam turned and peered out the window, her gaze instantly finding her lover. "I can't help it. I am totally, unequivocally in love. And isn't Ashley a great kid?"

"She's adorable. My God, I never thought I'd see you as a parent! But I think you'll be great at it. Kids have always loved you. I can totally see you with a family."

"Can you believe it? I never thought that'd be me, never. I figured I'd be single for life, and definitely no kids."

"Funny how life turns out. Here you're the one with a family and I'm the single one."

Ellen envied Sam, finding her true love and being so happy. She remembered what it was like, starting out a life together with someone you love and trust, the strength and hope that embarking on that kind of relationship gives you. Ellen wasn't sure she would ever find it again, or if she did, that it would be any more lasting than it had been the first time around. Would love visit her twice? And would the second time be the charm?

"Trust me, my friend, you won't be single for long. You're too good a catch for that." Sam winked at her. "And speaking of love, what's up with you and Courtney?"

Ellen didn't want to discuss her relationship with Courtney, mostly because there wasn't much to say. She had no clue what was going to become of them. Tomorrow by this time, she would be jetting back to Toronto, and Courtney, well, she supposed Courtney would go back to hanging out at that bar on Davie Street or maybe the casino, or maybe she would go back to the States. "Nothing's up. I'm going home tomorrow, and Courtney is either staying here or going back to Seattle, I guess."

Sam gave her an appraising look. "She looks at you like you're the most beautiful woman in the world, Ellen. Did you know that?"

Ellen nearly choked on the sudden sob in her throat. No, she didn't know that. Or maybe she did, but she didn't want to acknowledge it. "What's your point?"

"I think you know my point. She's in love with you."

Ellen shrugged, not really wanting to believe it, even though it was probably true.

"Come on," Sam continued, her beer bottle pointed accusingly at Ellen. "Don't try to tell me you think you've only been having a little vacation fling with her. You're not that stupid, and neither am I."

Contrite, Ellen had to turn her back for a moment. Sam was

right. So many times over the past couple of weeks, Ellen tried to convince herself that it was much less with Courtney than it really was. The sex was great, the companionship fabulous. They were having fun. In Courtney's presence, Ellen felt beautiful, smart, desired, needed. And yes, loved. Courtney made her feel truly loved, respected, cared for. A touch from Courtney could do that. Same with a look or a few simple words. Courtney was special, and so was what they had together. There was no denying they were falling hard for one another. To try to deny it was doing a disservice to them both. It was pure bullshit to pretend anything different. And yet Ellen couldn't find it in herself to fully admit it either. She wasn't there yet and might never be.

When Ellen turned toward Sam again, she had to wipe away a tear. "Dammit, I don't know what the hell I'm doing."

Sam stepped forward and drew Ellen in for a long hug. "Do any of us? Sometimes you have to put one foot in front of the other and trust that it's the right thing and that it's going to be okay."

"I know. I tried that for thirteen years, remember?"

"Yes, honey, you did. But somewhere it stopped being okay, and it took you a while to realize you were on a dead-end street. You're smarter now. You're more self-aware and better able to take care of yourself. You won't make the same mistakes again."

Ellen pulled away, wiped another tear from her cheek. "I don't know. And Christ, talk about complications. We're not even from the same country for one thing. And for another thing, we both have things to sort out in our lives. I mean, God, how can I even think of tangling myself up with someone when I'm not even fully untangled from Susan yet?"

"Give yourself time, El. You don't have to rush into anything. You don't even have to have any answers right now. It's about believing that the answers will come and that you *will* be happy again."

Ellen wasn't quite sure what she believed. And Courtney would want answers. She deserved some. *Dammit, why can't things be simple? Why couldn't we have met at a different time in our lives?*

As Ellen finished her glass of wine, Courtney strolled into the kitchen. She walked stiffly, as if a stern reaction from Ellen might break her in two. Ellen smiled at her and her relief was immediate in her body language.

"Hi, sweetheart." Courtney kissed her cheek. It was a simple, respectful act that told Ellen that Courtney had missed her.

"Hi."

Sam hastily made motions to retreat. "I think there are some folks hungry for dessert out there. I'll talk to you guys later."

Ellen nodded gratefully before turning her attention back to her lover. There was no more putting it off. They needed to talk, though Ellen didn't have a clue what she was going to say or how their conversation was going to end.

"I've wanted to get you alone for hours," Courtney ventured, her voice a little tremulous.

"I know. Would you like to go for a walk?"

"I'd love to."

The neighborhood was settling down in sync with the setting sun. The darker it grew, the lighter traffic became and there were fewer children's voices and barking dogs bubbling up from yards and parks. Courtney and Ellen walked in silence for a while, their arms linked like old friends or new lovers who needed to touch and yet act with decorum.

Courtney felt tense next to Ellen, as though she were bracing for a physical blow. Ellen did not want to hurt this woman, but there were certain realities they had to face. She wasn't the kind of woman to ignore her duties and responsibilities, to throw all caution to the wind, to give everything up in her life to blindly believe in some force greater than herself. And so while a part of her never wanted to leave Courtney's side, not even for a minute, that really wasn't a realistic choice. They each had their own lives to live, their own issues to sort out. As much as she wished it were otherwise, it was not their time.

After a couple more blocks, they came to a diamond where a women's team was in the midst of a softball game. Without speaking, they climbed up to an empty part of the grandstand

and sat down. The seats were dusty, but neither woman cared.

"Don't," Courtney finally said, her voice brittle, like a twig snapping.

"Don't what?" Ellen responded, startled.

It was a while before Courtney answered, as her eyes followed the action below. The batter hit a line drive double, the ball skittering past the right fielder. "Please don't tell me we're never going to see one another again."

It shouldn't have surprised Ellen that Courtney would get right to the heart of the matter. It was Courtney's way and her words were like an arrow piercing her. "Courtney, I—"

"I'm in love with you, Ellen." Courtney turned tortured eyes on her. "I don't want to be without you in my life."

Ellen's heart was in her throat. She didn't want to hurt Courtney, didn't want to hurt herself either. It was like walking on a frozen river and hearing the ice crack behind you. It was the most helpless of feelings, and yet she had to keep propelling herself forward. "I'm scared, Courtney."

"So am I." Courtney pulled Ellen's hand into hers. "Ellen, when I found out I missed being on that plane that crashed, I was relieved. I was happy as hell. And then I felt guilty for that and guilty for Danny. And then after that I began to wonder what was so special about me that I was chosen to survive. I knew that I could never find the answers unless I turned my entire life upside down, and that's exactly what I did. I still don't have all the answers, and maybe I never will. But I know that I need you by my side. I know that we were meant to be together. I was meant to find you and to find this kind of love for the first time in my life."

The words stunned Ellen into silence. It took effort to choke back her tears and compose herself. "I too pretty much thought the worst nightmare of my life had happened to me. I thought, what was wrong with me that would make Susan do that to me? What had I done to deserve all that misery? I blamed her, I blamed myself. For a while, I didn't know how to go on. And then I did somehow. Meeting you made me see that I can love again,

207

that someone can truly love me and respect me for who I am. Meeting you has meant everything to me." Ellen's voice cracked with emotion. "You've given me love and hope, Courtney. Two things I never thought would happen to me again."

"Oh, darling." Courtney put her arm around Ellen's shoulder and drew her close. Ellen cried into her shoulder for a few moments, her tears falling on Courtney's shirt in tiny round splotches.

"Don't let this be the end," Courtney pleaded softly.

"I don't want it to be the end." Ellen's voice slowly hardened. "But neither of us is in a position to begin anything deeper right now."

"Why not?" Courtney placed her finger under Ellen's chin and drew her face up until they were looking into one another's eyes.

Ellen faltered for a moment. Her eyes fluttered shut, her mouth quivered. She hated this. If she could wave a magic wand and change their circumstances, she would do it in a heartbeat. But she didn't believe in magic. No one had the kind of power that it would take to make their lives perfect right now.

"We are not at a point in our lives to be together, Courtney. I hate saying that, but you know it's true. I have things to take care of back home, things I need to do for myself. And you have a lot of things to figure out too. I can't be in a relationship with you right now. I'm sorry, but you have to know this is the right thing to do. For both of us."

Courtney shook her head. "I don't believe that not being together is the right thing to do, Ellen, I will never believe that. We can work the other things out. I know we can. Trust me, okay?"

"No." Ellen shook her head firmly. "I can only trust myself right now. Surely you can understand that."

Pain was etched in Courtney's face, visible in the way the muscles of her jaw tightened, the way her mouth drooped. Her eyes, watery now, looked lost and empty. Scared. She looked away, her shoulders slumping in defeat. When she finally spoke, her voice was rough with emotion. "Ellen, I won't give up. I can't.

And I won't stop loving you."

"Oh, sweetheart." Ellen's heart swelled and constricted. She was sad again. Excessively, inexplicably so. With Susan, her sadness had mostly taken the form of rage, anger and blame. This sadness was entirely different. Her very soul ached.

She was sure, though, that she was doing the right thing. They couldn't build a relationship when everything was so transient—when they weren't sure where they were either geographically or emotionally. "I love you too. But I know the time isn't right for us. I need to get my life together and so do you. I can't start a new relationship until I'm in a better, more solid place in my life, and neither can you."

"You know, one day you will be ready to love again, to be in a relationship again. And I know I've had such great luck in my life, but I'd trade all that stupid luck now to be the one who's there when you are ready."

Courtney's joyless eyes probed Ellen's. This was anything but the strong, cocky, reckless woman Ellen had first come to know. This was a vulnerable woman who was presenting Ellen her heart. Ellen wanted to take her in her arms and soothe her, but there was no consolation she could truly give to Courtney right now.

"How long will we have to wait?" Courtney asked tentatively.

Ellen released a long held breath. "I don't know. I just know we both need some time right now. I can't tell you anything more than that."

Courtney nodded curtly, resigned to Ellen's decision. "I won't come to the airport tomorrow to see you off. I can't."

It hadn't occurred to Ellen that Courtney wouldn't see her off. *Shit.* She should have realized how hard being in an airport would be for her. So many feelings swirled through Ellen now—fear, sadness, guilt, loneliness. A loud cheer roared beneath them—someone had probably hit a home run—and the incongruity of it shot through Ellen like a bolt of lightning. How dare people cheer while they were going through this horrible moment of letting one another go!

"I understand," Ellen finally said. "So we only have tonight."

Courtney couldn't make love with Ellen. Not tonight, their last night in Vancouver and maybe their last night together ever. Her body would have surely obeyed her if she'd commanded it to, but emotionally, she was too sad and too shattered for sex. Finally, she'd met someone she'd fallen head over heels for. A woman who had given meaning and dimension to her life, who loved her and made her feel so important. A woman who made her want to give up everything just to love her and be loved by her. A woman she finally wanted to share her life with.

Ellen slept and Courtney held her tight, not wanting to let her out of her arms, even for a minute. Tears slithered down Courtney's cheeks. Until now, her luck had been both incredible and dependable. Missing that doomed flight—that had been the biggest jackpot of her life. She'd also known good luck in cards, in her job, in practically every facet of her life. But losing Ellen— it was clear that her luck had finally deserted her...and in spades. It was like being handed one of the biggest gifts in your life, only to have it snatched away. It hurt all the more because there was nothing she could do about it. She was lonelier than she'd ever been in her life. The pain of it lanced through her, leaving her raw inside.

Dawn arrived and Ellen got up to collect her luggage at Sam's and get to the airport on time. Courtney and Ellen hugged long and hard in the hotel's lobby, both crying silent tears, both trying to be strong and not really succeeding.

It occurred to Courtney, despite the trauma of the moment, to wonder at the fact that they could show their affection like this, without anyone giving them a second look. In Vancouver, Canada, they were simply a couple saying goodbye and not a couple of freaks putting on a show as they would have been across the border. "I love you, Ellen Turcotte."

"I love you too, Courtney Langford."

Courtney kissed Ellen on the lips and summoned as much strength and confidence as she could. "We're going to see each other again, I promise."

Ellen didn't look so sure, but she smiled. "I will look forward to it."

As Ellen climbed into the back of a cab, Courtney stood rooted in place, unable to wave or even smile. In her soul, she hadn't felt this alone and abandoned since her mother died.

CHAPTER EIGHTEEN

Definition of "cold": A player or dealer on a losing streak is said to be cold.

Courtney drifted through the next few days, taking daily sessions with her therapist, reading, jogging and doing a lot of sitting around and thinking. Moping, more like. She hated having so little control. For nearly three months now, she'd been driftwood bobbing on the sea, waiting for the currents to take her somewhere. She'd given in to the unpredictability of it all, let the waves carry her to Vancouver, where she'd met Ellen and, for a while, seemed to have found purpose, a reason for her existence. But now Ellen was gone, and Courtney was adrift once again.

She talked about it with Jeff one night after his shift at the casino. She played a few rounds of blackjack while waiting for him to finish—and lost almost every hand, which amounted to something over a hundred dollars. She couldn't remember ever having lost so many times in a row. Her luck sucked all of a sudden.

"You're in a downswing right now, that's all," Jeff reassured her over a beer at a pub down the street. He seemed completely unconcerned, which thoroughly annoyed Courtney. He wasn't the one without his best friend and lover.

"I don't give a crap about the cards, Jeff, or the money. I've lost everything that matters. Everything." The chasm of emptiness within her grew deeper, threatening to swallow her.

"You haven't lost her, Court."

Courtney sipped her beer, anger now filling the empty well that was her heart. "How can you say that? She's gone. She doesn't want to be in a relationship with me. She hasn't even contacted me since she left."

"So? She needs space, that's all."

"Space, my ass." It hurt that Ellen didn't even want to remain friends. How could she just walk away like that from what they had? How could she not give them a second thought? How could she be so cold and distant? So final?

"Besides, she's right, you know."

Courtney scowled at her friend, mad at him for being such a smug bastard. "How can you say that?"

Jeff shrugged, and Courtney had the urge to slap him. "You told me she said that neither of you is in the right place for a relationship right now, and I gotta admit, she's right. A little more time might put everything right for both of you. You'll see."

"That little bit of time, as you so calmly put it, might put more and more distance between us until it's too late. You can't always recover what you've lost." The prospect of losing Ellen forever after only just finding her gave Courtney a sick feeling in her stomach.

"You'll have to take that chance. If you love each other enough—"

"Yeah, yeah, the stars will all align perfectly and we'll get back together," she snapped. "Bullshit. It was bullshit when you told me that at Sam's and it's bullshit now. Since when did you become the schmaltzy queen of romance advice anyway?"

Jeff deflected the insult with a grin. "I've been around the block a few times. Besides, you know I'm right. I can see how much the two of you love one another. You're meant to be together. There's nothing wrong with taking a little time to get there. You know, letting things simmer on the back burner while you each get your shit together. It makes total sense, don't you think?"

Courtney had been around enough to know when to pick her battles and how much energy to expend on them, how to tilt the odds in her favor and what to do when you were outgunned. It was a lot like card strategy.

"I guess I don't have any other choice, at least for now," she muttered. "Ellen is not the kind of woman who would want me to rush in on a white steed and carry her off or give her ultimatums and try to force her into anything. She's fiercely independent and she's made up her mind about this. There's not a goddamned thing I can do."

"So what's next?"

Courtney thought for a long time, searching for the answers in her diminishing beer. If Ellen wanted time and space, then she would have it. And what the hell, maybe Ellen was actually right about all this. Maybe they needed to sort their lives out first if they were going to have any chance of being together. Courtney certainly hadn't reached closure yet over the plane crash, nor had she figured out where her life was going next. And Ellen didn't seem to be ready to move on from her ex yet or, at least, was still in transition. What made it so frustrating was that Courtney could practically taste their being together, and yet it remained beyond her grasp. It was like trying to grab hold of a shadow. "I think I need to go backward," she finally declared.

"Backward?" Jeff looked perplexed. "I thought you're supposed to be going forward?"

Courtney shook her head purposefully. "Sometimes you have to take a step backward before you can go forward. I think there are things back in Seattle I need to make peace with before I can get on with my life."

"Wow," he said, shaking his head in wonder. "That's brilliant.

I wish I'd thought of that advice."

Courtney laughed cynically. "Maybe these therapy sessions with Liz are helping me more than I know. Shit. Courtney Langford, model shrink patient. Who'da thought?"

"But what are you going to do about Ellen? You're not going to let her go forever, are you?" He clearly didn't believe the last chapter about her and Ellen had been written yet. She hoped like hell he was right.

Courtney wished she had all the answers to the puzzle that was Ellen. If she could shake the answers out of Liz or some book, she would surely do it. For now, she had to look after herself and hope the rest of it would fall into place later. "I'll figure out that part eventually." Her eyes fell on her friend, and she imprinted in her mind the twinkle in his dark eyes and his infectious smile. She had great affection for him. He was like a kid brother to her. "I'm going to miss you, Jeff."

He winked at her, his grin presumptuous. "You'll be back."

Ellen had deliberately chosen her favorite Greek restaurant on Danforth for her meeting with Susan. Susan didn't especially like Greek food, while Ellen absolutely loved it. Italian had been their habit as a couple, and Ellen had decided to let her choice of restaurant send a message to Susan—the message that there was no more *us* and that Ellen now did as she pleased.

Ellen drummed her fingers on the table beside her glass of wine. She wondered whether Susan would show up drunk or sober, angry or pleasant, whether she would act hurt, apologetic, hopeful, bitter. Would she be cooperative or obstructive? Would things turn ugly or go smoothly? Susan's moods had become unpredictable over the last couple of years.

It struck her that she was back to her old habit of nervously waiting to see what mood Susan would be in. Thank God this part of my life is almost over, she thought with relief and resignation. It was time to live life for herself, to really try to be happy and healthy. And while it didn't mean all her dreams were going to come true or that even half of them would, it was time to at least start giving them a fighting chance.

Susan strode in, her eyes darting about anxiously. After greeting Ellen and sitting down across from her, she continued to exude tension. She squirmed in her chair and looked around for a waiter, probably so she could order a drink, Ellen figured. It shocked her when Susan instead ordered cola with lime.

"I don't drink anymore," Susan quickly explained.

"Okay. Well. Good for you. When did you stop?"

"Two months ago."

Ellen wondered if their separation had finally made Susan stop, or if something else had. She decided not to ask. It was good that Susan had stopped, but the why didn't matter anymore to her. "You're well then?"

Susan shrugged. "I guess."

Ellen wondered if the womanizing had stopped along with the booze. If it hadn't, well, it couldn't hurt Ellen anymore. So that was progress.

They studied their menus silently. It was incredible how little they had to say to one another after thirteen years, Ellen thought. There was a time when they couldn't wait to rush home and tell each other their news of the day, even the most trivial of things. For a while, they used to share everything, but that was a long time ago now. She wished she could remember when it had stopped, but it had probably stopped a sentence or two at a time, then an event at a time, until one day they only talked about the things they had to, like what bills had to be paid, what to get Susan's nieces and nephews for Christmas, that kind of thing. The process of closing up had been so slow and gradual that they'd hardly noticed—so slow and gradual that it hadn't even really hurt that much, Ellen realized.

Susan looked up from her menu. "I think I'll have moussaka."

"Wow. You've grown more adventurous with food."

"I've changed in a lot of ways, Ellen."

Ellen studied her former partner. She looked older, as though she'd aged over the few months they'd been apart. Her neck was thinner, the lines in her face deeper, her hair a touch grayer. She'd suffered too. "I've changed too."

The waiter took their orders, moussaka for Susan, stuffed eggplant for Ellen.

"Ellen, I've started going to a therapist. I've been really working on myself. I want us to get back together."

Ellen reeled for a moment. This wasn't at all what she had been expecting. Susan, of her own accord, had stopped drinking, had changed her behavior, had started therapy. She should applaud her, but dammit, why hadn't she done all of this sooner? Why had she waited until everything had turned to absolute crap before she got help? What Susan was doing now, she was doing for her own sake and not Ellen's. If she'd wanted to do it for Ellen, for their marriage, she would have done it a hell of a long time ago. It was too damned late now.

"Say something," Susan pleaded.

Ellen shook her head slowly but definitively. "I'm really glad you're straightening yourself out, but it's too late for us. I'm sorry."

"No, please. It's not too late. It can't be. We're still legally married, for Christ's sake. You can't just walk away for good without trying again."

Ellen didn't want to argue. She wasn't a prisoner. She wasn't trapped in any way. She could damn well walk away whenever she wanted. "Susan, don't."

Tears filled Susan's eyes, but Ellen felt nothing. There was no sympathy, no guilt, no love. It wasn't that she was uncaring or insensitive. There was simply nothing left in the well anymore.

"No, Ellen. Please don't tell me to give up on us."

"You have to. I already have."

The tears fell fast and furious. Susan would fight the inevitable for a while, but eventually her anger and feelings of rejection would flame out, just as they had with Ellen.

Their food arrived, but neither woman was hungry. They

picked at their meals, barely speaking, Susan's disappointment evident in her slumped shoulders and averted eyes. The worst of the unpleasantness would soon be over. They would pick at the carrion of their marriage until only the bones of it were left to scatter. Ellen had every intention of being fair, but she wanted it done, wanted it signed, sealed and legalized. *The sooner the better*.

At the end of the dinner, she handed Susan an envelope. It was a settlement offer, and she instructed Susan to take it to a lawyer and to get back to her.

On the street in front of the restaurant, Susan clutched the envelope with white knuckles, her face grave. Clearly she had hoped for something else from the evening. "I did love you, you know," she said in a shaky voice.

"I know you did." The sadness of it hit Ellen then. She turned before Susan could see her cry and stumbled back to her car.

Courtney stopped her motorcycle in front of the tidy brick bungalow and checked the address again. She'd called ahead, so they knew she was coming. She sat on her bike for a few more minutes, trying to rehearse in her mind what she might say, but it was useless. She really had no idea.

Courtney had seen them at the memorial service but hadn't introduced herself. She'd been deeply absorbed in her own denial then. But she remembered thinking at the time how they were older than she'd expected, maybe late sixties. They must have been close to forty when they had Danny.

"Hello, Mr. and Mrs. O'Leary. Thank you for seeing me."

If they were suspicious of her intentions or surprised by her request to meet, they didn't show it. They were nothing but friendly and welcoming.

"Any friend of Danny's is a friend of ours," Mrs. O'Leary announced cordially, ushering Courtney to a floral print loveseat.

The décor was very Seventies or maybe Eighties. Gold

appliances, floral fabric, lots of wallpaper. The coffee table and end tables were covered in cheap wood veneer, the draperies thick brocade. The place was well past its day, at least on the inside, but it was clean and neat. Courtney couldn't picture Danny growing up here. He had such vision with games and animation. Such creativity. On the other hand, maybe growing up in the dull, outdated house and with older parents was exactly why Danny had turned out the way he had. Maybe gaming and computers had been his escape; his upbringing had fueled his brilliance.

"We were making tea, would you like some?" Mr. O'Leary asked pleasantly.

"Sure, that would be wonderful."

It was served in a delicate china cup and saucer. Courtney noticed the handle was chipped.

"Danny talked about you all the time," Mrs. O'Leary said a little shyly. "He thought you were the greatest boss in the world. He said he learned so much from you."

"No," Courtney said quietly. "I learned a lot from him. He was excellent at his job. So good, in fact, that I often took his abilities for granted." Her voice cracked a little. It was more than his abilities she had taken for granted. She had taken *him* for granted. He was the little brother who wouldn't go away, the one constantly vying for her attention because he idolized her. She'd known it too, had even encouraged it because it made his work better. She sipped her tea, oblivious to the fact that it was scalding her throat.

The O'Learys both looked a little uncomfortable hearing how good their son was at his job. Mr. O'Leary smiled uncertainly. "Well, I wouldn't really know if he was good at his job or not. That computer stuff was not an interest we shared, but if you say he was good at it, then we believe you."

"We know it made him happier than anything in the world," Danny's mom added. Her eyes had taken on new life talking about her son. She was clearly proud of him. "He always had a childlike enthusiasm for those games. It was his whole life since the time he was about thirteen."

Courtney took a deep breath. This next part was tough for her. "I wanted you to know that his talent was very much appreciated. But there's more than that. Danny was a great kid. He did everything we ever asked of him and more. I'm sorry I never told him how much I thought of him. How much I cared, and how much I respected him. I should have told him those things. I miss him."

Danny's parents might not know much about his work, but clearly they understood the part about him being a great kid. They smiled broadly.

"Thank you," Mrs. O'Leary said. "I don't think Danny ever felt unappreciated at work. He certainly never acted that way with us and I know he loved his work. We were so very proud of him. He was everything we could have wanted out of a son."

"Would you like to see his old room?" Danny's dad asked.

Courtney didn't, but she complied, following them down the hall and into a bedroom still decorated like a teenaged boy's. There was a Seahawks poster, another one of Kurt Cobain. Computer manuals and textbooks were stacked on a bookshelf. The old IBM desktop computer looked to be at least ten years old, with its big clunky monitor.

"And how are you doing, dear?" Mrs. O'Leary suddenly asked her.

Courtney looked at the woman curiously, completely caught off guard by the question.

"We understand you were supposed to have been on that plane with Danny," Mr. O'Leary clarified, nervously clearing his throat.

Courtney sat down heavily on the single bed. Her legs would have given out had she tried to stay on her feet. She didn't know what to say. She couldn't tell them how many times she'd wished it had been Danny who survived, and alternately how many times she was glad she hadn't been on the plane. Some days it was the flip of a coin as to how she felt. "I'm sorry," Courtney whispered. She was not even sure what she was sorry about, just that she was.

"Don't be." Mr. O'Leary sat down beside her. "We're glad you missed that flight."

"In fact," Mrs. O'Leary added, "it gives us tremendous comfort that you're alive. Danny thought the world of you, and knowing that someone who was supposed to be on that flight was spared makes us feel like at least one good thing came out of it."

Courtney couldn't understand how they could be so gracious. Maybe grief makes you more human, more understanding, Courtney thought. *At least once you got over the toughest part of it.* She could understand that. She herself had lost a certain amount of stridency these last couple of months.

Courtney stood. She was ready to leave now. "I really wanted you to know that I miss Danny, and I thought the world of him too."

At the front door, they both hugged her. Before she could leave the stoop, Mrs. O'Leary looked pointedly at her and held her arm. "You do understand what this means, don't you?"

Courtney shook her head, not comprehending.

"Danny's gone, but you're not. It's up to you now to live for him too."

Yes, Courtney thought, it's true. She owed it to Danny to not give up, to keep on fighting, to keep living. That was what mattered now. Mistakes and regrets were only tools to help her learn and grow and to get her on her way. "I'll do my best."

Courtney sat on her bike a moment longer before pulling away. The O'Learys were a living example of how love never dies. Their love for their son would live as long as they did, just as Courtney's love for her mother remained in her heart. She had never really considered before the longevity of love, how it existed like its own living, breathing entity, even if the other person was gone. Whether through death or separation, love for another could continue indefinitely. *Yes, it's like that with Ellen. I will always love her even if I never see her again.*

The next day, Courtney met Nan for lunch. She wanted to apologize for the way she'd run out on her when she'd left for Vancouver. She'd been cold toward Nan, had treated her badly. Nan was a good woman, and she accepted Courtney's apology with humor and grace.

"Are you sure you won't stick around here?" Nan asked Courtney after she told her she was planning to leave Seattle for good. "Seattle's a wonderful city, and it's been your home for a long time."

"It is a wonderful city, but so is Vancouver, and I've made up my mind."

Courtney had decided to stay in Vancouver permanently. It was the city where she'd begun her transformation, the city where she'd met the love of her life, the city where she now belonged. It dawned on her that Jeff had been right when he told her she'd be back. She smiled at the memory, glad she had at least one friend waiting for her there. Maybe even Sam would be her friend too, eventually.

"I guess there's nothing that will change your mind?"

"Nope. It's where I need to be." It's where her heart was, for sure. There were so many memories of Ellen there, but there were new possibilities there as well. It would take some time and some red tape, but she would be able to get a work visa eventually. Either that or she'd have to get some nice Canadian woman to marry her, she thought with a smile.

"You will keep in touch this time, won't you?"

Courtney laughed. "Yes, I promise."

"And you're going to be okay?"

"Yes." One way or another, with or without Ellen, Courtney was going to be okay. She hugged Nan goodbye. She would miss her. She told her to be sure to visit some time, once she got settled. She had a lot to do in the meantime. Securing a condo would be her first priority. Then she could start looking for a job, see an immigration lawyer. There were plenty of game developers and animation companies in Vancouver, if she decided to go that way. Or she could put her skills to some other use. In any case, she had time to figure it all out.

Back in her hotel room, Courtney slid into deep sadness. She missed Ellen so much, like a dull ache that would not go away. Nothing she did could fill the emptiness. Her life was like a circle that didn't quite marry up. She hadn't wanted to pressure Ellen in any way, but it took all her willpower to leave her alone, to wait helplessly to see if she would ever contact her again. Each day she checked her e-mail and phone messages relentlessly, but always there was nothing from Ellen.

Courtney couldn't find anything on television to watch and she didn't feel like going out. A call to an old friend might cheer her up, though. Jordan Scott always made her laugh. She'd always been a fun distraction, whether it was hanging out on the softball diamond throwing the ball around or drinking a beer and watching girls. Her friend was as unpredictable as a firecracker near a match. They'd met several years ago. Jordan was a successful realtor who'd since moved back to her native Chicago, and they sporadically stayed in touch.

Jordan picked up after a couple of rings. "Oh, my God, Courtney! Is it really you, or is it someone doing a good imitation?"

Courtney laughed. "No, it's really me."

"Jesus, woman, I haven't heard from you since Christmas and Celine leaving and all that drama. I thought you'd died or something!"

Courtney winced. Jordan obviously had no idea how close Courtney had come to doing exactly that, but she didn't feel like filling her in. She wanted a normal conversation with someone for once—one that didn't involve Danny or the crash or even Ellen. "I'm afraid I'm still kicking, my friend. How's life in Chicago?"

"Well, why don't you get your ass over here for a real visit sometime and find out?"

"I will, Jordan, I will."

"Yeah, sure. You've been saying that for four years now. And that lunch we had a year ago on one of your business stopovers doesn't count."

"I know. You're right." Courtney had made all kinds of empty promises about visiting but never had. She'd been to Chicago on business plenty of times before but never pleasure. She tended to like something a little more exotic for vacation.

They talked for a while about old times, about what Jordan was up to in Chicago, which was pretty much the same as always— making money and making out with women. Jordan always teased her about how she could never keep up, and Courtney teased back that she had no desire to embark on a contest she could never win.

After more conversation, Courtney finally told Jordan that she'd quit her job and was looking for a new direction in her life. She was purposely evasive, though, keeping the conversation general, simply explaining that she'd been at the same company for too long and that it wasn't challenging anymore.

"All the more reason to come out here and visit me then. Or maybe even move out here! Wouldn't that be awesome?" Jordan's laughter was long and full of mischief. "Think of the trouble we could get into."

"Now you're scaring me! Besides, you know I'm a West Coast girl at heart." It was true. Courtney could never be happy in the Midwest, locked in by all that flat land, though at least Chicago had Lake Michigan going for it. Still, Chicago left a bad taste in her mouth, or at least its airport did. She didn't want to go near the place ever again.

"You're being stubborn. You can at least admit that much, can't you?"

"Hey, why don't we get together for a few days in Vegas or something as a compromise destination?" They'd gone there together a couple of times before, tearing up the casinos and the bars, staying out half the night and having a great time. A trip there with Jordan now would surely pull Courtney out of her funk.

"Now you're talking! But crap, I can't right now. I'm about to close a deal on a two-acre parcel of land a developer wants to build a thirty-story condo on. Probably my biggest deal of the year. It's going to tie me up for the next few weeks."

"Shit. I mean, it's great for you, I'm happy."

Jordan chuckled, clearly delighted. "It's a huge coup for me and is going to make me a shitload of money. But I love the challenge of it, you know?"

Courtney did know. She missed the challenge that work could bring, but her heart wasn't in video games anymore. "Yeah, I understand. I think it's great. Congratulations."

"Thanks, and hey, maybe after this project is over we could meet in Vegas for a few days of fun. In fact, I should think about buying myself a condo there. It'd be the perfect getaway for these Chicago winters, and you could come and visit me as often as you wanted!"

"Oh, my God, Jordan, I don't think Vegas would know what hit it if you started living there half the time. Certainly the women would be in for a big surprise!"

Jordan's laughter crackled through the phone line. "Well, you know what I like to say. Do it before you're too old to do it anymore."

"Yes, I remember your motivational little sayings very well. You should write a book!"

"Oh, hell, why write a book about life when you should be living it? But, hey, you've given me a great idea about getting a condo in Vegas. And I'm going to give myself a deadline of next March to have one."

"Why March?"

"Some good friends of mine are getting married in Vegas next March and they've asked me to be a bridesmaid. I could stay at my own place that way."

Courtney couldn't help but chuckle, picturing Jordan in a long, pastel chiffon gown with old lady hair and ridiculous shoes. "Okay, you as a bridesmaid? Are you kidding me?"

"Better that than to be the bride, my friend."

That was true. Jordan was not the type to settle down and get married. But who really knew. Courtney never thought she was the type to settle down either, and yet now she couldn't stop thinking about spending her life with Ellen. "A wedding in Vegas, huh?"

"Yeah. It's a great excuse for a party in the greatest city to party in!"

Courtney suddenly had an idea. She made her excuses and got off the phone as quickly as she could, then went online and began looking at flights. She had a little panic attack checking out the list of flights from Seattle to Vegas, her head growing dizzy and a hot spell flushing her, but it passed, thankfully. It was time to be bold, to act decisively and leap for that brass ring. And if she fell flat on her face, well, at least she'd tried. Doing nothing was no longer an option.

Courtney knew full well what she wanted for herself. And who.

CHAPTER NINETEEN

Definition of "blind bet": In poker, a bet posted without the player seeing any of her cards.

July was the most sweltering time of summer in Toronto. The humidity from Lake Ontario made the heat unbearable. It was the kind of heat that scorched grass to a brittle brown, like dead pine needles, and kept people indoors huddled close to their rattling air conditioners.

Staying indoors gave Ellen a good excuse to sit at her kitchen table and get a head start on her course curriculum for September. The loneliness that had crept into her soul was another good reason to immerse herself in her work. Since Vancouver, Ellen couldn't shake her pervasive melancholy, which seemed to follow her around like a cloud. It was because of Susan and giving closure to their relationship, yes, but it was also the acute absence of Courtney.

If Ellen could have written a script for her life, she would never have gotten into another relationship as quickly as she had with Courtney. It was insane, ludicrous, destructive, to jump from Susan to Courtney with barely time to breathe in between. It made absolutely no sense to prolong an intense relationship with Courtney right now. She should live on her own for a while, let herself heal, figure out what she wanted to do with the rest of her life. Lately Sam had taken to bugging her about moving to Vancouver. Ellen had to admit the idea appealed to her. There were plenty of colleges she could teach at there, and there wasn't much holding her to Toronto anymore. Vancouver was so beautiful, so clean, so outdoorsy, and Sam was there.

Ellen couldn't think of Vancouver, of course, without thinking of Courtney. The two now were inextricably linked. The mountains, the ocean, the quaint coffee shops, Granville Island, the casino, Whistler, Courtney's smiling face, riding together on Courtney's bike, Courtney's kisses, Courtney's touch, making love through the night, waking together. It was almost like a dream now, still strong in her mind, but no longer real. Even though it was all past tense, all memory now, missing Courtney was a deep cut that wouldn't heal. God, Ellen thought, I don't want to be one of these people who lives in the past all the time. I don't want the past to be the best part of my life.

Maybe Sam was right. Maybe she should move out there, start her life over. Courtney surely must have left the city by now, but perhaps she could capture some of Courtney's essence there, or the essence of what they had together. She might feel whole again, or something close to it. She sure wasn't very complete here, surrounded by the remnants of her old life—a life that no longer resonated with her. Her relationship with Susan was over, as it should be. She would be starting over no matter how she sliced it, and if she were ever going to undertake a total remodel of her life, now was the time. *Hell, if I'm going to do it, I might as well do it in a big way.*

Ellen scribbled a note to herself. Tomorrow she'd try to find a real estate agent. Next month she would tell her department head that the fall semester would be her last. This would give her time to sell her condo and inquire about teaching jobs in Vancouver while still bringing in a paycheck until Christmas. It all sounded complex, and yet when she wrote it all down as a list, it looked shockingly simple. It was positively energizing to act decisively. Finally, she was taking charge of her life and mapping out her own direction.

Sam's going to die when I tell her!

Ellen was e-mailing back and forth with a real estate agent when Courtney's name popped up in her inbox. Every muscle in her body tensed, especially her heart. It pounded madly before lodging squarely in her throat. *Courtney.* It was a sweet pain. The kind of pain that almost felt good. They'd had no contact since Ellen had left, which was exactly the way she wanted it. Writing or calling one another would only have prolonged the pain, and Courtney had respected that. Until now.

Ellen stared at Courtney's e-mail for a long time, wondering what she wanted, wondering if, whatever it was, it would bring her more pain and loneliness, would remind her how empty her life was without Courtney, make her regret that they hadn't finished what they'd started. She couldn't keep staring at it, nor could she delete it and pretend it had never popped up. She needed to be brave and open it. She tapped a key.

Hi, Ellen!

I hope you are well. I won't waste your time with idle chatter because that's not what we're about. I think about you all the time because you are a part of me, like breathing or walking. I think about our love and know how special it is, how special we are to each other. I have never loved anyone the way I love you, Ellen. Our time apart has not changed that.

In fact, every day we are apart feels wrong, and it feels like I am just going through the motions of my life until we are together again. So I will get to the point. I want to be with you...forever. Yes, Ellen, I want us to make a life together. If you feel the same way, meet me in Las Vegas on the 6th. I'll be at a blackjack table at the MGM Grand, hopefully winning a nice little jackpot. I will wait for you for the rest of my life, but I will start by waiting for you at the casino. I don't want you to reply to this e-mail, I want you to please come.

Your Courtney

August 6th was only nine days away. *Crap! Vegas? Make a life together?* Ellen's head spun as she read Courtney's words again and again. Courtney was reaching out, offering her a chance to be with her, encouraging her to throw caution to the wind and totally go for it. *To make a life together.* Ellen had already made one of the biggest decisions of her life this week by deciding she would move to Vancouver. Now Courtney was asking her to make an even bigger decision. Not only was she faced with putting job security and geography on the line, but now her heart too. The first two things she could remedy if moving was a mistake. The last one, not so much. She breathed in deeply and considered all the possibilities and consequences, sweat dripping down her sides suddenly. She got up to see if the air conditioner was still working.

Well, Ellen Turcotte, I guess it's time to really see what you are made of.

Courtney broke into a cold sweat the minute she entered the airport. Her legs turned to lead, each step a painful reminder of the last time she was in an airport. Regret was instant, like a punch to the stomach. Maybe she'd overestimated her ability to do this. Maybe, in fact, she could not get on an airplane. She had considered riding her motorcycle to Nevada, but had rejected the idea because it was a long and potentially dangerous trek on a bike. Ironic, though, because flying sure as hell wasn't safe either. She commanded herself to breathe, to keep walking, to pretend she was someone else, perhaps someone heading to a high school reunion in Atlanta or on the way to do business in D.C. Millions of people flew all the time and most, if not all, of them lived to fly another day. Why the hell should she be any different? She could do this. She could be one of these anonymous passengers hurrying to their gate, anxious to get to their destination, and, by God, reaching that destination. It was just another day, just another airport, just another plane among the thousands in the air at any given time.

Courtney looked around, watched people rushing or meandering through the long, wide, sterile corridors. Funny how airports tried to give the impression of lots of wide open, bright space with high vaulted ceilings and expansive corridors, lots of natural light and chambers that echoed with the noise of life. Perhaps it was to fool passengers or calm them before they became prisoners in the tight confines of an airplane.

Courtney plodded ahead and checked her bag, then went through security. If there wasn't the possibility of meeting Ellen at the other end, she would not be doing this. Ellen made tackling her fear worthwhile. And if Ellen didn't show? *Well...shit.* If Ellen didn't show in Vegas, Courtney would find a way to move on, to start some kind of a life, regardless, though she would never ever give up the hope that Ellen would one day come to her. Courtney had already decided to move to Vancouver, and now it was a matter of figuring out what kind of work she wanted to do and getting settled there. With Ellen, her life could be rich and full of love and hope and meaning, the way it had been when they were together in Vancouver. Without her, well, Courtney didn't really want to think about that possibility right now. Without Ellen, she would simply be going through the motions, same as she'd been doing for years, only with the knowledge of what she could have and once had, but didn't any longer. She supposed it was a bit like tasting something exotic and wonderful that you would never again be able to eat, always remembering that taste and never replicating it.

On the plane, Courtney settled into her aisle seat. She stuffed headphones in her ears, switched on the little television screen on the seat in front of her and ordered a drink as soon as the plane was off the ground. She would get through this if she could zone out and pretend she was somewhere else. Disappear for a while. *It's only a couple of hours out of the billions of hours in a life. I will do this, dammit!*

Vegas sweltered. Its desert heat shimmered from the ground up, making everything in its midst almost crackle, like a match being struck. Courtney cursed herself for choosing Nevada in August. What the hell had she been thinking? And yet strangely, it felt a little like coming home. Or a homecoming, with luck. As for the heat, well, hopefully she would be spending all her time indoors. *Making love to Ellen.* The thought gave her a little jolt. Heat of a much more pleasurable kind washed over her. Wishful thinking or not, she needed to believe there was a good chance Ellen would come. She couldn't get to her hotel fast enough, as if Ellen might be waiting for her right by that big ol' golden lion statue in front of the MGM Grand. Of course she wouldn't be, and Courtney tried to prepare herself for that. Still, as she carried her bag up the steps, she couldn't help but glance at the big lion, blinding in the sun, its gold promising great riches inside. Courtney would love to leave here rich, but not with money.

In her room, Courtney quickly changed into fresh clothes. She hadn't given Ellen a time, only a date, and had said she would be at a blackjack table, waiting. She moved fast, not taking the time to shower, and practically ran to the elevator. She had to apologize to an elderly couple she nearly knocked over in the hallway.

The casino was crowded, its inhabitants looking grateful to be in air-conditioning, moving slowly, as if they were there for the long haul. It might be tough to find a seat at a blackjack table. Courtney hoped the only vacancies weren't at the fifty-dollar tables. She'd be broke if she had to play for hours at fifty bucks a pop!

Courtney glanced around for signs of Ellen, and, seeing none, hovered until she found a seat at a fifteen-dollar table. She pounced on the empty chair and bought two hundred dollars worth of chips. She stacked the chips, solid and smooth in her hand, into neat towers, then sized up her tablemates, trying to gauge whether this would be fun or boring. The fat guy beside her smelled of too many free drinks and was trying too hard to be best friends with everyone at the table, as though they were at summer camp. The barely smiling woman on the other side of her was playing blackjack like it was her job, methodically and without joy. A young couple at the table seemed more interested in each other than the cards, exchanging intimate looks and touches. *Oh, well.* She would put up with whatever she needed to because she would stick this out until midnight if she had to. Hell, who was she kidding. If Ellen didn't show today, she'd probably keep haunting this place all week, waiting for Ellen.

The dealer, a good-looking woman in a serious, seen-it-all kind of way, was probably talked out from the drunk beside Courtney and worn out from trying to make conversation with the robotic woman on the other side of her. She made eye contact with Courtney as she waited for the automatic shuffler to do its job, her gaze communicating that she too was gay and might be up for a little side action. Courtney shook her head lightly.

"Waiting for someone?" she asked Courtney.

"That obvious?"

The woman lifted one shoulder in an insignificant shrug. "You do look a little distracted." She leaned closer and smiled slightly. "And taken."

I hope so, Courtney thought.

She played without much enthusiasm, raking in the chips when she won, pushing them back out for a bet, checking her cards, doing the math in her head, deciding on her next move. A tap on her shoulder startled her. Her heart raced. She turned slowly, afraid it was Ellen, afraid it *wasn't* Ellen.

"Care for a drink?" It was only a barmaid with a big smile and a small waist.

It took a moment for Courtney to calm down again, her heart still a jackhammer in her chest. She ordered soda water with lime. Her hand was still shaking when she handed over a tip. *Oh, God, Courtney, you need to get a grip or this is going to make you crazy.*

She stopped looking at her watch every ten minutes, stopped looking over her shoulder too and played on. "A watched pot never boils," her mother used to tell her. Soon, with the repetition of playing cards in the constant din and under artificial lighting, she lost all sense of time. She had successfully tuned out sound and peripheral movement when her nose suddenly picked up a familiar perfume. It tickled her senses and awakened her, as if from a dream. Beautiful Love. *Ellen's scent!* She whipped around so fast that her stack of chips went flying.

Ellen's smile was the rising sun over a beautiful valley. Courtney's heart leaped and so did she, leaving her chair so abruptly that she knocked it over. She flew into Ellen's arms, and suddenly the world was back on its axis. In one moment, everything in Courtney's life suddenly fell into place, like the automatic card shuffler coming to a stop. It was sublime order. Perfection.

"Oh, my God, Ellen. You came!" Courtney covered Ellen's face with kisses. She held on tightly to her, afraid to let her go.

"How could I not?"

They looked at each other, their foreheads touching. There was no mystery or question in their eyes, only happiness and love, desire, relief, all there, plain for anyone to see.

"I wasn't sure," Courtney admitted, the old fears and doubts rising momentarily. Though Ellen stood before her, Courtney could still hardly believe she'd come.

Ellen raised a teasing eyebrow. "All you had to do was ask."

Courtney laughed, relief quickly snuffing out any lingering doubt. "Goddamn, I should have asked a hell of a lot sooner then."

The dealer was staring at Courtney, a discernable twinkle in her eye.

"Let's get out of here," Courtney said to Ellen, still holding on to her arm.

"No, wait," Ellen implored. "I want to try blackjack at a *real* casino!"

It took a moment for Courtney to realize Ellen was joking. "The minute I get you alone, you're going to get it for that."

"I hope so," Ellen said slyly.

Courtney gathered up her chips as quickly as her fingers would allow, then whisked Ellen up to her room. They were silent and simply stared at one another on the elevator up. It was as though both could hardly believe the other was standing there.

"Wow, nice," Ellen observed, checking out the suite. Courtney was glad Ellen liked it because she hadn't gone cheap on it. She would never go cheap on anything when it came to Ellen.

"There's only one part of this room you need to worry about checking out." Courtney challengingly cocked her head toward the bed.

They raced to it, laughing and discarding their clothes along the way. Courtney fell on top of Ellen. She'd been so afraid she would never see her again, never hold her like this again. She rained kisses down on her like a monsoon.

"Oh, baby," Ellen said. "It's okay. Slow down. I'm not going anywhere."

Courtney lifted her head. "I'm sorry, sweetheart. I was so afraid I'd never have you in my arms like this again."

"I know." Ellen's fingers swept a lock of Courtney's hair from her face. "I wasn't sure we would ever be together again like this either."

Courtney's tears suddenly burst from the dam that had been holding them back. Ellen was finally here, in her arms, but would she stay? Was she here for good? Courtney didn't think she could handle it if Ellen left again, but for now, it was too difficult to verbalize her thoughts.

Ellen held her tight, stroking her face and hair, wiping her tears with a tissue from the bedside table. "It's okay, honey," she soothed. "I promise you, everything is going to be okay."

"How can you be sure?" Courtney wanted so badly to believe her.

"Courtney, look at me. What do you see in my eyes?"

That was easy. Love. Confidence. Desire. Strength. Faith. Serenity. Courtney smiled through her tears. "What made you change your mind about us?"

Ellen traced a finger along Courtney's collarbone. "I realized that with you, I'm alive. Without you, I'm just going through the motions of my life. And I didn't want to do that any more. I've been doing that for years, and it's time to stop. Your e-mail to me last week forced me to do some really hard thinking. I mean, I really looked at my life and what I want out of the rest of it. I decided I want to live, Courtney. I want to be happy, and being with you makes me very happy. And I think it's time we both deserve some happiness."

"Wow." Courtney brightened. "I can't say I don't know what you're talking about, because I do. You're the color in my black-and-white life, Ellen. The pot at the end of that damned rainbow! And God, yes, we deserve to be happy."

Ellen laughed heartily and nipped Courtney's neck. "You're quite the poet, aren't you?"

"I hear being in love can make a poet out of anyone."

"Yes, it can." Ellen kissed her, the kiss familiar and yet brand new. Their first kiss as a true couple. "There is one snag, though."

"What?" Courtney asked, instantly worried.

"I've already begun making plans to move to Vancouver. Sam's been on me about it and I agreed to do it. I mean, nothing's written in stone. But that's what—"

"Oh, Ellen, I love you so much!" Courtney kissed her, hard and possessively. Both of them moving to Vancouver. *What a wonderful coincidence!*

Ellen smiled up at her afterward. "The word Vancouver certainly has an effect on you. Is that our new word whenever I want to get you excited? Kind of the opposite of a safe word?"

Courtney snuggled tightly into Ellen and nuzzled her neck. "You don't have to say anything to get me excited, silly. It's quite the coincidence, though."

"What?"

"Vancouver. I'd already decided to move there too. I've got an appointment to look at condos next week."

"Get out! Seriously?"

Courtney nodded and smiled against Ellen's soft skin, enjoying how all the pieces of the puzzle seemed to be coming together, as if it were all part of some grand design. *Finally!* Maybe, Courtney considered, this was the point of it all—loving Ellen. Perhaps that was why she'd been spared from the crash, to find the love of her life, to reach this pinnacle. She kissed Ellen again. "Maybe you would like to look at the condos with me?"

"Courtney Langford, are you asking me to move in with you?" Ellen's eyes widened and her mouth opened in shock. It was hard sometimes to tell if she was joking or serious.

"I guess I am. Crap, is it too soon? I mean, you haven't been on your own long and so I understand if—"

Ellen placed a finger on Courtney's lips to silence her. Her smile told her that she couldn't be happier. "It's fine, sweetheart. More than fine! I would love to live with you."

"You would?"

"Don't sound so shocked."

"Jesus, I guess I am. I mean, I was worried you would want more time. And it's totally okay if you do."

"I'll be having a little more time anyway. My place is going up for sale as I speak and I've committed to teaching the fall term in Toronto, so I won't be ready to move until Christmas."

Courtney's spirits dropped a little, but it sounded like the sensible thing to do. And maybe by Christmas she would figure out what she wanted to do for a living. She doubted Ellen wanted a housewife kicking around all day. "That's okay, honey. I can get us settled while you finish your job. And besides, I'd wait forever for you if that's what you wanted."

"Really?" Ellen stared at her in wonder before kissing each eyelid, then Courtney's nose and finally her lips. "Oh, Courtney, I love you so much." She pressed her cheek against Courtney's. They lay like that for a while, wrapped in one another's arms, every part of their naked bodies touching.

"You know what?" Courtney whispered after a few minutes.

"What, sweetheart?"

"We've been in this room for over a half hour and we haven't even made love yet!"

Ellen's chuckle was low and sexy, almost a growl. "Well, I think we need to do something about that."

Ellen moved on top of Courtney. Their breasts touched softly, then their stomachs and thighs. Their skin was soft and warm with the heat of their desire. Ellen ran her tongue down the center of Courtney's chest. "I love the muscles in your chest. You're so strong and sexy."

"Oh yeah?" Courtney purred. "What else do you love?"

"These!" Ellen licked her lips before planting her mouth on one of Courtney's nipples. She coaxed it alive quickly with the sure, stiff strokes of her tongue, and Courtney squirmed beneath her. Her desire was already red-hot, pulsing through her in a demanding pleasure-pain, and she reached for Ellen's hand to push it between her legs. "Ahh, you're wet for me already," Ellen replied, grinning.

"Baby, I've been wet since I turned around and saw you at the blackjack table."

"Mmm, I like you wet, but I especially like it when you're wet and I have you all alone like this."

"I like it too when I'm wet and I know you're going to take care of things."

Ellen moved her hand firmly over Courtney's throbbing center. Her fingers plucked at the most sensitive parts and began expertly massaging them, mixing up the pace, motion and firmness of her touch until Courtney began to wriggle excitedly. Her hips indulgently arched up to meet Ellen's hand, undulating against the pressure, demanding more.

"Damn, I've missed you so much," Courtney blurted out between deep breaths, suddenly overwhelmed by her emotions. She had to still Ellen's hand for a moment, take another deep breath and collect herself.

"Sweetheart, I can tell." Ellen's voice was soft and sultry, further unlocking Courtney's passion.

There was nothing like her lover's voice warming her soul, her touch setting Courtney's senses on fire. She didn't think it was possible to love anyone more than this.

"Are you okay?" Ellen asked worriedly.

Courtney nodded; she couldn't speak.

Ellen moved down the length of her body, her warm breath tickling Courtney's thighs. Courtney snapped her eyes shut, arched her head into the pillow at the first touch of Ellen's mouth on her. It was like coming home and at the same time traveling to a different plane of existence, one where the power of her pleasure and the depth of her love for Ellen were all that mattered. She could stay in this place forever, sizzling inside, the rush of physical and emotional bliss poised to completely engulf her.

Ellen began alternately sucking and stroking Courtney with her tongue. She slipped a finger inside her, and Courtney lost all composure. Her orgasm crashed through her body all at once. She clutched Ellen's head, pushing her harder into her, rode Ellen's perfect mouth until her orgasm finally ebbed. By the time Ellen crawled up to her, Courtney was crying.

Ellen stroked her face tenderly. "Oh, honey, what's wrong?"

Courtney shook her head, unable to speak. Ellen nestled into her, holding her, letting her spend her tears.

She had never cried during sex before, Courtney realized, and though it should have surprised her, it didn't really, not with Ellen. She'd never felt the power of love like this before. It was vulnerability and safety at the same time, longing and fulfillment too. She couldn't fight it and didn't want to. They silently held each other for a long time, not wanting to let go, until Courtney finally moved onto her lover and began kissing and touching her in ways that made her intentions obvious. She made sweet love to Ellen like she was the most precious woman on Earth.

"I love you, Courtney," Ellen repeated over and over as she came.

Courtney smiled through fresh tears.

It was late into the evening by the time they realized they'd skipped dinner. They ordered soup and sandwiches from room service and consumed their meal in bed, glancing periodically at the brightly lit hotels and casinos on the Strip outside their window. The imitation Statue of Liberty glowed green, the mock New York City skyline of New York-New York danced with lights of blue and pink. Ellen wanted to experience Sin City in all its glory, but not tonight. Tonight she wanted Courtney all to herself and in the confines of their room. They awoke in the middle of the night to make love again before falling back asleep in one another's arms.

In the morning, Courtney rose early, slipping down to the Starbucks in the hotel lobby. She returned with aromatic stores of coffees and breakfast sandwiches as Ellen was opening her eyes.

"Oh, my love." Ellen yawned. "You know how to take care of your woman, don't you?"

"You're just learning that now?" Courtney grinned, proudly bringing the food and coffee to Ellen like hard-won prizes. "Shall I feed you too?"

Ellen pulled herself up to a sitting position. "Oh, my God, you might have to. I feel like I've run a marathon or something."

"Me too! We're out of practice, that's all." She kissed the tip of Ellen's nose, then passed her a steaming cup of coffee.

"Oh, this is a lifesaver, thank you."

"You're welcome. So, my sexy woman. What do you say we explore the town a little after breakfast and showers?" Courtney wiggled her eyebrows. "Or we could stay in and explore a few other things."

Ellen laughed heartily and drank her coffee like much-needed medicine. "As much as I would love to feast on your body all day, I think I need a little break to restore, um, certain things."

Courtney winked. "Wimp."

"What?" Ellen exclaimed. "Who you calling a wimp? I'll have you know that I could easily go a few more rounds today. But I figured the results might be better if we store it up a bit."

"All right, all right. I admit I could use a little restoring myself. But I can't promise to leave you alone in the shower this morning."

"I should hope not," Ellen said over a bite of her egg sandwich.

After a long shower during which they brought each other to orgasm again, Ellen and Courtney dressed, kissed lingeringly at the door, then sauntered arm-in-arm down the hall. Outside it was hot, at least ninety degrees, Ellen figured, but she was dying to see the Strip and its plethora of opulent hotels. She didn't mind getting hot and sweaty. After all, it meant they could shower together back in their room later.

"What are you smiling at?" Courtney asked as they began to walk the Strip.

"Thinking about showering."

"Past or future?"

"Both, because I expect the same results."

"Ah, now you're talking, darling," Courtney whispered in her ear. "I can't wait to get you alone again."

Ellen delighted in the shiver racing up and down her spine. She entwined her fingers with Courtney, needing to touch her. It was wrong to draw comparisons, but she couldn't help herself. She couldn't ever remember feeling this physically turned on, this needful of a touch, with Susan or anyone else.

They barged past outstretched hands trying to give them cards for sex phone lines or prostitutes. The soliciting was annoying, but Ellen tried to ignore it as best she could. She smothered a smile. She had her own hot babe right at her fingertips.

"You need to see the Venetian," Courtney enthused. "It's incredible, but I have to warn you, everything else is going to pale in comparison."

"Well, I know all about that."

"What?"

"Things paling in comparison."

Courtney smiled. "So do I, sweetheart, so do I."

Courtney was right about the hotel, which strived to look like a street scene from Venice, Italy, with its marble columns, shops and ceiling murals.

"Oh, my God, there's a river in here!" Ellen exclaimed. "With little boats in it!"

"Gondolas," Courtney corrected with a laugh. "Will you go for a ride in one with me later?"

"I can't believe this place!"

"The best that a billion dollars can buy. I want to take you shopping before we do anything else, though."

"Oh, Courtney, I don't need anything, honestly."

"Yes, you do." Courtney steered her up the stairs and along the aisle of shops until they came to a jewelry store.

Courtney led a protesting Ellen inside to the display of diamond earrings. She asked the clerk for a close look at several pairs, asking knowledgeable questions about the cut, clarity and the carats. Even the cheapest ones had to be several hundred dollars a pair, Ellen figured.

"Honey, there's no point in me looking at these."

"Yes, there is." Courtney looked at her with serious eyes. "I want to buy you a pair."

"No, I couldn't let you do that."

"Why not?"

"They're expensive and I don't need them."

"Look, I can afford them and you *do* need them. You would look absolutely beautiful in them and you deserve to feel good about yourself, Ellen. And believe me, you will feel good in these. I'm getting them for you and that's that. Beautiful diamonds for a beautiful woman."

Further objections would certainly be ignored, so Ellen acquiesced and chose a pair. She'd always wanted some fine jewelry, and she wanted to look beautiful because she *felt* beautiful. Courtney beamed as the clerk put them in a little box. Ellen nearly cried. They were exquisite, and she would wear them tonight, getting dressed up so Courtney could show her off. "Thank you, my love," Ellen enthused outside. "They're gorgeous."

"So are you."

Over lunch, Ellen marveled at how happy Courtney seemed. She knew full well that her presence here was largely responsible for that. She made Courtney happy, that was evident, just as Courtney made her happy. She gasped a little as she thought how close she'd come to letting the love of her life go. If Courtney hadn't sent her that e-mail and if she hadn't gone for it the way she had...

"Are you okay, Ellen?" Courtney tenderly closed her hand over Ellen's on the table.

"Yes. I'm so happy to be here with you. I'm so happy you asked me to come."

"Me too. I'm thrilled you took me up on it. You've made me the happiest woman in the world by coming here."

It occurred to Ellen then that Courtney had to have flown to Las Vegas. Her stomach turned over as she wondered how Courtney managed to get past her fear of flying and what memories the journey must have conjured. She felt the blood drain from her face. "Oh, my God. How did you get here? Did you fly?"

Courtney swallowed visibly. "Yes."

"Is it the first time since what happened in the spring?"

"Yes."

"Oh, crap. Are you okay?"

"I'm okay, but I admit, the only thing that got me on that plane was the prospect of seeing you here."

"Dammit, I wish I'd been with you on the flight."

"Don't worry, you were. Or at least, you were in my heart and in my thoughts the whole time. I closed my eyes and tried to imagine you were sitting next to me, holding my hand."

Ellen smiled at her lover. She would have given anything to have been able to do that. "How are you doing with everything?"

Courtney beamed. "Much better now that you're with me."

"Seriously. How are you doing in general?"

Courtney sighed, hesitating before she answered. "Some days are still a struggle, but the good ones outweigh the bad ones now, thank goodness. I'm over the worst of it now."

"Really? Oh, Courtney, that's wonderful."

"I still work at it. I still have phone sessions with Liz twice a week, and once I move to Vancouver I'll probably resume seeing her." Courtney recounted her visit to Danny's parents in Seattle. "Seeing them gave me some closure, you know? They don't hold me responsible in any way, and I think I needed to see that for myself. And I needed to apologize for not treating Danny better. I needed to let go of the guilt."

"And have you?"

"Mostly, yes. I decided I don't want to waste any more time going through life without really living it, you know? 'Fear not death but fear a life never lived.' I read that somewhere once."

Ellen nodded thoughtfully. "Words to live by. I know exactly what you're saying. And I'm very proud of you."

Courtney squeezed Ellen's hand. "Thank you, and I'm proud of you too, sweetheart. Are you doing okay?"

"I'm doing much more than okay. I'm more than ready to move on with my life. Deciding to sell my condo and move to Vancouver was huge for me. It really cemented it for me that my new life is just beginning."

"I'm so pleased. I knew you would get to this point eventually. But I have to tell you, Ellen Turcotte. I have plans for us to be ridiculously ecstatic for the rest of our lives."

Ellen took Courtney's hand and kissed it, then giggled wildly, as though living her life was suddenly the simplest thing in the world to do. "I think I'm already there."

EPILOGUE

Eight Months Later

Courtney turned the manila envelope over in her hands before holding it up to the light. There were documents inside from the Ministry of the Attorney General of Ontario. She didn't want to think about what might or might not be inside, so she set it back on the kitchen counter, anxious for Ellen to get home and open it.

Courtney worked on her computer for the rest of the afternoon, only stopping when she heard Ellen coming in the door.

"Hi, honey." Courtney greeted Ellen with a kiss and a long hug.

"Hi, yourself, sweetheart. Can I have another one?" Ellen leaned in for a second kiss.

"How was your day?"

Ellen shrugged out of her jacket and hung it up. "Fine. The students are all looking forward to the semester ending and summer coming, of course, so it's hard to keep their attention."

"I'm looking forward to the semester ending too, since it will mean having you around more."

Ellen leered at her. "You're sure you can handle that?"

"Oh yeah. I can more than handle that, little girl. Question is, can *you* handle it?" Courtney drew Ellen in for another hug.

"I look forward to it, my love. And remember our deal. You're not going to work too much yourself this summer, right?"

"Yes, dear. But starting a new business is—"

"Ah-ha!" Ellen pulled back and shushed Courtney with a finger on her lips. "Deal's a deal."

Courtney rolled her eyes good-naturedly. "I know, I know."

"I'm glad you know, because I'm not going to let you forget it."

"Oh, this envelope came for you today." Courtney reached for it and handed it to Ellen, trying to be as casual about it as she could, even though her hand was shaking a little.

"Not trying to change the subject, are you?" Ellen said with narrowed eyes.

Courtney laughed. "Oh no, dear, I would never do that!"

Ellen took the envelope and opened it, a slight frown on her forehead. She pulled out the papers and absently walked away as she studied them, shutting Courtney out. When she turned around again, the tiny frown was still there but also a small smile that took on shades of both happiness and puzzlement.

"Everything okay?" Courtney asked, worried.

"Yes. It's my divorce papers. It's official now."

Courtney closed the distance between them and wrapped Ellen in a loving embrace. "Are you okay, sweetheart?" Courtney was ecstatic, but she wasn't so sure Ellen was, and so she didn't want to act too excited.

"I'm okay," she said after a while in a weak voice. "It's a little sad, that's all."

Courtney's mouth went dry. She'd hoped Ellen would do a

little happy dance and maybe even talk about the two of them getting married now. She'd hoped Ellen would greet her divorce as wonderful news. "Um, okay. Can you tell me more about the feeling sad part?"

"It's sad because I went into it with such hope for the future. Marriage is a very hopeful statement two people make, Courtney. They are in love and they are optimistic about being together forever, sure that their love will survive no matter what trials and tribulations they might come across. Can you understand that?"

"Yes, I think I can."

Ellen pulled away enough to look into Courtney's eyes. "And when it doesn't work out, there's a feeling of failure, of lost hope. It's not that I miss Susan or have any regrets about the divorce. I need to be able to be sad for a day or two, for myself, you know?"

"Yes, I do know, darling." Courtney kissed her lover on the forehead. "Take all the time you need for this, and then I want you to be ecstatically happy for the rest of your life."

Ellen smiled. "Thank you for understanding."

"Thank you for loving me." Courtney kissed Ellen tenderly on the lips. "Are you going to be okay for our party next weekend or do you want to cancel it?" They'd organized a party over a month ago to celebrate the company Courtney had begun with her therapist, Liz.

"Yes, I will be more than okay by then, and I can't wait for the party."

"Me too, and in more ways than one," Courtney said, intentionally cryptic.

"Courtney, honey, you're the best!" Jeff wrapped her in a bear hug. "I couldn't be prouder of you."

"Thank you, Jeff. I owe a lot to you, you know. You were a friend when I really needed one. And I still need one!"

Jeff beamed at her and handed her a box wrapped in gift

247

paper. "You made that part very easy. And of course you still need a friend. You're not getting rid of me that easily."

"Hey, what's this? The invitation said no gifts!"

"Yeah, well, since when do I ever listen to you anyway?"

Ellen joined them, greeting Jeff with a kiss on his cheek. "Welcome, Jeff. And Courtney's right, you shouldn't have. We really just wanted to get all our friends in one place and to celebrate Courtney and Liz's new company. You being here is your gift to us."

Jeff shook his head. "Okay, enough of the butt kissing. Open the damned present and get me a beer, would ya?"

Courtney laughed before tearing through the wrapping paper. It was a beautiful, chocolate brown leather briefcase, embossed with her initials. "Wow, this is awesome. I love it. Thank you so much! It's gorgeous." The leather was soft and smooth as butter.

"Well," he replied with an aw-shucks grin, "I figured you'd want to look professional when you met with clients."

Courtney kissed him on the cheek. "Thank you, my friend. I'll use it all the time. It's perfect. Now come in and sit down and let me get you that beer."

Sam and Rebecca were already there. So were Liz and her husband. Another lesbian couple they'd befriended through Courtney's work, both of them cops, was also there. A colleague of Ellen's from the college was on hand too. It was a small group but plenty big for their two-bedroom condo.

Moments later, Ellen opened a couple of champagne bottles and poured everyone a glass. She raised a toast to Courtney and Liz and saluted their new company. Called "We Are Survivors," it offered those with PTSD at-home computer-based workshops to help them deal with their demons and aid them in their healing process. It also linked them to other help agencies and support groups. Liz was providing the counseling expertise, of course. Courtney had developed the software for the program and was responsible for its marketing and distribution. It was important, Liz said, because so many with PTSD suffer alone at home and need help that is available without having to leave their houses. The company was in its infancy but so far showing a lot of promise. Courtney was now working on a cell phone application for the program.

First Liz and then Courtney took turns thanking their friends with a little speech. When it was her turn, Courtney pointed to Ellen, then took her hand. "I wouldn't be here today, doing work that I love and being so happy and healthy if it weren't for this woman."

Ellen smiled sheepishly. She was so cute when she tried to deflect attention from herself, thought Courtney.

Ellen drank to the toast, then cleared her throat nervously and stepped forward. "I don't want to take anything away from Courtney and Liz, who are doing wonderful work and have worked hard to make their new business a success. I couldn't be prouder of Courtney. And since all of you are our friends, I have my own little announcement to make."

Courtney's heart beat a little faster. She'd hoped Ellen would do this tonight, but she wasn't sure. Ellen had been pretty quiet since she'd received her divorce papers in the mail.

"Everyone, I want to tell you all that my divorce became final this past week. And while a divorce is always a sad time, it's also a time to embark on a new and wonderful stage in my life." She looked at Courtney and gave her a private smile that was bursting with love. "And I hope that Courtney will be with me every step of the way for the rest of my days."

Courtney squeezed Ellen's hand. "You can count on it, my love." She would love Ellen for the rest of her life.

The group cheered them and raised their glasses for another toast. Courtney was barely able to restrain herself from getting the gift she'd hidden away from Ellen and giving it to her in front of everyone. But she knew that would embarrass Ellen.

Later, after everyone had gone, they stood out on the balcony under the moonlight. Courtney put her arm around Ellen. "That was very brave of you, telling everyone tonight about your divorce being final."

Ellen leaned into Courtney. "They're our friends and I

wanted them to know. And I wanted them to know that I plan to spend the rest of my life with you."

Courtney kissed the top of Ellen's head. "Good, then you won't mind that I got you a little gift."

"You did? When did you do that?"

Courtney reached under the patio chair for a wrapped package that was lying there with a fresh red rose resting on top of it. She handed the rose to Ellen first, then the package. "I had a feeling about tonight. I had a feeling you would be ready for this."

"But I don't have anything for you. I—"

Courtney silenced her with a kiss. "Just open the damned thing."

"All right." Ellen lifted the rose to her nose and inhaled deeply. "Mmm, I love roses."

"Okay, but that's not really the best part yet."

"My, aren't you impatient," Ellen answered, laughing. She opened the package quickly. It was a book. She flipped it over to see the cover. Her eyes widened and her jaw slackened when she saw the title. *An American Wife*.

"Well?" Courtney prodded.

"Oh, my God. Is this what I think it is?"

"If it's a proposal you're thinking, then yes."

Ellen threw her arms around Courtney, crushing the rose between them.

Courtney spun Ellen around, laughing and twirling her. "Is that a yes, my love?"

"It most definitely is!"

They kissed under the moonlight, the mountains in the distance swallowed by the night.

Publications from Bella Books, Inc.

Women. Books. Even better together.

P.O. Box 10543 Tallahassee, FL 32302 Phone: 800-729-4992

www.bellabooks.com

TWO WEEKS IN AUGUST by Nat Burns. Her return to Chincoteague Island is a delight to Nina Christie until she gets her dose of Hazy Duncan's renown ill-humor. She's not going to let it bother her, though…
978-1-59493-173-4 $14.95

MILES TO GO by Amy Dawson Robertson. Rennie Vogel has finally earned a spot at CT3. All too soon she finds herself abandoned behind enemy lines, miles from safety and forced to do the one thing she never has before: trust another woman.
978-1-59493-174-1 $14.95

PHOTOGRAPHS OF CLAUDIA by KG MacGregor. To photographer Leo Westcott models are light and shadow realized on film. Until Claudia.
978-1-59493-168-0 $14.95

SONGS WITHOUT WORDS by Robbi McCoy. Harper Sheridan's runaway niece turns up in the one place least expected and Harper confronts the woman from the summer that has shaped her entire life since.
978-1-59493-166-6 $14.95

YOURS FOR THE ASKING by Kenna White. Lauren Roberts is tired of being the steady, reliable one. When Gaylin Hart blows into her life, she decides to act, only to find once again that her younger sister wants the same woman.
978-1-59493-163-5 $14.95

THE SCORPION by Gerri Hill. Cold cases are what make reporter Marty Edwards tick. When her latest proves to be far from cold, she still doesn't want Detective Kristen Bailey baby-sitting her, not even when she has to run for her life.
978-1-59493-162-8 $14.95

STEPPING STONE by Karin Kallmaker. Selena Ryan's heart was shredded by an actress, and she swears she will never, ever be involved with one again.
978-1-59493-160-4 $14.95

FAINT PRAISE by Ellen Hart. When a famous TV personality leaps to his death, Jane Lawless agrees to help a friend with inquiries, drawing the attention of a ruthless killer. #6 in this award-winning series.
978-1-59493-164-2 $14.95

A SMALL SACRIFICE by Ellen Hart. A harmless reunion of friends is anything but, and Cordelia Thorn calls friend Jane Lawless with a desperate plea for help. Lammy winner for Best Mystery. #5 in this award-winning series.
978-1-59493-165-9 $14.95

NO RULES OF ENGAGEMENT by Tracey Richardson. A war zone attraction is of no use to Major Logan Sharp. She can't wait for Jillian Knight to go back to the other side of the world.
978-1-59493-159-8 $14.95

TOASTED by Josie Gordon. Mayhem erupts when a culinary road show stops in tiny Middelburg, and for some reason everyone thinks Lonnie Squires ought to fix it. Follow-up to Lammy mystery winner *Whacked*.
978-1-59493-157-4 $14.95